A Curse That Bites Deep

Thomas Fenske

A Curse That Bites Deep

The Mossback *was* her life. She glanced at the old calendar over by the register when one of the lights drifted past it like a spotlight. It had been there since 1971 and her dad never took it down. It was his way of reminding her. The date circled was the court date for her first divorce. Her dad had forbidden her marriage, but she had done it anyway. Less than six months later he took her back in when she couldn't take the verbal and physical abuse any more. Not a word was said about it; he just accepted her bad choice as fact and moved on.

She related her experience to her current problem and drew from the lesson she had learned. Deep inside, she knew she had to accept Sam's choice, but she didn't have to like it. She trusted Sam because she loved him, but her love didn't mean she had to stop worrying about him... or, for that matter, stop worrying about herself.

"Sam, I wish you knew how much I hate this," she said as she put her head down on her folded arms and sobbed.

Then she abruptly raised her head. She had heard a strange sound. The old building often creaked and groaned in the dark but this was different. She looked around.

"It came from the kitchen," she said and she darted to the door where she saw a glow through the diamond shaped window. The door was hot but she opened it anyway and saw flames leaping up the back wall, near the door. She let the kitchen door swing shut and ran to the phone. It was dead. Her purse was under the counter and she grabbed it and ran to the front door where her keys still hung in the deadbolt. She unlocked the door, grabbed her keys and ran outside. She was out of breath by the time she got the few steps to her car. In moments she was speeding down to the nearest place she knew was open, the Dolings Motel. She threw open the door and was relieved to see Darcy was working late. Darcy, the owner, was one of her of her oldest friends.

"Darcy, The Mossback's burning! Call the fire department."

Darcy grabbed the phone and started dialing even before she managed to exclaim, "Oh, dear!"

Soon, they heard the sound of sirens and Smidgeon drove back to the restaurant. The volunteers had quickly arrived, and were hard at work. The front of the building was dark but the glow of fire in the kitchen was visible through the windows and billows of smoke rose from the rear of the building. The sound of breaking glass and a combined roar of water and steam punctuated the otherwise quiet darkness. Smidgeon was in tears as Fire Chief Lyndon McDonald, approached her.

A Curse That Bites Deep

BY

Thomas Fenske

Mystery/Adventure Novel

Originally published by Wings ePress, Inc.

Edited by: Jeanne Smith
Copy Edited by: Leslie Hodges
Executive Editor: Jeanne Smith
Cover Artist: BJ Haynes

Published In the United States Of America

Dedication

I dedicate this book to my awesome and talented daughter, Audrey

One

"If I start hiking now, I'll be way too early."

Sam was mumbling to himself in the clammy darkness. He had snapped awake two hours earlier than planned.

"Might as well do something," he continued, as he began gathering his tools.

He shined a light down the lower shaft.

"That's what kept me awake," he said. "Might as well take one last crack at it."

All he could think about was a boulder blocking that shaft, the rock that had thwarted him all day Sunday.

He found one lantern with good batteries and lit a candle in what he called the anteroom. It was a depression midway through the mine, an opening that had likely been the result of a cave-in. He made his way down the deeper shaft and confronted the source of his frustration.

"You're the reason I can't sleep," he said as he reached out and tried to budge the obstruction.

He examined it again with his small light.

"Something's gotta give," he said.

He lifted his ancient chisel and hammer and tapped at the rock, trying to find a weakness. It was too big to drag out so he had been working to find some way of fracturing it into smaller pieces. It wasn't hot but it was humid and he was sweating profusely.

"Just a few whacks," he muttered. "I still have a long hike, can't afford to get too tired."

He was on his side with the chisel in his left hand and he placed the business end of it firmly against the rock. The shaft was cramped but he managed a good swing with the hammer and heard a tell-tale dullish ring of the chisel and he was elated because he knew the last hit had finally cracked the rock. He wiped the spray of gravel from his face and examined the small crack with his light.

"Good, just one more," he said and he set himself to repeat the process.

A few grains of material filtered down from the ceiling of the small shaft as he reared back to make another swing. The chisel rang clear as the rock split in two.

"Got it!" he yelled just before the ceiling came down on him.

He dropped the hammer and chisel, covered his face with his hands and tried to snake his way out of the cavern but only made it a few inches before he was completely covered in an avalanche of rock and gravel.

He was lucky. It hadn't been a hard fall. He coughed against the cloud of dust covering him and reached out and tried to find his lantern in the debris. He waited a few minutes, trying to suck precious oxygen through his protecting fingers, gasping in shallow breaths to avoid inhaling too many of the dusty, settling particles of mountainside. A glimmer of light fought through the haze and he knew he had found the lantern. He spread the dust and rocks to the side and rescued it.

"Chisel and hammer must be close," he muttered and he shifted his body forward, back into the shaft, moving material until he found his precious tools. He examined the rock he had been working on. It was broken into two somewhat smaller pieces.

"Great. I wasted almost an entire day on it and it almost kills me in revenge," he quipped. "I'll leave the rest of it for next time," he added as he pulled his lantern and tools behind him into the dim light of the anteroom, where everything was covered in a thin layer of dust from the cave-in.

"And *that* is why I don't do this in the morning before I leave," he said.

He silently stowed his tools, grabbed his pack and pushed it ahead of him, up the tunnel on the other side of the small room until he was outside. The night was clear and the stars twinkled. The cool early spring air was a relief after another night in the dark confines of the mine. After a few deep breaths, he proceeded to tilt the flat rock back into its place to seal the mine entrance and then he started hiking toward the wide end of the cut.

"It's still a little early but I'll just take it easy," he said, "I've had enough of the Sublett Mine for one weekend."

~ * ~

Sam paused to catch his breath and scanned ahead, studying the dim, dawn-tinged landscape for the ribbon of road he knew had to be there. The sun struggled against a crust of overcast but managed to allow just enough light for him to speed his hike.

He heard a truck before he saw it, an eighteen-wheeler moving from the south. Its headlights flickered in the distance as it sped down the deserted highway.

"Less than an hour more," he rasped, thankful he finally had a firm bearing on his destination.

He pulled out his canteen and took a swig. The moisture relieved his parched throat and revived him somewhat. He increased his pace toward the rendezvous point.

It had been a tough weekend. The rocks did not easily give up their secrets but he had known it would not be easy since the beginning. When he had found the depression in the wall of a hidden arroyo two years earlier, it had seemed like the end of his long search, but here he was, still at it. The only difference was that now, instead of endless hiking trips, he spent his time clawing into the earth, trying to find the end of...what? Was it really Ben Sublett's lost mine?

"I can honestly say I have no idea," he mused out loud, "but it's something and the clues fit."

It was a small consolation. The hole in the ground was highly unstable, and he had struggled to shore up the walls with lumber he had to haul in a few boards at a time. In two years he had managed to stabilize the entrance tunnel and what he called "the anteroom," a larger chamber about seven feet across.

"No doubt the result of another cave-in," he muttered as he walked.

It had a ceiling high enough to allow him enough room to stand upright, at least in the central area. The hollow was wider at this point and he used it as his base of operations. It sheltered him in all weather and provided a place for him to store tools and supplies.

Now he was working on the lower tunnel and it was even more unstable. The danger was emphasized on this trip when he suffered through another collapse as he worked. All it took, it seemed, was the slightest touch to the low ceiling of the lower tunnel and rocks would pepper him. Smidgeon had fussed at him about a hard hat, but he always thought one might cause even more trouble in the tight space.

"A hard hat sticks out, makes it hard to judge where it is," he said, repeating the same phrase he had used on Smidgeon many times.

This time luck had held. The smattering of pebbles foreshadowed a bigger collapse and somehow he managed to set himself before the rocks rained down. The worst he had suffered was a fit of hacking and coughing as the dust settled.

"All it will take is one time," he said. "I'll find myself buried down there... and it will be hopeless because nobody knows where I am."

He stumbled over a rock and mumbled a few bad words, then instinctively looked around, embarrassed, but there was no one to chastise him. Smidgeon didn't much appreciate his past inclinations toward profanity and had focused on it as one of the first things she had tried to change. Sam regained his composure and started walking again, this time thinking about her.

She had dropped him off after dark Friday evening and he had hiked in. Working the mine was another of his bad habits, but it was one she had learned to tolerate.

"I guess she knows me too well," he said. "It is not negotiable." He smiled after he said this, then added, "Well, up to a point, I guess."

His obsession had served to introduce them, when he had made her café a regular stop after his forays into the hills. The Mossback, in Van Horn, was one of his favorite places to have breakfast during his early fruitless searches for the mine.

Those trips had been different. He didn't know exactly what he was looking for, so he trespassed aimlessly, trying to make some sense of the elusive clues Slim Longo had given him. When he finally thought he had deciphered one of the clues, he made the fateful December trip to try to verify it. He'd never hiked in the winter because of the uncertainty of the weather, but that one time he broke his own rule and as a result he had almost died.

"Pure dumb luck," he said to himself as his thoughts turned to the small box in his pack. It still contained the good luck charm given to him by the old Hispanic witch-woman in a Fort Stockton parking lot. "Well," he chuckled, "if you can call a beating luck."

Drunken ranch hands had happened upon his camp and robbed him of most of his supplies and equipment. After beating him, they dumped him off a small cliff, expecting him to die of the elements. But he wasn't hurt as badly as they assumed and he'd managed to flee, making his way to a safe haven in another of the many hidden gullies in these rugged hills. He miraculously found himself facing the solution to the riddle.

"The clues fit," he again repeated to himself then his mind flashed on the small talisman again and muttered. "Luck?"

He considered the word as he thought about his lonely hike, trying to escape with the knowledge of his discovery.

"Followed this same path, to the same highway," he said.

When he had made a hasty escape across the strip of flatland between the mountains and the highway, his intent had been to flag down a car in the early morning. He assumed it was the only way he could get a ride back to Van Horn and safety. When Smidgeon magically appeared in the first car traveling from the north and whisked him to safety, she seemed almost like a guardian angel. That moment had changed both their lives.

"Can one moment change a person's entire life? Or does it take a lifetime of such moments?" he mused.

His mind raced back to the dark and depressing Travis County Jail block where he'd met a dirty, homeless alcoholic who was dying on the floor. The jailers and the other prisoners were uninterested, but Sam had tried to help him as best as he could.

"Of course," he muttered, "was it luck or was it fate? Fate is what put me next to Slim."

A broken and injured derelict of a man, Slim Longo had wheezed and rasped the incredible statement that had transformed Sam's life.

"Ya gotta follow the Devil until you see the table, then turn around and you'll see the why of it."

Sam had labored ten years to no avail to make some sense out of Slim's revelation. At least until he was directed by a sidelong comment made by his friend Sally. She was randomly looking at one of his maps one day and mentioned a feature he had somehow overlooked many times: Diablo Rim. *Diablo*! It was so obvious, yet he had missed it.

He had to wonder if it was fate or luck when the crusty old trapper confronted him in The Mossback's parking lot. Loot Meldings quickly transitioned from suspicious interloper to adviser and confidant.

"More than that," Sam said, "Loot became my friend."

It was Loot he was expecting to meet shortly along the deserted highway.

Sam squinted and could just discern a long thin line of pavement in the distance. He brushed the dust off his watch and pressed the button on the side to turn on the light.

"Sunrise soon," he said. "I hope he's on time."

Sam had taken a big chance by allowing the old man into his confidence, but their shared friendship with Slim had bonded them like a band of steel. Despite his age and his alcoholic past, Loot had proven to be a valuable partner. Sam was, after all, still trespassing. The mine, such as it was, was on private land. It was basically just a man-made hole, one he hoped was following a vein of gold that had accumulated long ago into a fault. The fault had been the "why" part of the clue, a "Y"-shaped intersecting fault line. So far Sam had managed to extract only a smattering of gold from fragments of rock he had found while trying to dig down the far tunnel, trying to make it stable enough to get farther in.

"If I ever expected to get rich," he laughed to himself, "it is definitely a losing proposition."

The highway was much closer and the sight of it spurred him to walk faster. Sam was relieved to discern the outline of his rendezvous point, a shallow culvert. When he verified the location of the culvert, he veered off in a random arc so he would not run the risk of wearing a path. It was a genuine concern so close to the highway. He tried to do the same thing when he entered and exited the arroyo, too.

The culvert allowed him just enough cover to duck down out of sight. He and Loot had a prearranged signal, a brief toot of the ancient Jeep truck's horn as it passed and then the old man would turn the truck around and Sam would blink his flashlight to show he was there and the Jeep would approach the culvert slowly to meet the younger man. If Sam was late, Loot would drive down a couple of miles and repeat the procedure. Occasionally they'd be interrupted by another vehicle and Loot would zoom on past while Sam scooted back down to hide.

Sam was relieved to find the culvert floor dry, so he dropped his pack and sat in the opening. He was tired and may have been dozing when he heard a familiar single "beep" as a truck whined past.

Sam stood and looked over the edge.

"Loot," he said and grabbed his pack. When the truck turned around, he blinked his light.

He looked both ways, out of habit mostly, but the road was empty except for the truck, so he got out of the depression and waited on the side of the road. Loot slowed as he approached.

"Right on time," Sam said as he threw his pack in the bed of the truck, nestling it into the debris in the back.

"Mornin', Sam."

In the two years Sam had known Loot, he always seemed to have the same, sparse salt and pepper growth on his face and the same crimson-tinged eyes.

"How you doing?"

"Great, buddy. Got you just in time. Supposed to rain before too dang long. How'd it go up there?"

"Slow, really slow."

"Well, since you have to carry everything in, tools, lumber, food, water...gonna take a long time, Sam. I told you that from the beginning."

"I know...frustrating, though."

"You're lucky the whole thing ain't caved in on you. You really should get some walkie talkies with enough range to git out here. Then if you was in trouble, you could at least call out and maybe let me know."

Same thought about the most recent cave-in as he said, "Yeah, but those cost money. I don't make much at the café."

"I reckon your gal would buy 'em for you if she thought it would help keep you safe."

"Yeah, she might, but then it would just remind her of how dangerous this is and we don't want to do that."

"Exactly why I hain't been tied down all these years." Loot finished with the distinctive cackle he always used when he was telling one of the private jokes and, to Sam, the accompanying sly grin seemed to provide a murky glimpse into the old man's secret past.

The two men sat in silence the rest of the way as the old truck rattled down Highway 54 toward the flickering lights of Van Horn.

Two

The truck hit the outskirts of town just as dawn reached a point where it was more light than dark.

"Where you want me to drop you off? The house?"

"Yeah, I need to get cleaned up," Sam said. "Then I gotta go to work at the café."

"You must be tired," Loot said. "Still, it is a far sight better than what you used to do."

Sam laughed, remembering the long drives he used to make after hiking the hills north of Van Horn.

"Yeah, it was a real grind. And back then I usually hiked even farther... and then I'd have to drive to Austin."

"Close to five hunnert miles," Loot added with a low mumble.

The truck stopped in front of a neatly trimmed stucco house near the edge of town. The closest house was a couple of hundred yards away, but Sam glanced around nervously after he emerged from the truck and grabbed his pack.

"Thanks, buddy," he told Loot. "I'll come around later in the week."

"You bet...I best get out and check my traps now," he chortled. Then he put the truck in gear and rattled off.

Sam fumbled with the watch pocket on his jeans and extracted the house key. He never took too much with him on these expeditions except for the key. The porch had two doors, one entering into the living room and the other into a front bedroom. This was the room Smidgeon had bequeathed to him when he moved in.

"Everybody needs their own private space," she had said. "It was my daddy's study, but I'll let you use it now."

He hung his pack on a hook and grabbed some clean underwear from the dresser he had brought from Austin. A multi-colored tabby rubbed against his leg and he crouched down to scratch her head.

"Good morning, MamaKat."

There was no other sound in the house except for the motorboat purring of the cat. Smidgeon was already at the café.

He knew he was running late, so Sam quickly showered and dressed and got into his aging VW beetle, The Clunker, to make the short drive down to the restaurant. The parking lot had a good crowd for a Monday, so he scooted around the back and entered through the kitchen. The smell of hot biscuits and bacon made his stomach growl as he grabbed his apron.

Chuy looked up from the flat grill, "Sam! *Que Alivio!*"

"Sorry I'm late, what do you need me to do?"

"The boss been asking about you three times already; you better go see what she needs first."

In the dining room he noticed several tables needed bussing so he grabbed a plastic bin and went right to work. Smidgeon was taking an order and he picked a table near her as his first task.

She came by as he cleared the table, "Thank heavens. We've been slammed," she said. "How are you doing, sweetie?"

He pursed his lips to mime a kiss as he answered. "Good, sorry I'm late," he whispered.

"Oh, you aren't really late, we're just busy," she said as she took the order back to Chuy in the kitchen.

Sam was hungry but breakfast would have to wait. He quickly cleared a few tables and when he took the dishes to the kitchen he could see a pile of dishes waiting to be washed, so he began to rinse some of them in the first of the triple sinks as the middle one filled with clean soapy water. His primary job at The Mossback was to do whatever needed to be done. His life was a tradeoff. He had the convenience of being able to follow his obsession with the mine but it had to be balanced out with Smidgeon and her restaurant.

Sam reflected on these facts as he washed the dishes. He thought about the early days when The Mossback had been a regular stop for him. He and Smidgeon maintained a casual flirty repartee until the day she had rescued him out on the highway. Over the next several months he'd made quite a few trips to Van Horn and their casual flirtation gradually grew more serious.

In previous years he never stopped, skulking through town under the cover of night to sneak into the hills, but he began to use her place as a base. She would take him out to the same spot on the highway so he could hike to the mine without leaving his car on the side of the road.

"That's how Loot figured out what I was doing," he mused under his breath, "he noticed my car."

Before he had found the mine, all his trips had involved blind searching. but it was simpler when he had a specific destination. His hike was shorter; he could sleep in the mine so he didn't need to haul as much gear, and he could even hike out after sunset. Smidgeon would pick him up around midnight and he'd stay the night. It didn't take long before he found his attention diverted between those piercing brown eyes and that dusty hole in the ground. It turned out Smidgeon had a plan.

One weekend she parked on the way to the culvert, "just to talk," she said.

"Why don't you move out here, Sam?" Her voice was shaky as she blurted out those words. "I mean, you can't keep making ten hour trips to just spend one or two nights in a hole in the ground like you've been doing for the past several months. I love you, Sam, and I want you here all the time. I've got the room and Lordy, I could sure use your help at the cafe. I think it is time you just moved here."

"I love you too," he said. It was the first time he had said it out loud and her eyes beamed back at him. In truth, she had beat him to the punch. He had considered broaching this same subject with her. On his long drives back to Austin, he often mimed out scenarios and he had played out this same general scenario numerous times but he was always afraid she'd say no.

A rush of thoughts and emotions flooded his mind. He was making more frequent but shorter trips than in the earlier forays and they had become a real grind. He realized in that moment, the best thing about his most recent trips was *her* and he decided not to go out to the mine at all.

"You know what? Let's just turn around," he said.

She was a little shocked, but she smiled as she headed her sedan back home. It was the first time they had spent the entire weekend together.

On Monday he left Van Horn with the big issue still unresolved, but he thought about it all the way back to Austin and when he got to his apartment, Sam knew it was the best thing for them both. He usually called her to tell her he had arrived safe and sound back in Austin, but when he called her this time, he told her he would move to Van Horn.

"If you still want me to," he stammered.

He could hear the background clatter of the café as there was a long pause on the phone.

"Of course I do," she said and he could almost see her smile on the receiver.

Then he spluttered, "Do you want to get married?"

It wasn't as much a proposal as it was a question. He knew Smidgeon had been married a couple of times before and wasn't sure about how far she wanted to take things.

"Let's just ease into this for a while," she said. "People will talk but, you know what? They'll just move on to other subjects. They're sort of used to seeing us together already anyway."

He began reviewing his belongings and his finances and decided he had nothing much keeping him in Austin except for his job, and it was no lifelong career, it was just a job. The worst part was leaving his three best friends: Godson, Moll, and Sally. All three knew about the mine and had stood by him through thick and thin for years.

Moll was home alone when he told her about his plans.

"Seriously, Sam?"

She blinked back at him as her blue eyes brimmed with tears.

"I don't think I want you to go," she said as she gave him a tight hug. Then she added, "But I guess I've been expecting this. I haven't met Smidgeon, but from the way you talk about her, I'm surprised you've waited this long." After a pause and a sadness-tinged sigh she said, "You are happier now than I've seen you in a long time. At least it will be a relief you aren't making all those long trips. It's just a matter of time before a big rig runs over you. Something like that would change all our lives forever in ways I can't even imagine."

Sally took the news a little better, but expressed similar thoughts. "I don't know what I'll do if you leave. I mean, we've spent all these years working together and we've developed a real rhythm. I guess I'll just have to train somebody new. At least you'll be off the road. You'll never know how much I've worried since you started going out there so often."

Godson took things a little more pragmatically.

"I figured you'd do this. A woman, a job, and a gold mine...of course you're leaving. Who wouldn't? Don't worry, I'll be out to visit before too long," he said. "But you better take me out and show me this thing when I do." They shook hands and hugged and he agreed to the condition. He figured Godson would be good for another load of wood.

So Sam quit his job and moved out west. He had twice moved across Texas and both times the moves involved a bit of culture shock. This time, occupied as he was with Smidgeon, the café, and the mine, it was different. His found life was full.

"Sam!"

Chuy had broken him out of his daydream.

"Oh, man, I was in the zone," Sam said, looking up from his work. Chuy was holding a plate and a cup of coffee.

"I figured you needed some breakfast, so I made you a breakfast taco."

Sam dried his hands and grabbed the plate. He was starving so he immediately took a bite of the taco.

"Potato, egg, and bacon!" he managed to say with his mouth full.

"Your favorite, right?"

Sam nodded, still chewing and Chuy handed him the cup of coffee and smiled broadly, showing off his gold tooth.

Chuy's name was actually *Jesus* but Chuy was a common nickname for Jesus.

Sam took a quick sip of coffee, then put the cup down and gobbled the rest of the taco. "I was hungry," he said.

"Want another one?"

"Naw, I better finish up these dishes and get back out front."

The morning rush had dwindled a bit and after Sam had cleared a couple of tables, he and Smidgeon met in the small hall by the restrooms where they found enough privacy to hug and talk.

"I missed you, baby," she said.

"I missed you, too."

"Everything okay out there?"

Sam hesitated momentarily, thinking of a way to avoid directly mentioning the cave-in. "I got in a little farther but...well, I need to pack in more wood," he said, "I worry about shoring the thing up. I mean, I've got the front part in pretty good shape but I need to keep stabilizing the next section. It's slow work."

"Yeah, I worry about you when you're out there. What if you get stuck in there, like a cave in?"

"Loot said the same thing this morning," Sam said with his best poker face.

He had been working with Loot for two years, but he could still see Smidgeon bristle slightly whenever the name was mentioned. The crusty trapper had proven to be a good friend to Sam and had even come and helped Sam make some repairs to Smidgeon's house, but of course she was always at the café whenever that sort of thing was going on.

"Like how?" she asked.

"He said I should get some walkie-talkies."

"Hmmmm, do you think that would work?" She was taking it better than he had imagined. The café did okay but financially they always seemed to be struggling. Sam basically worked for free and he knew she suffered through his frequent absences.

"Well, cheap kid ones probably wouldn't work. I'd have to get really good ones, need something with some range. And even then, they might not work when I'm down in the hole."

"Well, I like the idea, Sam. If you got stuck, there's no way for anybody to know."

"Just can't tell for sure without trying, I guess," he said, but a van full of tourists came filing into the café like a mini parade.

"Oops, better get back to work," she said. "We'll talk more about this later, okay?" She gave him a peck on the cheek and went to greet the newcomers while he retreated to the back to kitchen area to wash more dishes. Chuy had left a plate with another taco on the shelf above the sink. He wolfed it down before he dipped back into the dishwater.

After he finished with the dishes, he spent the rest of the morning working in front, ringing up customers, clearing tables, and refilling coffee. There was always something to do in a restaurant. About nine-thirty the place was almost empty and Smidgeon came over to him as he cleared the last table.

"Whew, busy morning, but at least we've made some money today. You want some breakfast? You must be starving."

"Well, Chuy made me a couple of breakfast tacos."

"Oh, eating up the profits behind my back," she laughed.

Smidgeon had an infectious smile and when she laughed she brightened up the room. Her long dark hair framed her face, but there always seemed to be a strand or two that escaped her tie-band. He reached out and smoothed one back in place.

"I guess I could stand another taco and a cup of coffee," he said.

"I'll fix us up something," she said as she turned to the kitchen, her long ponytail making a graceful arc in her wake.

Sam always loved to watch her walk through the café. In the early days it was one of the first things he had noticed about her as she gracefully navigated her way through the chairs and tables, almost as if she were floating a half inch off the ground. He filled a couple of cups with coffee and grabbed a table near the coffee station. It would allow either of them to jump up and help any customers who might come in.

Just as Sam sat down, Smidgeon returned with two plates.

"*Chorizo con Huevos*," she said.

Sam smiled. The chorizo had been one of his first contributions to the restaurant. Smidgeon had been buying premade chorizo but he suggested they make it fresh. He worked to fine tune the recipe over the course of a week. It wasn't a difficult recipe, but it took a little experimentation to get the balance of spices and ingredients just right, especially the amount of vinegar. Good chorizo always has a bit of vinegar, adding an acid tone to the blend of spices. Smidgeon had been an immediate convert to his final version and it was a good seller.

As she took her first bite she reminded him, "I never much liked chorizo. I had it on the menu because people expected it, but I've got to say, after you came here and came up with *this* I pretty much crave it."

Sam smiled and looked down, almost embarrassed by the compliment.

"I was happy I could make a contribution,"

She reached under the table and rubbed his leg suggestively and he blushed. "Oh, you've made big contributions, honey."

He laughed, "Now don't be starting nothing..."

He stopped at the sound of a car door. One of the local deputies walked in.

"Clay, good to see you," Smidgeon said.

"Morning, Jo."

Sam still couldn't get used to some locals calling Smidgeon by her old nickname. Her daddy's name was Joe and people used to call her "Little Jo" because her middle name was Josephine.

She was already on her feet and walking toward the coffee station, "Coffee?"

Clay sat at the table with Sam. "Sure, just have a minute. Morning, Sam."

"What's up, Clay?" Sam asked. He detected the hint of something official in Clay's voice.

Smidgeon brought a steaming cup to Clay and sat down.

"Bad news, I'm afraid. Well, to some I guess," he nervously laughed. "Lucius MacGregg is dead."

"Really?" Smidgeon's expression was a combination of surprise and shock. "What happened?"

"He slammed that plane of his into the prairie outside Odessa last night. Was flying there on business."

"Oh, my. Nobody has said a word this morning."

"It hadn't been reported yet. Next of kin, you know? I just finished with the official notification. My least favorite part of the job. Not much left, I'm afraid. They were finally able to track down the ownership of the plane based on a piece of the engine they found. It was a bad crash."

"Oh, the poor family."

"Not many people around here cared much for the old cuss," Clay said, "but nobody deserves to die like that."

"I know," she said.

"Tim's on his way from Abilene to take over the ranch."

"Gosh, I haven't seen him in at least seven years," Smidgeon said, "since he went away to go to school."

"Who's Tim?" Sam asked.

"He's their son, Sam," she said.

"Oh." Inwardly, Sam felt a bit disconcerted. The mine was on a rugged and somewhat forgotten corner of their ranch and he hoped that any change in management wouldn't affect him.

Deputy Clay finished his coffee, "Well, I best be getting along."

"Thanks for stopping by, Clay," Smidgeon said. "If you see Mary, give her my condolences."

"I will, Jo. You two take care."

After the tourists left, the café quieted down for a while and they chatted a bit about the latest news as Sam swept and Smidgeon stocked sugar and salt.

"Interesting news about old man MacGregg, isn't it?"

Sam looked up from his sweeping. "I only know stories, well, except for my one experience with his hands."

"That pretty much tells the tale," she said. "He always ran the place with an iron fist. You know that's why Tim stayed away after school. He was sweet when he was a little boy, but he eventually became pretty much a jerk himself, but I guess he couldn't deal with the old man so he went away to college and afterwards just worked in Abilene."

"I have to wonder if this will have any influence on, well, you know." They both tried to never mention the 'm' word out loud.

"I doubt it. It's a big ranch," she smiled. "And Tim's not much of a rancher."

Three

Most evenings, Smidgeon went home and left Sam to run The Mossback. Breakfast and lunch were the busier services, but the dinner traffic was enough to justify staying open, at least until eight. For years Smidgeon had worked seven days a week, open to close, and when Sam started working there he insisted that she take a break. They also traded occasional weekend days when he wasn't scratching his way into the mountain. Van Horn was small and she was never far away, so if the café got busy, Sam would call and she'd come running.

Smidgeon spent her time at the house tidying up the place. They never seemed to be around long enough to actually create much of a mess but the arid climate made for a lot of dust, so she usually concerned herself with sweeping and vacuuming. She peeked into Sam's room while she worked.

"Lordy, that man," she said as she picked up his dusty trail pants and took them to the wash room at the back of the house.

She decided to take them outside so she could empty his pockets. Dirt always made its way into them while he crawled in and out of the tunnel. "I've told him to leave these in the washroom," she said, smiling as she added, "but I suppose he was just in a hurry to get to the café."

As she dusted the shelves and bookcases throughout the house, she reflected on the past two years. She remembered their early, flirty customer/waitress banter. Her friendly demeanor was one of the things that made her restaurant work, but in Sam's case it had evolved into more.

"I felt something the day I picked him up," she said out loud, almost daydreaming as she dusted. "I'd always kind of liked him," she said, "he was cute and funny, but he only came in every now and then. Out camping he said. When I found him on the side of the road I was stunned, then I got a little mad when he told me the real story." She paused in her dusting. "No one likes to be lied to," she murmured out loud.

But once she understood what he had been doing and he showed her a nugget, she realized it was just part of who he was. "I could see the reason," she said.

That particular trip had ended in a blur. Town gossip speculated about a trespasser discovered at the MacGregg place. Sam had arrived under the cover of darkness and he needed to leave the same way to avoid suspicion. She asked her friend Marcy if she could use a room at Doling's Motel. It was a questionable favor, but it pointed more toward something amorous than anything else. She knew Darcy could keep her mouth shut about the favor.

"And it wasn't the first time," she laughed, "if Marcy blabbed about every romantic liaison in her motel, well, she'd go out of business."

But this had been no romantic dalliance with Sam. He simply needed a place to rest and lay low until night. She had thought about taking him to her place but at that point she didn't really know him and she was worried someone might see them together. It was a small town and everybody in town knew her. It was not as if she cared if people knew she had a gentleman caller, but she assumed MacGregg's men were scavenging around and might have gotten wind of it. There was no telling what lengths old man MacGregg might go to if he thought he might have been duped. The back side of the motel provided cover and she got Sam out of sight quickly and safely.

She smiled as she remembered the kiss they shared before he left to go back to Austin. It had been an impulsive kiss on her part but Sam tenderly returned it and lovingly touched the side of her face. It was a spark for her, but as he headed away from her car in the dark toward Loot Melding's place, she felt the same worry and dread she still felt today whenever he traipsed across the desert scrub in the dark to crawl back to that hole.

Her feelings intensified when Sam called to say he had arrived safely back in Austin.

"Smidgeon? I'm back safe and sound," he had said.

When she heard his voice, she felt her heart race and she knew she was smitten.

She went back into his room and vacuumed up the trail dirt where his pants had been.

"I wish he'd take me out there some time... I want to see this thing," she mused.

She had asked a number of times, but Sam always insisted on going it alone. These days he went out frequently, but it depended on the weather and the moon. He said he needed some light for his night hikes. He usually hauled loads of whatever he needed out there: supplies, water, and wood. Stockpiling he called it.

"It's a long hike across open ground and it's dangerous," he told her. "There is always danger. One person can be inconspicuous, but two? Not as easy to avoid being seen. And the mine is...well, it is dangerous too. Maybe one day, when I get it more stable and can get it more organized. Right now there is barely room for one person."

Smidgeon sighed as she worked. "He's probably right. I'm not much of a hiker and anyway, I can't afford to close the café. But I still worry."

She knew there was a lot to worry about like snakes, coyotes, and cougars, and worst of all, MacGregg's ranch hands. The day she'd saved him she brought him some food at the motel after the breakfast crowd died down. Sam had his shirt off when he opened the door and his body was so bruised it looked like he was wearing camouflage.

At first, when he came to town he parked his car at Loot's place and she would take him out and drop him off so he could hike to the mine. Those early trips were awkward. They never had a chance to spend quality time together. He'd stayed at her place a couple of times when the weather had unexpectedly changed, but he slept on the couch and everything seemed superficial. Of course, she had to spend most of the day at the café, but he always did some little thing like mop the kitchen floor or clean the bathroom. He was a gentleman and it was something she really liked about him.

But the more she knew Sam, the more she knew she wanted to be with him. One weekend she surprised him by parking in a spot she knew, a place where they could be alone for a few minutes. That was where they began to probe the possibilities of a relationship.

"What's this?" he asked.

"Just a small detour, I guess. I want to talk for a few minutes."

"Sure," he said, fidgeting in the seat a little. She couldn't tell if he was uncomfortable being alone with her or was just anxious to be on his way.

"Sam, the next time you come out here, I want you to forget about the mine, just one time," she had told him.

"What?"

"I mean, how about maybe just coming out here to spend some time with me? Sam, I want to be with you. If you're going to keep going to the mine, that's fine, I get it, but...why don't you move out here?"

She remembered being afraid of making such a bold move, but she had given it a great deal of thought. She knew she had fallen in love with him, but so far he had been just like a shadow figure in her life, breezing in and out so fast they both had no way of actually learning more about one another. At the time she wasn't sure if he felt the same way because his focus was always on the darned mine.

"I mean, deep down I knew he cared, I just wanted more," she mused.

There had been a full moon that night and it illuminated the interior of the car. It was quiet as they looked at each other and Smidgeon was afraid she had possibly scared him away.

"I'm sorry," he said and her heart skipped a beat. "I...Smidgeon, uh, you know I'm an idiot. This stupid mine just messes with my head."

Her eyes were beginning to tear. She knew she had probably blown it but then he surprised her when he took her hand in his.

"Hey, I'm here right now. I don't have to go out there this trip. It can wait. I mean, if you want."

She flushed and her heart raced; she almost couldn't catch her breath and her voice wavered as she tried to stifle waves of emotion.

"Oh, Sam," she said.

They had embraced in the car, hugging each other tightly and then they kissed. They had kissed before, but this was different. It was a long, deep, very passionate kiss.

~ * ~

Smidgeon giggled, remembering them making out in her car like two high school kids.

Sam had stayed at Smidgeon's house that night. His car was safely tucked away at Loot's place so there was no worry of gossip. But the morning came too soon and although tired, she had to get up and go open the café. When she got home, she found Sam had vacuumed and dusted and straightened up and had dug into her freezer and found the makings of a steak dinner.

"You know, you're a pretty good cook," she had said as she sampled the steak.

"Bachelor cooking," he said. "I'm not very sophisticated, but show me a Texan who doesn't know their way around a good steak."

"Well, there isn't much problem getting good meat out here...this is ranch country and owning a restaurant, well, I have the pick of the litter."

They both laughed and after talking for hours in the quiet west Texas evening they spent another passionate night together.

~ * ~

She shivered as she remembered his soft warmth against her skin, and the way he gently caressed her until she almost whimpered.

~ * ~

"I...I think I'm falling in love with you, Sam," she had blurted out that evening.

"Really?"

She had nodded in the dim light of the still full moon and he said, "Well, you know what? I love you too."

As they cuddled and snuggled before sleep overcame them, she considered how happy she felt to have finally expressed her feelings to Sam and she was overjoyed he had responded in the same way.

He gently cupped one of her breasts as they spooned and said, "Good night, sweetie, guess you've got an early start."

"Yeah," she responded, but then she remembered something she had forgotten to tell him. "We're open early for breakfast but

I'm closing at nine-thirty. Big doings at church tomorrow...a sort of pot luck celebration. Go with me?"

~ * ~

Smidgeon continued dusting as she remembered that special day. Sundays were always a problem for her but she had staff she could trust so she usually left the cafe in capable hands for a couple of hours while she went to church. While she dusted, she glanced at the picture of her father on a nearby shelf and teared up. She picked up the picture.

"You never opened on Sunday did you, Dad?" she asked, touching his face on the picture. "But the economy was different then. I just can't afford to keep it closed. I need the breakfast and lunch crowd, and people, especially travelers, need a place to eat."

She dabbed at the area where the picture had been and then replaced it and continued dusting as she remembered their magical weekend.

~ * ~

A few eyebrows were raised when they walked into the sanctuary together. She still attended the local Roman Catholic church even though she was twice divorced, but she thought the raised eyebrows were more associated with his status as a stranger than her status as a divorcee with a man in tow. She had lived outside the church for a while after her first divorce and second marriage and this had distressed her parents. She couldn't take sacraments, but she could still pray, so she went back to appease them. She hadn't talked with Sam at all about religion before that day, but he calmly worked his way through the Mass and then cordially greeted her church friends and acquaintances. He engaged in conversations as if he had known them for years.

Later when they talked about the day, he explained his religious views to her.

"I was raised a Catholic."

"Really?"

"Yeah, Catholic school, catechism, Confirmation, the whole bit."

"But what happened?"

"I don't know, just sort of let it slip away. I was a bit surprised when I saw it was a Catholic church. I mean, I knew you were divorced and all."

"Yes, it's a problem, I know. I can't fully participate but...well, you know, it doesn't mean I can't be a part of the church family."

"I hadn't been to Mass in years...the last time was when I was visiting my mother in Houston. She sort of expects it still, even though she knows I've let it slide."

"I wonder sometimes if I should go ahead and have my previous marriages annulled so I can belong."

"Yeah, it sort of gets in the way. You know, I'm not a total heathen. I've gone to other services like Baptist, Episcopal, and Methodist. Methodists have an open Communion policy. I like that," he said.

"Really?"

"Yeah. Kinda like you don't have to be part of the secret club. But I don't know, I believe in God and all, but don't go anywhere regularly, I'm afraid."

"Shame on you, Sam."

"I know," he smiled, looking down.

"But you didn't take Communion today...why not?"

He laughed. "Guilt, I think. When I first took open Communion in a Methodist church I remember thinking maybe I was crossing a line. I got over it that time, but, well, here? I sort of had the same feeling, like I had crossed one line so far it was hard to go back over it. I was thinking I needed to go to Confession or something first. I guess all the strict Catholic training got to me."

They both laughed.

That evening she formalized her previous suggestion and asked him to come out and move in with her. She was sure of her feelings so it just seemed a natural thing to say.

"Not much for me to do for a living out here," he said.

"You could teach maybe...you have a degree."

"But no teaching certificate. I'd have to go back to school and that would mean Sul Ross or UT El Paso or something else I couldn't afford."

"You could help at The Mossback. I'd pay you," she said, adding with a laugh, "and there would be fringe benefits!"

Then she got serious and hugged him tightly. "I just don't want to lose you and, well, I worry about you on those long road trips. I really do. You exhaust yourself...how long before you fall asleep at the wheel or even worse, get crushed by a truck driver who is even more exhausted than you?"

"Yeah, don't think that isn't something I worry about. It's a tempting thought," he said.

"Look, I know you are obsessed with this mine thing. If you lived out here, you could work on it more often...it's something we could work out, you know?"

Sam looked out into space as he answered. "Like I said, it's tempting. Heck, I don't even want to go back right now," he added as he lifted her hand and kissed it. "But I've tried small town life once before and it was a disaster."

"Really? Where?"

"Northeast Texas. Mount Vernon. It was with another woman several years ago. She had moved there for her job. There wasn't much for me to do out there. I felt empty."

"But that was then...this is now. And you have a reason and a purpose for it." She hugged him again and kissed him on the cheek. "Plus me!"

"It's a big thing to consider," he said. "Let me think on it."

Early the next morning he packed his car and left and she remembered being depressed all day, barely going through the motions at work. She was really afraid she had scared Sam off and she had the added worry about him driving alone those six hundred and fifty miles back to Austin. About seven o'clock the café phone rang.

"Mossback," she said.

"Smidgeon? It's Sam."

"Hey, sweetie! You back home?"

"Yeah, safe and sound. Look, I need to tell you something… I couldn't think of anything else the entire trip. Let's do it, I mean, if you still want me."

A flush of blood rushed into her face and she almost dropped the phone but she managed to stammer, "Of course I do."

He even followed it up with a lame proposal, which she had side-stepped.

"Let's just ease in together for a while," she said. "People will talk but, you know, they are sort of used to seeing us together already anyway."

A customer came up to the register as she was talking.

"It will take me a little while to figure it all out, okay?" he said, "It is a long move, but I'm in."

Tears welled up in her eyes as she said, "Oh, Sam…hey, I have a customer, I'll call you later from home, but…well, I'm really happy."

The customer, a regular, noticed her tears and asked, "Everything okay, Jo?"

She blinked most of the tears away and brushed the rest with her hand. "Couldn't be better," she said.

~ * ~

Smidgeon found she had sprouted a new crop of tears as she finished her recollections and retired to the bathroom to freshen up before Sam came home.

Four

It was almost closing time at The Mossback when the door opened as Sam was clearing what he had hoped was the last table of the night. He didn't recognize the man, but unfamiliar faces were not uncommon in the evening, usually people passing through and staying the night in a local motel. The stranger sat at a table near the window.

He seemed nervous and worried when Sam brought him a menu.

"I don't need a menu," he said. "Just some coffee?"

"Sure," Sam answered. "Cream?"

"No, I take it black. I just got in from a long drive and don't know what to expect when I get home. I just needed a few minutes to collect my thoughts."

"Oh, you're a local?"

The stranger was about Sam's age, medium height and build, sandy brown hair with dark brown eyes. His face lacked the weathered texture evident with most ranchers.

"Yeah," he said, "but I've been away for quite a while. Don't get back much." He extended a hand. "Tim MacGregg," he said.

"Sam Milton." Sam noted the handshake was limp and unsatisfying.

"You're not a local; I'd know you from school or something."

"No, I haven't been here for very long. I've heard of you, though. Look, I'm sorry about your father."

"The old fool deserved what happened to him."

Sam was a bit taken aback by the comment. "Well, I can't say I ever met him, I just knew about him from local talk."

"All of it bad, I assume." Tim looked down at the table. "Can I get that coffee?"

"Oh, I'm sorry. Coming right up." Sam hurried off and returned with a steaming cup. "You're in luck... it's fairly fresh."

Tim took the cup. "Thanks," he said. "I'm surprised Jo isn't here."

"I usually work evenings during the week to give her a break," Sam said.

"So what brought you to Van Horn? You look like a city boy." Tim laughed.

Sam shrugged. "Love, I guess."

Tim MacGregg's face flashed with realization. "Wait, you and Jo? Are you kidding me?" He laughed out loud.

Sam was beginning to see the family resemblance. His face flushed. "Something funny?"

Tim looked up and realized he had struck a nerve. "No, well, geez...look, man, I'm sorry. She was just a bit of a wild filly back years ago."

"People change," Sam said, then added with a smirk, "Well, most people do. She does all right with this place."

"I'm sure she does. Look, I said I'm sorry." He extended a hand again and Sam shook it briefly, anxious to release the clammy lump of flesh. One thing he did not like was a weak handshake.

"So you're back for the funeral?"

"Yeah, and to take over the ranch. My mom can't run it, so I had to quit my job in Abilene. I used to hate that ranch, but I was thinking while I was driving, maybe it was him I hated. My dad and I didn't get along at all."

"Like I said, I never met the man, but me, well, I try not to speak ill of the dead."

Tim looked down at his coffee. "That will be tough for me. Might take some time."

Sam had an abiding interest in the fate of the ranch himself so he tried to remain aloof. "So you're not a rancher?"

"No," he said, "I've got a business degree. Was working at a bank in Abilene when I got the call. My mom asked me to take the ranch over for her so I quit my job. As soon as all this funeral stuff is finished, I'll have to take a look at the whole operation. I never much liked some of the people my dad usually hired so maybe there will be changes. I've already called an old college buddy of mine who majored in Animal Science to see if he'd like to take over as foreman. Hoping he'll take the offer." Tim looked pensively out the window and laughed under his breath. "If he comes, he's sure to shake things up around here. It's funny, you know? He always wanted to come down here to check it out, but, well, I guess I didn't want to inflict my dad on anybody I knew."

Tim sighed loudly.

"I do need to talk these changes over with my mom, but she pretty much kept in the old man's shadow all these years. She's a good woman but he was overbearing, so she just learned to keep her place. It's probably why she asked me to come back. I guess she's more comfortable with a man running things."

Sam listened intently and the café wasn't busy so he had the time. "Well, I hope it all works out for you. I'm not from around here but from what I see, ranching is ranching...a combination of business and just plain old hard work."

"Things like streamlining and diversification are what I'm talking about. Saving money and increasing the profit. My dad made more money than he ever admitted to but he wasted it. Like the plane. You know what he was doing? Flying to meet up with some girlfriend. Cheating on my mom. That's why he bought the damned plane and learned to fly. Oh, he scouted lost cattle with it and made a few business trips, but most of his 'business' was with *her*."

Tim looked up at Sam. "I want to change things," he said.

Sam put a hand on Tim's shoulder, "Well, I know you have mixed feelings about things, but like my grandmother always said, it is best to take care of first things first. I'm sorry for your loss."

"You sound educated. Where are you from? You didn't say."

"Houston, originally," Sam said. "But I lived in Austin for a while before coming here."

"You left *Austin* for this dump?"

"Austin was okay, but I wanted a slower place."

"Geez, but Van Horn? It's not just slower, it's almost crawling backwards. You must have it bad for Jo. I mean, working in this broken down place must be a real let down for a city boy. So you went to college?"

"University of Houston, liberal arts degree."

"I went to ACU, Abilene Christian," Tim said.

"So you have stayed pretty much in Abilene."

"Right, just far enough away to live my life, close enough to visit my mom from time to time," Tim said as he swigged the last of his coffee. "Well, Sam, I guess I had better head out to comfort my mom."

"I've never met her, how is she doing?"

"She seems to be doing okay so far. Dad's infidelity had taken its toll on their marriage but she had stuck it out because, well, that's what people from her generation do. I mean, he never beat her or anything. She liked the ranch and he kept her pretty comfortable. Still, pretty much everyone is glad he's gone. This is just a ritual we all have to get through to get on with business, you know? The crash was so bad there isn't really too much to bury anyway. "

Sam gave a half nod.

"I'll be interested in talking to you some more, Sam," Tim said, "it will be a relief to have somebody more educated and sophisticated to talk to. Who knows, it might make life out here more bearable."

"Oh, and your buddy, the new foreman, don't forget about him."

Tim laughed. "Yeah, but if he comes, he'll be...well, he's different, you know? Black guy. Like I said, he always wanted to come out here to see the place, but earlier I kind of side-stepped the real reason I never brought him here. Seriously, my dad would never have allowed him in the house, but, you know... I thought about doing it anyway it a couple of times, you know, out of spite, just to tick the old man off," Tim chuckled at his own private joke, "then I decided there are some lines you just don't cross, not with the old man at least. Hell, I heard he had a trespasser killed just a couple of years ago. I believe it. He was *that* mean."

Sam raised an eyebrow at this statement, as Tim continued, "It's too bad. Lance took school a lot more seriously than I did, very polite and smart. He was an athlete until he got hurt but he kept up at school and toughed it out. We didn't really hang together, especially after graduating, but we'd see each other in town from time to time. With all this going on, I figured, what the hell, maybe he'd be a good fit. I prefer somebody I at least know to help run the place. He knows ranching a heck of a lot better than me." Tim laughed before repeating, "And he's sure to shake things up."

Tim stuck out his hand again and Sam felt as if he were shaking a cold fish.

"Bye, Sam."

"Yeah, so long, Tim. Once again, please accept my condolences."

Tim nodded and headed out the door. Sam looked up at the clock and could see it was closing time. Manny, the relief cook came out of the kitchen.

"So, *that one* has come back."

"That one?" Sam asked.

"Tim," Manny said. "I listened from the door. Saying such bad things about his father. I mean, we know, *Señor* MacGregg was a bad man but, well, he's dead now. I was raised to never speak of the dead in such a way, Mr. Sam."

"I know, Manny. I was raised the same way."

"And I tell you this, Mr. Sam. Bringing a new foreman could cause trouble."

"You think?"

"You wait and see. A black man? Crazy stuff."

After the closing duties were complete, Sam and Manny went their separate ways. On the short drive home, Sam wondered what impact the new management at the ranch would have on his own association with the MacGregg place.

Smidgeon waved at him from the door as he drove up. It was a rare treat for Sam because he thought she looked particularly attractive in the dim porchlight, the shadows adding a sultry, sexy look he really liked.

"Hey, sweetie," she said as he came up on the porch.

Sam embraced her and they shared a brief kiss. "You seem chipper tonight."

Smidgeon laughed and her eyes sparkled. "I don't know why, but yes, I'm feeling really happy tonight and I'm glad you're home. I fixed us some dinner, so come on in and let's eat. You better not have let Manny fix you anything."

"No, no, no, I'm starved. Let's eat!"

Sam went in and Smidgeon immediately switched off the overhead light and he could see the glow of candlelight in the small dining area. A familiar aroma wafted in from the kitchen. Smidgeon gently directed Sam to his usual chair and said, "Sit yourself down and relax. Was it busy tonight?"

"Not at all. Minor rush around six, so I think we made some money but business died down and we managed to get a head start on cleaning the place."

Smidgeon emerged from the kitchen carrying a large dish. "Here, Sam, I made that chicken casserole you like."

"The one with the mayonnaise and potato chips?"

"Yes." She smiled broadly as she set the dish down. "It just seems so wrong, yet I really like it too. It works."

"I know. It was an old recipe I got out of the Houston newspaper years ago. I love it."

She retrieved a salad bowl from the kitchen then sat down. Smidgeon bowed her head and said the Catholic grace like she always did, and Sam softly joined her.

As they ate Sam spoke up, "Oh, just before closing Tim MacGregg came in."

Smidgeon had just started chewing a mouthful of casserole and she abruptly stopped and a mild wave of shock and surprise swept across her face. Then she hurriedly chewed and swallowed before saying, "Tim MacGregg? What did he want?"

"Coffee," Sam chuckled.

"No, silly. Did he say anything?"

"I think he was looking for a psychiatrist. He said he hated his father and didn't have much of a relationship with his mother, yet he dropped everything from his life in Abilene to come here to take over the ranch."

"Not a big shock there. Old man MacGregg never much got along with anybody. It was no secret Tim couldn't wait to get away and he has pretty much stayed away. But there's money in the ranch, so I'm not surprised he came back."

"He seemed interested in the fact that a city boy like me would want to stay out here with a country-fried girl like you. He actually laughed when I told him about us."

"He's a jerk. At one point he chased after me. He pretty much ran through as many girls as he could when he was here. Football team star and all of that, and once he had run through all of the girls his age, he started looking around in other places. I had a sketchy reputation for a few years and although he was younger than me, I think he thought he'd make me another notch on his belt. Sure, I had my flings, but I knew I didn't want to have anything to do with the likes of him. Didn't stop him trying, though. I thought maybe a few years out in the real world might have mellowed him."

"I'd say...all in all...he is probably still a jerk. I didn't know him back then, but now he's probably got more sophistication in his jerkiness. It's just a guess, but I figure once he settles down and gets back to business, I'm sure people will realize the apple didn't fall far from the tree."

Smidgeon giggled as she munched the last of her dinner. "Oh, I know people here, they probably already know."

She got up and rubbed Sam's shoulders for a few seconds then bent down and nibbled his ear and whispered, "What say we turn in early tonight?"

"What has gotten into you?" Sam mumbled with the last of the casserole in his mouth.

She giggled, "I, well, I've just been reminiscing about how we first got together and, well, you know, it makes me all butterflies and roses inside."

Five

The miles drifted past as Lance pushed the battered Chevy truck down the interstate, the wind buffeting through the windows. He shook his head to clear a bout of momentary deafness.

"The road noise does tend to get a might tiresome after a few hours," he said.

"Rowl."

He looked down at the mottled furry figure on the floorboard in front of the passenger seat. "Hold on, girl, we'll be stopping soon."

The dog was bigger than average and she looked at him with her soulful dog eyes and put her head back down on a piece of rolled up towel.

"Coming up on Monahans," he said as he passed a road sign.

Soon, the exit loomed and Lance pulled off. He instinctively glanced at the gas gauge but realized his mistake and then looked at the odometer. The gas gauge had been broken for years and he had to estimate his fuel needs by mileage. He patted the dashboard.

"Best not to push her too far," he said, then adding as he squinted down at the dog, "don't want to push you too far either, do I, girl?"

He found a place for gas with a vacant lot next door so he could run the dog for a few minutes. He stopped at the side of the parking lot and said, "C'mon, Prewash!"

He opened the door and the dog blinked, almost in disbelief, then stirred. Lance patiently waited while she dutifully dragged herself out of the truck and onto terra firma and stretched her hind legs as she made a few tentative steps forward with her front legs. Lance had a small plastic bag and followed the dog as he looked around warily. He was well aware of what a lone black man could expect anywhere, especially in west Texas.

As if on cue, a patrol car soon pulled up next to his truck.

Lance thought inwardly, "Here we go." He looked down and tried not to shake his head in disgust but he silently sighed.

"Prewash! Finish up your business, girl! We got to be on our way."

He walked over to where she was squatting and waited patiently, watching the police car out of the corner of his eye. He knew the cop was probably checking his plates. When she was finished, Lance gingerly draped the bag over her droppings. It probably wasn't necessary out there, but he had long ago learned to anticipate any unwelcome attention.

"C'mon, girl," he said and waved his arm and she obediently headed back to the truck. In the back of his mind he intoned his favorite prayer, "Lord, give me patience and help me to be the kind of person my dog thinks I am."

The officer had exited the patrol car and was standing next to the weathered truck as he watched them approach. Lance could see he was a typical paunchy, small town, good-old-boy cop, probably bored to tears. Finding a verified black man out running an untethered canine was no doubt the highlight of his week. "Might even make the local paper," Lance thought to himself.

"Morning," the cop said. "Glad you seen fit to pick up after your dog. Ain't many, uh, *tourists*, who do that around here."

Lance played along and laughed. It was a practiced routine, playing a game he didn't want to play, but deep down he had been raised to know he had to.

"The place where I lived in Abilene was picky about such stuff, Officer. I guess I got the habit."

"Just passing through?"

"Yes, sir. Need some gas and she needed to, uh, stretch her legs as you saw."

"So you're from Abilene?"

Lance nodded as the cop eyed the household items sticking out from under the tarp in the back of his truck. "You said 'lived'...where you headed?"

"Oh, got me a job in Van Horn."

"Van Horn? What kinda job you got in Van Horn?"

"Foreman at the MacGregg Ranch."

"The MacGregg place," the deputy raised his eyebrows. "I hear'ed the old man got hisself killed just up the road from here. How'd you come by *that* job?"

"Went to school with the son. He got a business degree but I got a degree in Animal Science. My granddaddy worked ranches out here when he was younger. Moved to Houston later and, well, after growing up hearing all his stories, I always kinda hankered to learn the life he had lived."

"You got an ID? I already checked yer plates...just want to see if everything matches up. Just routine, you understand."

Lance fully understood the nature of this routine and although he was disgusted, he mustered up the courage to be nice about it. "Name's Lance Norton," he said as he pulled out his wallet and extracted his license.

The officer went back to his car and talked on his radio and waited a few minutes. Lance took the opportunity to get the dog's bowl from the truck and poured her some water. After a quick drink, Prewash sauntered around the patrol car sniffing for a minute then nosed around the scrub in the empty lot. "Don't be going too far, girl," he said.

Presently the officer returned and handed him the license. "Everything looks good. You can get your gas and be on your way. You be careful out there in Van Horn," the officer said, ending with an almost imperceptible pause.

Lance could tell the officer had managed to stifle the 'boy' that used to be hung onto the end of such sentences. An older cop would have probably still let it slip but this younger breed of police officer had learned to exercise a little more finesse.

"I will, Officer. I'm more on the business end of ranching, but I'm not afraid to get my hands dirty. I *worked* my way through school. C'mon, Prewash!"

"Interesting name."

"It's been her main job since she was a pup. Disgustin', I know but ain't no way I can stop her from wantin' to lick plates and bowls now. I just washes them extra clean." Lance smiled...he was playing it up for the cop.

The officer shook his head laughing and after the cruiser drove away, Lance sighed. He paid for his gas and pumped it and was soon back on the road, the wind drowning out every sound again.

"Van Horn will probably be worse," he told the dog. "Tim told me there are almost no blacks, and even whites are a minority." Then he screamed out the window against the wind noise, "But I bet they don't *feel* like no minority," and laughed his way down the road.

He drove his truck a little below the speed limit so it took him about two more hours to get to Van Horn, not long after Interstate twenty connected with ten. Lance had directions to the ranch, but he was hungry and he knew the dog was hungry too.

As he drove through town he looked for a place where he could get something to go, maybe a burger for him and one for the dog. He spied a local joint and laughed as he read the sign out loud.

"Mossback! Good name for a place out here in boondock west Texas." He looked down at the dog, who had raised her head when he laughed, and explained, "Prewash, a Mossback is an old wild cow or bull, like they used to have all over out here in the olden days. Also, my granddaddy would say the same thing about any cantankerous old fool that crossed his path. Either meaning probably fits this place," he said as he stopped and let a fine cloud of dust settle around the truck.

His old truck seemed to fit right in with the array of different vehicles in the parking lot. He offered Prewash a splash of water in her bowl but she seemed content to wait for something more substantial. It wasn't a hot day and the windows were down so he figured she'd be fine. The door to The Mossback creaked ominously when he went in.

Everything seemed to momentarily stop as he entered. He had learned to pretty much expect this reaction every time he walked into a place like this, but it was still a bit of a shock every time it happened. All eyes were on him and the din of conversation paused. The only person still moving was a guy clearing a table, who glanced up but hadn't missed a beat in his work. The moment passed and the background clatter of the café returned to normal.

The guy busing the table seemed to be the only person working. Presently he carried his bin of dirty dishes and dropped it on a counter near the kitchen door and came over to Lance.

"Can I help you?" Lance thought he could almost detect the hint of a familiar accent. He figured the guy was probably not a local and not quite as impressed at seeing a lone black man as the others had been.

"Yeah, I was hoping I could get like a couple of burgers to go. Oh, and some information."

"Okay," the guy said. He had a nametag haphazardly pinned to his apron that said 'Sam' and he pulled out a pad and pen and wrote down the order. "How you want them?"

"One all the way, with mustard. One just meat and bun."

"Cheese?"

"Naw, just burgers. Maybe some fries with one of them."

"Okay, you want to pay now? Good idea since from my experience once your order is ready the register is usually stacked with people paying and your food gets cold."

Lance laughed. "Okay, sure."

Sam rang up the ticket and completed the transaction, then took the order back through the kitchen door. Almost immediately, a pretty woman with a long dark ponytail came out with Sam trailing. She had a nice smile and shining eyes that seemed to reflect her smile as well.

"Sam said you wanted some information? I probably know pretty much anything you might want to know, at least concerning the area."

"Looking to get to the MacGregg place."

There was another momentary dip in the background chatter when he said this. The guy, who he assumed was Sam, had already resumed his work but even he seemed to hesitate at the word.

"You got business up there?"

"Here for a job," Lance said.

Sam spoke up, "Oh, you're Tim's college buddy?"

Lance answered, "Yeah. You know about me?"

Sam chuckled, "He said he was bringing in an old college friend to shake things up. I'm Sam Milton. This is Smidgeon Toll, this is her place. "

Lance returned the laugh. "Shake things up, huh? I reckon I can see that, but mostly I just aim to be his foreman, keep the ranch on a paying basis. He got the business degree, but me, I got the degree in Animal Science. I'm Lance Norton," he said, extending his hand, first to Smidgeon, then to Sam.

"Pleased to meet you, Lance," Smidgeon said.

"Yeah, be nice to have someone new in town...it'll take some of the pressure off me," Sam joked.

Lance looked up as a short Hispanic man emerged from the kitchen with a bag and handed it to Smidgeon.

"He's already paid," Sam said.

"Oh, I didn't tell you how to get to the MacGregg place," she said as she pulled out her pad and proceeded to sketch out a few landmarks and roads on the back of one of the order blanks.

"Too bad you can't sit down and relax a few minutes," she said as she finished her note.

"Well, I got my dog in the truck...the plain burger is for her. And they're expecting me so I had better be on my way. Just starving so I thought I'd scarf this down. Hate to arrive too hungry and, well, the dog, she's hungry all the time anyway. Thanks for the hospitality. I guess I'll see ya'll."

Back at the truck, Lance unwrapped the plain burger for Prewash and saw Sam walk out with a bag of garbage. After taking it around the side of the building, he returned and approached Lance, who was already half finished with his burger and fries. The dog's burger was long gone.

Sam smiled as he said, "You know, there aren't a lot of blacks here."

"No, I reckon not," Lance answered. "Is that a problem?"

"I doubt it. But some people will probably be uncomfortable for a while. I still get the same thing, I mean, not like you will by a long shot, but people here are slow to accept strangers. Came here from Houston by way of Austin. Even though they see a lot of tourists passing through, they are wary of new people."

Lance's eyes widened. "Houston?"

"Yeah."

"I'm from Houston too."

They both laughed.

"Look, most weeknights I'm here alone and after seven it isn't usually busy. Come for dinner some night and we can talk, you know, reminisce about the old country."

"Old country," Lance chuckled, "I like that. Okay, Sam, it's a deal," and Lance extended his hand again and they shook on it.

Lance gobbled the last bite of burger and started the truck.

"Best be on my way," he said.

"You think you got a cold reception here," Sam smiled, "wait until you get to the ranch."

"I know that's right," Lance said. "Time to go face the music, I guess."

Sam waved as the truck headed on down the road.

Six

The phone rang, interrupting the lunch rush at The Mossback. It wasn't unusual, usually somebody in a hurry wanted to place an order.

Smidgeon answered it, then flagged down Sam, who was busing a table.

"Sam, it's your friend Moll."

With the restaurant so busy it was definitely not a good time for a personal call and she managed a disapproving frown as he took the phone.

"Moll? What's up? This isn't a good time."

"Godson's been in an accident."

"What? In Austin?"

"No, they said near Sonora. He was coming out there... wanted to surprise you. I don't know anything else. Sam, I really need you... I'm heading out there right now...can you meet me?"

"Of course, Moll. You said he was coming here?"

"Well, he was going to El Paso. His sister just had a baby, but he was going to swing by and see you on the way. Sam, it doesn't sound good. Can you leave right away?"

"I'll get there just as soon as I can," Sam said. "Moll, you're upset. You should get somebody to drive you."

"There's nobody, at least not on such short notice, Sam. Look, I've got to go. He's in the local hospital there. I'll see you when you get there."

"Sure. I need a few minutes to get ready and it's a least five hour drive for me. It's a little more than halfway, so I think you'll probably beat me there. Be careful, please? I'll get there as quick as I can."

"I will. You be careful too. Thank you, Sam. See you soon."

Smidgeon had just taken an order into the kitchen and had noticed the wave of gloom sweep across Sam's face as he talked on the phone.

"What is it, Sam? You look like your favorite dog just died."

"Close," he said, "Godson was in an accident. Moll wants me to meet her in Sonora."

"Sonora? What in heaven's name was he doing in Sonora?"

"He was heading to El Paso to see his sister ...she just had a baby. Smidgeon, she said it doesn't look good."

Smidgeon wedged her order pad into an apron pocket and hugged Sam tight, then backed off with her hands still on his shoulders.

"You think he's going to be okay?"

"She really didn't know much else, but I have a bad feeling about this, Sweetie. She was pretty upset...I've got to go see what I can do. We've all been through a lot together and they're two of my best friends. "

"I'm so sorry, honey. Sam, we'll manage okay. You go on and do what you need to do. I'll get a ride back to the house," she said. "Your car okay to drive or do you want to take mine?"

"Oh, the Clunker will make it," he said. "It already knows the way."

"Grab some cash out of my butter and egg money, okay? Just let me know what's going on."

The stray strand of hair that always seemed to loosen from Smidgeon's ponytail extended down her face and as she looked at him she tried to blow it away. Sam appreciated the look of concern in her eyes and he hugged her and kissed her right in the middle of the dining room.

A few catcalls ensued from the customers and Smidgeon blushed a little before saying, "You get going, we'll be okay here." A tear rolled down from her eye as she pecked at his cheek one more time.

Back at the house, Sam packed a few clothes and toiletries and grabbed some money from Smidgeon's stash of what she called her butter and egg money. He took more than he thought he'd need, knowing he would return any he didn't use. As he headed out the door, he stopped and went back to his dresser and rummaged around behind his socks and underwear until he found the small, battered jewelry case. He opened it and looked at the small cross-shaped rock inside.

"Just in case," he muttered.

He hadn't driven The Clunker in a couple of weeks and hesitated as he reached to turn the key, but the dusty old Volkswagen started right up. He let the engine idle for a minute while checking his maintenance log.

"Looks good," he whispered to himself. "I couldn't remember where I was on oil changes."

He glanced at the house as if to take a mental picture of it, then put the car in gear and puttered down the road. He was soon on the Interstate heading east. Sam instinctively checked his watch as he began the long drive; it was one o'clock.

"That will put me in Sonora around six or so," he said to himself.

He thought about Godson as he drove and felt guilty he hadn't talked to his friend in several months. He and Godson and Moll had been friends for years, ever since college. As he drove he remembered their stint working at Trotsky's, the dingy college bar where he and Godson had first met Moll.

"Those were fun times," he mused, "until somebody burned it down."

They celebrated the anniversary of the fire every December twenty-third, Christmas Eve-Eve they called it.

"It was the last time I called," he said. "Months ago...some friend I am!"

He had spent the last two Christmas seasons in Van Horn with Smidgeon. She didn't understand the whole Christmas Eve-Eve thing and it just seemed too far to make the holiday trip, even to see his family in Houston.

Smidgeon had grown to depend on his help and the café was just barely getting by. She tolerated his trips to the mine but taking extra time for the holiday seemed too much to ask. Besides, he found he liked the low-key, quiet Christmas time they managed to share.

Sam smiled as he thought about Smidgeon's effect on his life. They got along well together and their few moments of relaxation were tender and loving. They talked about closing the café for a vacation, but it was just talk. Things were just too close to the edge to even consider it.

His reflections about the holidays spurred another conversation with himself.

"If I go to Austin, I had better make the side trip to Houston too, to see the folks," he mused. He felt guilty because he had not seen his family in such a long time.

"Just can't seem to work it in,"

Of course it wasn't just because of The Mossback. The real reason there wasn't any extra time because any spare moments he managed to extract ended up being spent on the mine. He was no longer limited to just the spring and fall like he used to be. Now he hiked out there all year, whenever the weather was even moderately acceptable. Shorter trips were used to stockpile equipment and supplies. Longer trips involved digging, as he tried to make his way farther into the shaft. It was slow work.

"Two years!" He slammed his hand on the steering wheel. "But at least the entrance and the anteroom are stable," he said. "I spent most of my time on those two things."

It was frustrating, but every time he seemed to make a little progress, more rocks would fall. His thoughts flashed to the recent conversation with Loot about walkie-talkies and he shook his head.

"I don't think anything I buy could get through the rock and down to the highway. Besides, nobody else knows exactly where the mine is, so what good would it do?" he said.

Loot had a general idea, but Smidgeon only knew the spot on the highway where the rendezvous occurred, and the fact that it was 'out there' from that point. Diablo Rim was long and meandering.

In Fort Stockton, Sam decided to top off his tank at one of his usual haunts. These regular stops served as landmarks on his trips, and allowed him to rest for a few moments and stretch his legs. It was good for the car too, allowing the engine cool off a little. It was all part of his well-practiced routine of long drives across Texas. He got some coffee then checked his oil ... it had been a while but he fell right back into the old habits as if it had only been a few months. As he sipped his coffee in the parking lot, his thoughts turned to an incident at this same store.

"The talisman," he mused as he remembered the strange warmth and power emanating from the old Hispanic witch-woman's hands as she gazed down into his soul with her milky eyes. She and her family had sent him on his way with the cross-shaped rock in his hand along with a battered scraper they had foisted upon him as part of the deal.

"Heck, I ended up *needing* that scraper too," he said as he recalled the ice storm waiting for him just beyond the horizon.

When Sam got back on the highway, his thoughts turned toward his friends and the accident. When he first met Moll he had been quite attracted to her inner strength and sense of purpose. She was an awesome woman...pretty, friendly, personable, totally in charge of a bar called Trotsky's. He'd been too shy back then to ask her out or make any kind of move. It didn't matter in the end because before too long she and Godson had hit it off. He chuckled as he remembered.

"Hah, I brought Godson to Trotsky's in the first place!"

Now, with Godson hurt, Sam worried about her state of mind. He knew tragedy provided a severe test to a person and it didn't matter how strong someone was internally, a catastrophe involving a loved one just might break them. She obviously knew this too, which is why she wanted him there. Sam tried to avoid thinking beyond the possibility of his friend being severely injured, but he became increasingly anxious as the miles blurred past his window. He kept The Clunker to the speed limit but as he got closer he let his speed creep up a bit. When the Sonora exit came into view he gulped slightly. His heart raced as he exited the highway and turned toward the center of town.

As he navigated the streets, he realized he had no memory of ever driving through the town. For Sam, Sonora was one of those landmarks along the highway, a place he had passed countless times, always on the way to someplace else.

"Just another gas stop," he mumbled as he looked around. Then he remembered he had visited the famous local caverns once.

"But that was basically just a side-stop too."

He paused at a store to inquire about the location of the hospital, then headed there where he felt a wave of apprehension followed by relief when he recognized Moll's car in a parking space.

She was sitting on a bench just inside and looked up as soon as he opened the door. The moment their eyes met he knew he was too late.

"Oh, Sam," she said.

He took her in his arms and as she buried her face into his shoulder he realized she had been crying for quite a while because his shirt was instantly wet. They stood there for several minutes, Moll sobbing softly and Sam holding her tightly. He deferred his own feelings and concentrated on trying to give her what comfort he could.

Finally she released her hold on him and looked at him with swollen, glistening blue eyes.

"I'm so glad you're here."

"Sorry it took so long."

"Sam, this is a long way from anywhere. They told me right when I walked in the door. I've just been numb."

"I am too, Moll. I am too."

"Why, Sam? Why?"

"I don't know. How can anyone know?"

They sat on the bench in the quiet waiting area for a long time, their hands entwined, not saying anything.

Finally a deputy came by to speak with Moll.

"You the wife?" he asked. To Sam the question seemed a bit coarse, but then he reconsidered. There really wasn't any other way to deal with this type of tragic business.

"Yes," Moll answered and she followed him a few steps away where they whispered. When she returned she said, "The details are pretty awful."

"What happened?"

"Big truck changed lanes right on top of him. The officer said he never had a chance."

"Poor Godson," Sam said, looking down as he struggled for words.

"They need someone to identify the body, Sam. I don't know if I can do it."

Sam took a deep breath, "I'll do it."

A couple of people from the hospital returned with the deputy and Sam followed them down to the room he guessed was the morgue. A sheet was lifted and he immediately recognized Godson, but his friend was torn up pretty badly and obviously there had been a fire too because there were severe burns. Sam had to fight an impulse to just turn and run down the hall and puke his guts out, but he stayed and did what he needed to do. He noted the familiar contours of his friend's face and the singed remnants of his long hair, but just to be sure Sam asked to see the upper right arm near the shoulder. Thankfully, they covered the face again while they manipulated the body and finally he saw what he was looking for, the small peace sign tattooed there, a remnant of Godson's stint in the Navy during the waning days of the Vietnam War. Sam finally nodded and turned away, fighting back his tears.

The news had been devastating enough, but the reality of seeing his friend had completely overwhelmed him. When Sam returned to Moll, he nodded slightly and she embraced him again and cried into his shoulder.

"I could tell from your face," she sobbed.

They sat alone together, silent, each with their thoughts, until the deputy returned.

"We'll hold the body until you decide what you want to do, but I recommend using the local mortuary service to prepare the body. We're holding the truck driver. We have witnesses that it was his fault and we are verifying our suspicion alcohol or drugs were involved. I'm so sorry, ma'am. I know it is tough, but you have a lot of decisions to make." He looked at Sam. "Are you a relative or a friend of the family?"

"Friend," Sam answered.

"It's good she has someone to help her. Look, we're arranging a room for her... do you need a room too?"

Sam hesitated. He'd brought some money, but wasn't sure if he could afford it. He had no idea how long he'd be staying, but he knew he had to stay for his friend."

"Sure."

The deputy returned with the motel information and said, "A local church is covering the cost."

They walked back out to their cars.

"I don't know if I want to be alone,"

"I'll stay with you as long as you need me," Sam said.

At the motel, Moll made several difficult phone calls, to Godson's folks in the Houston area and to his brothers and sisters and to her own family members.

Sam called Smidgeon as well. She could tell he was quite upset when he told her the news.

"You just do what you need to do, Sam. I'm so, so very sorry," she said. "Please tell Moll too. I know this is just devastating to her."

"Yeah," he said. "I'll tell her. I'll be in touch. I love you, Smidgeon."

"I know, Sam," she said, her voice wavering. "I love you too."

It turned out Sam didn't need the motel room because he sat up with Moll in her room, gently rubbing her hands and caressing her hair until she finally sobbed herself to sleep and he dozed in the chair beside the bed.

The next day was a blur as Sam helped Moll deal with the details of death. Godson's parents were going to help with the funeral costs but wanted their son's remains buried in a family plot they had in Houston. They were a bit shocked when Moll told them of Godson's wish for cremation.

"Godson always said he didn't want to be a bother to anyone," she told Sam.

When the arrangements were complete, Moll drove back to Austin with Sam following.

While he drove, he finally allowed his own emotions to bubble up.

"Why didn't he tell me he was coming?" Sam asked himself, adding, "...as if it would have made any difference."

His recent conversations with his friend had been sparse, but Sam remembered the last time they spoke Godson had said, "Man, I sure wish I could see you and how you're making out. Maybe if I do manage to get out there, you could show me around." The implication, of course, was that Godson had wanted to see the mine.

At the time, Sam had said, "Just let me know."

Of course, he hadn't. Sam smiled as he remembered Godson's fondness for pranks and surprises.

"This has turned out to be the biggest surprise of all," Sam said, with a tear rolling down his cheek.

In Austin, Sam called Smidgeon from Godson and Moll's house.

"Hey, just checking in."

"Sam! How is Moll doing?"

"She's coping," he said. "We're back in Austin. I'm helping her deal with the details."

"Oh, Sam, I almost couldn't sleep... I've been thinking about you all night. I'm so sorry."

"Yeah, same here. We're still a bit numb from the shock of it all. And there is hardly any time to recover from something like this because there are so many particulars that need to be taken care of."

"I know. Nothing about death is easy. Well, you just do what you need to do. You going to be okay?"

"It's been tough...I had to identify the body...it was pretty bad. He never had a chance. I'm glad Moll didn't have to see him like that."

He heard Smidgeon gasp as he said this.

"Oh, dear. How horrible for you... for you both."

"I know, Smidgeon, I know. The funeral will be in Houston in a few days. His parents live there. You handling things okay?"

"It's busy but we're making do. I brought in my cousin Hezekiah to help out for a few days so we're doing okay. Do you know what happened?"

"Eighteen wheeler changed lanes right on top of him. Like I said, he never had a chance. I think maybe the driver was drunk."

"Lordy, drunk drivers."

"Yeah, pretty awful all around. Look, I had better go. I'll call you first chance I get."

"Okay. Sam, I miss you something fierce; wish I could be there to help."

"I know you do, honey. I'll call later. Bye, now."

Moll had been standing in the doorway, listening. "You really love her, don't you?"

"Yeah, I do. Not many women would put up with me the way she does."

Moll laughed and it brightened her face a little. Her eyes were still red but it made Sam happy to see her laugh, even a little.

"I'm not hungry at all but we should eat," she said. "You've been away for a while. There anyplace you miss? I owe you a good meal for all your help.

"You'll hate it. The Stallion?"

"The Stallion? Ugh. You're right. How about El Patio?"

Sam thought for several seconds. El Patio was a good second option. Both were Austin landmarks, although The Stallion owned the seniority.

"Okay, I could do with some classic Austin Tex-Mex," he said, smiling.

The small Mexican food eatery was in the shadow of the University of Texas and had a loyal following among the school community. Inside, savory aromas sparked his taste buds, which he thought was odd since he was bombarded with similar smells virtually every day at The Mossback.

Moll ordered a beer, but Sam opted for water.

"No beer, Sam? That is so unlike you."

"I just got out of the habit. I figure I've had enough, you know?"

"You might have a point, there. Still, this is more Smidgeon, I think, isn't it?"

"Her second husband was an alcoholic. I think there was violence too. She said there wasn't much room in her life for another drunk. I was headed down that path, Moll."

"Well, you've had your moments," she joked. "You don't mind if I have a drink, do you?"

"Not at all. I'm just tending away from it. No big deal."

They munched on saltines and hot sauce. The saltines were a throwback to the early days of Tex-Mex when fried tortilla chips were not automatically part of the meal. Moll quickly finished her beer and started on another. Sam could tell she was already feeling the effects but decided to let her go her own way. She was having a tough time and he knew it wasn't going to get any better for a while.

"Sam, what keeps you out there? Is it her or is it that silly mine?"

He hesitated for a moment to think about his answer and his thoughts were interrupted by the arrival of plates of steaming food.

She picked at her dinner as Sam started eating. "Sam, you never answered."

He finished chewing and laughed.

"You're right, I didn't. I guess it's a little of both, Moll. You know, I could have continued to fiddle with the mine from here... but Smidgeon, well...I think we really have something. When I got jumped and beaten and left for dead, after she picked me up on the highway and helped to hide me, well... she *took care* of me in a way that really got to me. I mean, I had been attracted to her before, but this became something more. Don't get me wrong, the mine is part of it. Being out there *has* helped me to a great extent. I'd be working forever trying to do it from here. Sure, she suggested I move out there and it meant leaving a good job..."

"Sam, you hated that job."

"Yeah, no contest, right? At least I was starting to hate it... but working in the cafe is no picnic either," he laughed. "But, well, it is a routine. Every day has its struggles, but when the closed sign goes up, it's all over, you know?"

"But I have to wonder...is it good she's trying to change you, Sam? I can tell," Moll stared at him intently with her red-rimmed eyes. "Look at you, eating Mexican food with no beer. And you used to curse all the time. It's been two days and I don't think I've heard a single bad word!"

Sam smiled. "Those aren't bad things, Moll. Are they?"

"No, I guess those aren't bad things at all. Just seems weird. Don't forget, you sort of picked up with her on the rebound from that other woman. What was her name?"

"Loretta. It was hardly a rebound... we were together just a couple of weeks. She just sort of swept into my life and was gone... and it was months before I really took up with Smidgeon."

Sam took Moll's hand in his. "You're getting sloshed. And on an empty stomach. Eat," he said, pointing at her plate.

Moll sighed and slowly started to eat. She managed to complete about half her meal. As she was slowing down, Sam ordered coffee and Moll ordered another beer.

"Another one?"

"I need it tonight, Sam."

"You're right. Sorry, no more arguments from me."

The waiter cleared the table and they relaxed and continued to chat.

"Sam, why didn't we ever get together? You know, all those years ago at Trotsky's."

"That was a long time ago, Moll."

"Of course it was... but I want to know."

"You got together with Godson. Was I supposed to interfere?"

"You want to know a secret? I had a crush on you first, I mean, when you first started to come in, before you brought Godson to the bar... before you worked there. We had nice chats and I really liked you. That's why I told you about the job. I liked you a lot, but you never made a move. Not one." She traced the lip of the longneck with her finger.

"You had a crush on me?"

"Yes." She took another sip from her beer but her eyes never left his.

"Hah, *now* you tell me," he laughed. "Back then I think I valued friendship more than sex."

"You had sex."

"Not as much as you might think."

"Then what was it?"

Sam looked down at his coffee cup. "I was really shy."

Moll laughed out loud. "Come on, you?"

"No, seriously, and I was never good with the first move. I was a clueless idiot so I guess I dismissed subtle messages or missed them entirely."

"Early on, I tried to get you to come over after work, remember?"

"I thought you were being friendly, but it was late. School, remember?"

She smiled. "So you *were* just an idiot. Let me ask you... if I had been a little bolder, insisted, would you have come home with me? You know, I thought about it but figured, well, there was something about me you didn't like."

Sam was getting uncomfortable with the conversation. "Oh, no, it wasn't anything like that at all. You were awesome. Well, you still are. Yeah, probably, if you had pushed me. I did like you, Moll. A lot. But you know, you're still one of my best friends. That probably wouldn't be the case if we'd... well, you know." Then he added, "And even if we had ended up together way back then, you would have still had to contend with the Sublett Mine."

She smiled, then sighed deeply. "Maybe, but... well, who knows. Anyway, this was a long time ago, all in the past. To time!"

She held up her beer for a toast and Sam clinked his coffee mug against it. "To time," he said.

"You know, Godson and I were not getting along very well," she said as she put her beer down.

"I didn't know. I'm sorry. I've been so out of the loop. Life is a blur of mediocrity out there."

"But it's true. Look at this last trip. We fought about it. I think he mostly really wanted to see you. The nephew thing was just an excuse. He probably wanted to talk to you about it. I guess I was a little jealous because I would have liked to see you too but he didn't even ask. It hurt me," she said, looking looked down at her clasped hands, tears brimming in her eyes. "The hell with him."

This comment took Sam a bit by surprise but then he remembered something about the stages of grief, and anger being one of those stages, so he just let it go.

"I hope we aren't going to toast to that," he quipped, trying to redirect the emotion a little.

Moll smirked. "No, I guess not. Look, let's get back to the house. I need to make up your bed...the spare bed doesn't have sheets right now, just a bedspread."

"Don't go to any trouble for me, Moll. You know I can fiddle with the linens."

"Nonsense," she said. "But I would prefer if you'd drive. I think I'm feeling those beers."

When they returned to the house, Moll struggled to pull a set of sheets from a hall closet and Sam took them from her.

"Here, I've got this. You go on and get to bed."

As he made the bed in the spare bedroom, Moll appeared at the door in a long robe, the ruffles of a nightgown framing her neck and face. "Looks like you've become very domestic out there. I guess she's had a good influence on you after all."

Sam chuckled, "Well, I just didn't want you falling over."

"Now, Sam, I'm not *that* drunk," she said in a huff, turning away. She looked down as she walked, as if she had seen something out of place on the floor of the hall. Suddenly she stumbled slightly and tried to regain her balance by reaching out to the wall but failed and she collapsed in a heap to the floor. "Or maybe I am..." she said as she reached out and groped at the floor. Sam guessed she was trying to figure out a way to get back up.

"You're okay," he said as he helped her up and led her to her bedroom. "You're just tired. We both are, and we have a long day tomorrow. Go get some sleep."

The room was dark, but he stood in the doorway and watched through the shadows for a minute to make sure she got in bed, which she did after first putting something in the nightstand drawer. He hadn't noticed her holding anything earlier and he briefly wondered what it was but decided it was her business.

When she was safely under the covers, he said, "That's better. Sleep tight, Moll," and he left the door slightly ajar and returned to the guest bedroom.

~ * ~

Later, Sam stirred from a sound sleep as he became aware of some movement. A soft warmth slid under the covers next to him.

"What's going on?"

"It's me, silly."

"Moll?" Her breath reeked of stale wine.

"Yes. I'm making a bolder move, Sam," she said as she put her arms around him and snuggled in close.

"Moll!" Sam sat up. "We can't do this."

"Why not? Godson's gone, Sam. The way I see it, we should have done this a long time ago. Better late than never."

"You're drunk."

"So?" Moll blinked up at him in the dim light.

"I know you're upset and... and you've had a lot to drink. You are scaring the heck out of me right now."

"Is this really *that* bad?" She giggled and stroked at his leg lightly with her foot under the covers.

Sam reached out and turned on a small light next to the bed. "It just isn't right. Moll, think about it. It isn't fair to Godson, it isn't fair to Smidgeon, and it isn't fair to me."

She threw the covers back and revealed her naked body.

"So, you don't want me?"

"Moll! It isn't that, it's..."

"Oh, so you *do* want me."

"Stop it. This just isn't an appropriate thing to even think about. I mean, well, I'm sure you know what I mean, or you would if you weren't..."

He pulled the bedspread back to cover her and tried not to think about the contours of her body. "Listen, I understand this is a hard time for you. It's hard for all of us. If you're lonely, I'll sit up with you like I did at the motel."

"I liked that. I liked it a lot. I wanted more."

"It just isn't right. Not now."

"You worried about your *girlfriend*? She's hundreds of miles away and besides, *you're* not married, so what does it matter?"

"Geez, Moll. It would matter to her. Think of poor Godson, his family, your family, what would people think?"

"They aren't here. I only care about you. What do *you* think?"

"You know what I think. You're great, one of my best friends. Yes, in the past, under different circumstances I would have responded to a move like this but not now, not like this."

Those were the words he was saying but in the back of his head he was imagining a little Sam on his left shoulder, just like in the movies, enticing him to "go ahead, man..." while a second little Sam with a halo stood on his right shoulder and reminded him to be good.

She sat up and leaned over to him and put her head on his shoulder. Her nipples stood out as her breasts moved gently with each breath she took. "I don't understand you, Sam."

He stood and motioned for her to get out of the bed. She complied with a pout and he draped the bedspread around her. "Maybe you'll understand in the morning."

He led her back to her bedroom. "You want a nightgown or something?"

"Humph," she said as she emerged from the bedspread and slipped back underneath her own covers. "You said you'd stay with me."

"Okay, okay, just a second," he said and he went back to his room and slipped on his jeans. He returned and sat on the bed next to her, outside the covers, propped up with a pillow behind him.

It was chilly in the bedroom, even with his pants on and he tried not to think of her nude body as he covered himself loosely with the bedspread from his own bed. He gently caressed Moll's hair as she snuggled closer to him. He reached over for the light and it was only then he saw the half empty bottle of wine on the side table.

"Several beers and half a bottle of wine..." he thought to himself as he turned off the lamp.

In a few minutes Moll was snoring softly and it wasn't long before he was dozing himself. At some point he got up in the dark and retreated to his own bed. The entire experience had confused him but he mumbled under his breath, "It's probably just another stage of grief."

He wore himself out thinking, trying to remember them all before he fell back asleep.

~ * ~

"Hey, sleepyhead. Time to get up. I made some breakfast."

It was Moll, fully dressed, bending over and shaking him gently.

"Right. You feel okay? You were pretty drunk last night."

"You know, I have a slight headache this morning but I feel pretty good, considering. Godson's mom called. They have a reception at the funeral home at six and a small private service tomorrow at two. I told them Godson always said he never wanted much fuss and I think they've accepted that. The cremains are being shipped today by bus."

Godson blinked groggily at the news. "Today? Will they get there in time?"

"Apparently. It doesn't really matter, I guess. It is the spirit of the thing, don't you think?"

"I guess so," he said, rubbing the sleep out of his eyes.

They ate in an awkward silence over breakfast until Moll finally spoke. "Sam, I want to apologize about last night. I don't remember a lot of details, but I know I acted a bit foolish."

Sam was stammering through his words. "It...It... well, I mean, it just wasn't right, Moll. I figured you would regret it."

"You were a perfect gentleman, Sam. I wouldn't expect less from you, because you always have been. I really think that's one reason I've always had an underlying attraction for you all these years." She smiled. "Godson knew it. He always knew it. Truth is, I talked about coming out to visit you too. I even wanted to come this time, but he wouldn't hear of it." She sighed deeply. "We'd both be dead if I had."

She put her fork down and reached over to touch his arm. "And you're right... I would have regretted it. Well, I wouldn't have regretted making love so much but I would have regretted the timing. Thank you, Sam."

Sam grasped her hand and said, "You're welcome, Moll."

They took Moll's car to Houston, where they knew a whirlwind of activity awaited them. But a trip to Houston also gave Sam a chance to see his family. Moll dropped him off there while she went off to see her family, and of course, Godson's.

Sam's mother went with him to the funeral home and agreed to accompany him the next day to the funeral. He had been friends with Godson for a long time, so she knew him and liked him. Driving to the services she asked him a question she hadn't asked him before.

"When are we going to meet this girlfriend of yours?"

"Smidgeon, Mom, her name is Smidgeon. We've talked about it. But, you know, it's hard to get away. The restaurant business is tough. It's open seven days a week," he said. "But we'll try. Soon, if business picks up enough to where we can hire extra help or maybe even close the restaurant for a vacation. I'd really like you to meet her."

"That's good. I'd hate to think you were keeping some sort of dark secret out there."

~ * ~

The morning after the funeral, Sam and Moll returned to Austin.

"So, you're going back today?" Moll asked.

"Yeah, I think I had better get back home, unless of course you need me to stay."

"It's tempting; I know it's going to be tough for a while, but I think I'll be okay. You should eat before you go. I know you mentioned The Stallion before...why don't we go there?"

"You sure? I know it's not your favorite."

"I'm fine with it, as long as a speaker doesn't fall off the wall and release a hoard of creepy crawlies."

"Oh, wow, I forgot...that really happened to you one time." Sam giggled, "Sure, if that happens, I'll be happy to leave. Hey, I couldn't reach my old co-worker Sally before we went to Houston. If she's home, could I invite her along?"

"Oh, I remember her. Sure," she said without much enthusiasm, "the more the merrier."

He did manage to catch Sally and they all met at The Stallion. It gave Sam and Sally a chance to catch up and gave Sam a chance to feast on The Stallion's wonderful fried chicken and share one of their legendary pyramidal towers of fresh breaded onion rings. Moll kept quiet through most of the meal as Sam and Sally talked, but she occasionally made small talk.

"I promise to do better job trying to keep in touch, Sally," Sam said as they walked out to the parking lot.

"I've been bad about it too," she said as she started her car. "Hey, Robert and I might be going to California soon, at least he's talked about some work out there, so I'll let you know. You might be seeing us sooner than you think."

"Oh, that would be great," he said, "Van Horn is pretty much just a place to stop on the way to someplace else," he laughed and waved as Sally drove away.

Back at Moll's house, as he got his bag from the spare bedroom, Moll came up and hugged him hard.

"You have been wonderful with everything, Sam," she said, then she grabbed the back of his head and drew him to her and kissed him.

"Consider this one more attempt at a bolder move, Sam," she said as she broke off the kiss. "The next time we meet anything goes."

The sudden kiss had shocked him but as the shock wore off, the memory of Moll's sudden kiss continued to roll around in his mind as he drove across the vast west Texas landscape.

Seven

Loot Meldings sipped a cup of coffee in his cluttered den while he watched a game show on his small television. He looked up at the sound of knocking on his front door. He was expecting Sam at some point, but the old man squinted at the clock and could see it was early...the café would not be closed yet. He fumbled with the lever on the recliner and as he stood he hesitated slightly to let his head clear. His dizzy spells were becoming more frequent and he had learned to augment any sudden movement with a short pause.

"Nobody comes out here besides Sam, 'cepting maybe Gil Osmond, and even then it's only if he's got a reason," he muttered as he weaved his way through the narrow passages of his small house, being careful not to disturb the stacks and piles of debris.. He took each step deliberately because he was still feeling a bit shaky. The last time he had fallen he thought he'd never get himself up. It had been like some nightmare, as every time he reached up trying to find a handhold he dislodged more and more of the delicately balanced junk.

"Almost buried myself that time," he grumbled to himself. "I guess I'm just going to have to dig in and start cleaning this mess; I just don't know where to start."

He reached for the shotgun he kept next to the door. At the start of another gentle knock, Loot set the ancient hammer and brandished the weapon at the ready as he opened the door. Daylight streamed into the dark house, revealing a young black man, in a worn plaid shirt on the small porch. The jeans, boots, and tattered cowboy hat in his hands indicated to Loot the man worked for a living.

"Whatcha want here?" Loot asked.

"Hold on, ain't no call for a gun. Are you Mr. Meldings? Loot Meldings?"

"Who wants to know?"

"Can you put down the shotgun? Uh, please? It sort of makes me nervous."

Loot peered down the long barrel. "State yer business and I'll think about it."

"Name's Lance Norton. I work down at the MacGregg place."

"MacGregg place? That ain't helping yer case none. What do you want?"

"Mr. Meldings, seriously, I don't want no trouble. I think you knew my grandpa. Thaddeus Norton. He used to work out here. He said you was buddies in the old days, so I wanted to look you up."

"*Thaddeus*? Look, stranger, I don't recall no..."

Loot stopped as a wave of recognition flashed across his face.

"W-wait, you don't mean *Scamp*, do you? Scamp Norton?" The barrel of the gun had dropped about eighteen inches as Loot squinted into the bright late-afternoon framing the unfamiliar face.

"Yeah, Scamp Norton. Sorry. To me he was always just Grampa Thad."

"Scamp Norton! Hain't hear'd that name in a coon's age. How's he doing?"

"He passed about a year ago, Mr. Meldings. Had a touch of the sugar. Lost a foot first, then the leg, then got an infection and it just all got the better of him. I used to sit and listen to him tell his stories about working ranches and such. I loved the ones about Loot and Slim the most. He always said you were too cantankerous to die before him."

Loot put the gun back in its place by the door and laughed. "Damn, old Scamp. Him and me and Slim Longo, we was..."Loot hesitated as the emotion of his memories swept over him. "Wait, you said you work at the MacGregg place? Don't seem possible. I mean, the MacGreggs don't seem like the type to hire no..."

"You don't have to say it, Mr. Meldings. No, you're right. But since the old man died, Tim MacGregg is running things. He brought me on. I knew him in college. I'm the new foreman. I think things out there are changing, little by little." The young man smiled broadly. "So, you gonna ask me in?"

"Oh, I'm sorry, young fella. What was your name?"

"Lance."

Loot stepped back after nervously glancing from side to side outside the front door. "Sorry about the gun. I get a little spooked out here by myself sometimes."

"Hey, you're old and alone, I don't blame you for being careful. Thank you, Mr. Meldings."

"You can call me Loot, young feller. Mr. Meldings is what some danged preacher will probably call me over my corpse."

As they walked through the canyons of junk, Lance said, "Grandpa said you was something of a packrat. You use all this stuff?"

Loot laughed. "Not as much as I'd like. Guess I'm a might worse than I was when Scamp was around."

In the den, Loot turned down the sound on the television and cleared a spot on the couch next to his recliner. He motioned for the younger man to sit.

"So you're working for Tim at the MacGregg place. That young'un was a wild one when he was still here. Heard he's been in Abilene."

"Yes, sir. I guess I was pretty wild too. Wasn't you wild when you was eighteen or nineteen?"

Loot chuckled. "I spent a goodly portion of those years hunkered down in foxholes in North Africa, Sicily, and Italy. The worst was Anzio. Now *that* was a wild old time, if'n you consider the notion of being constantly shelled and shot at by the Germans as something wild."

Lance widened his eyes a bit at this revelation and continued, "No, I don't suppose it was. Anyway, Tim and me, we both went to college there, in Abilene, I mean. What about Slim? I don't reckon he's still around?"

"Naw, old Slim died a while ago, back in Austin. Things weren't going well for him, I'm afraid. Let the booze get to him."

"Oh, too bad."

"Yep. Slim and Scamp was particularly good friends...they used to pal it around quite a bit until..."

An ashen look crossed Loot's face.

"I know about the incident, Mr. M..., uh, Loot. Grandpa didn't much like to talk about it but he told me a little of what happened."

"You know, it was *on* the MacGregg place. Does Tim know? I mean, that your grandpa..."

"Nobody's put it together. Not so far. All the regular hands are Mexicans...all they know is horses and cattle and drinking in town on their days off and Tim's too young. Only one who might be there from those days might be Tim's mom but she's not well and I don't think the old lady knew much of the dealings of the place."

"I haven't even told Sam the whole story," Loot started and then realized he was saying something he shouldn't and stopped.

"Sam? The guy at the café?" Lance asked. "Why should he know about it?"

Loot froze for a moment, thinking about his words carefully. He knew he had slipped up and wanted to protect Sam's interest in all things MacGregg. "Oh, nothing. Sam and me is buddies, that's all. I tell him lots of stories about the old days. Like you and your grandpa. He's a college boy like you, likes to hear them stories."

Lance leaned forward and clasped his hands. "Yeah, the old days. Pretty much why I'm here, Loot. I wanted to ask you something about grandpa and Slim. What were they doing when they were beaten up? I guess you weren't with them that day?"

"Naw, I was getting drunk pretty regular on my days off back then and the day they was roughed up was no different. I was trapping a lot back then and I'd get me a bottle and go check my traps. Them two was always out poking around in the hills. Hunting, I guess. Trespassing, most likely. Bad idea for them to go onto the MacGregg place...especially mixed as they was. Most of us hands, we didn't care much about color as long as a man worked. Ranching is hard work. White, black, brown...no matter. Lazy is what we hated. But MacGregg wasn't lazy, he was just a callous S.O.B. He always had a bad reputation. Didn't even hire Mexicans in those days, but economics softened him on that score, I guess. I still don't rightly see how you're going to fit in."

"New management, I guess. I know what I'm doing on a ranch, but that's not why Tim wanted me."

"No?"

"I think he hired me out of spite for the old man."

"Ha! Makes sense. Old man MacGregg was even harder on his own kid. Always hired tough hands, too. Especially foremen. You don't rightly fit the profile."

"I'm tougher than you might think. And it hasn't been an easy time so far. Jose, the old foreman, was rightly miffed at me replacing him. It's hard to move from foreman to just a hand again. He tried to pull something with me... had to knock him down on his rear end. He high-tailed it off back to Mexico, I guess."

"Watch out for him, might make his way back."

"I will, but I think he was a bit intimidated by me. Heck, I'm a heck of a lot bigger than he is and I'm pretty handy with a gun too."

"You know, after the beating, MacGregg's boys just dumped poor Slim and Scamp on the side of a back road. Those boys was lucky I was driving by after checking some of my traps. They was a mess and it was really early in the morning when I found them. Drove them to town and the only place open was The Mossback."

"Really? The same place where that Sam guy works?"

"Yep. The same. Old Joe Toll owned it. It was kinda new then. I was pretty drunk, like I was most of the time in those days. Tried to take them in there to clean them up. Wanted to call the cops. He wouldn't let us in the front door. Not sure if it was because they was hurt, or because of Scamp, or if it was because I was drunk. Looking back, I guess it was probably a mixture of all three. I got mad and threw a rock and busted out a window. Ended up getting arrested."

"Grandpa didn't mention anything about a window or the law getting involved."

"He was out of it. I hated getting arrested, but it was a good thing the law came. *They* saw Sam and Scamp and the condition they was in and called in an ambulance for 'em. Saved their lives, I reckon. I was too drunk to even think of something so obvious. I never saw either of them again after that."

"What happened to you?"

"The usual. Drunk and disorderly. A few months in jail. Tried to come back and pay Joe for the window but he kicked me out, told me to never come back. I've pretty much stayed away from the place even to this day."

"But you're friends with Sam."

"Yeah. In spite of our friendship, he took up with Joe's daughter. She's a decent gal but she seems to have inherited a certain dislike for me. But...well, she's come to sort of tolerate the notion of old Loot because her beau and me are friends. You go there? The Mossback, I mean."

"Just one time, when I rolled into town. Didn't seem too friendly a place, at least to a black face."

"Probably more a strange face. Times are different now."

Lance chuckled, "Not much, but maybe a little. Still, I can see the stranger angle and Sam tried to tell me the same thing. Basically, I've learned I shouldn't try to push it. I just keep to myself and do my job."

"Why you so interested in what Slim and Scamp were doing? Didn't your grandpa tell you?"

Lance looked down. "Said pretty much what you said, that they was poking around out in the hills. Some fool notion of a gold mine."

Loot tried not act surprised. "Gold? Hah. Ain't supposed to be gold in these hills. Maybe a smattering of silver and a few other things, but gold? Naw, I don't think so," Loot lied.

"Well, it was a long time ago," Lance said, as he slapped both knees and stood. "Loot, I best be on my way. Grandpa Thad always spoke highly of you. Now I see why. You saved his life and I'm grateful for that."

"Just an old drunk trying to do the right thing as best as he could. Not sure getting arrested qualifies as a life-saving event."

Lance adjusted the brim of his hat as he added, "Whatever works, right?"

Loot led Lance back through the pathways of clutter.

"You know, Mr....uh, Loot, this is pretty much a fire hazard."

"Oh, I know, I know...I really need to start clearing out some of this crap," he cackled. "I fell a few weeks ago and almost started an avalanche!"

A scarlet sunset flooded the sky as Lance Norton started toward his truck.

"You need some help with cleaning up, let me know. Two trucks can haul twice as much stuff. Nice to finally put a face to the stories, Loot. I'll come back real soon," he said.

"Okay," Loot said, waving at the sunset-framed shadow.

Loot returned to his den and muttered to himself. "Kid knows something. Glad Sam is coming over in a bit. He should know."

Then Loot remembered his mistake in mentioning Sam. "Gol-dang-it! I hope I didn't mess anything up there... shouldn't have mentioned him at all. "

About an hour later, there was another knock, followed by the sound of a door opening. Loot looked at the clock and assumed it was Sam and he knew he had given the younger man a key.

"Loot? It's me, Sam!"

The crusty old trapper smiled. He had always liked Sam, ever since the first time they had met in the parking lot at The Mossback. He still never knew why he felt compelled to stop and confront the young man when he recognized the car. He had seen it numerous times and somehow, deep in his heart he knew it had something to do with gold. It had been a hunch. Like driving that particular road the morning when he found the two crumpled, beaten figures or the day he instinctively called to the major to turn the half-track to the left, allowing them to avoid the minefield and flank that German patrol. Every now and then he just got a feeling.

"Come on back, Sam...come on back."

Sam emerged from the darkness into the dimly lit den. He had a bag in his hand. "Brought you dinner," he said.

"Aw, you didn't have to do bring me nothing."

"What'd you eat today?"

"Nothing much, some crackers, maybe. Hain't been hungry."

"Then I *did* have to do it, you old fool. You have to eat!"

Loot accepted the bag and set it aside. "I'll eat this after you leave. So, I heard you went back east."

"Yeah, one of my best friends died. Godson, from Austin. He was on the way here, got crunched by an eighteen-wheeler near Sonora."

"Aw, what an awful shame. Yeah, you'd mentioned him before. He was married, wasn't he?"

"Yeah."

"How's she doing? The wife, I mean. Tough business for a wife to lose a husband."

"She's managing okay. Funny thing, though, she was ready to jump into bed with me, almost right off the bat."

Loot did not seem surprised. "Not the first time I've heard of that, Sam. Grief messes a lot with a person's mind. A woman sort of panics at the loss of a husband. Did you...?"

"No!"

Loot laughed. "Probably for the better. She'd likely hold it against you later. Such things can get a might complicated." Then Loot changed the subject. "So, what's the plan? You ready to go back out to the mine?"

"Yeah, still need to work on the bad section."

"There's a slight snag you should know about. The MacGregg's new foreman."

"I've met him. Black fella. Seems to be a decent guy. I thought it might be an improvement."

"He came to see me today. Just a while ago."

"What?"

"Sam, he knows something about the mine."

Sam was wide-eyed. "How could he...?"

"His granddaddy used to work out here. I knew him. Scamp Norton. Scamp knew Slim too. We was all three buddies but

Scamp and Slim, well they was like two peas in a pod. Remember me telling you Slim was beaten real bad one time?"

"Yeah, I remember."

"He was with Scamp. They both ended up in the hospital. I saved them, picked 'em up when they was dumped on the side of the road. But I was drunk, didn't know what else to do, so I took them to that damned café where you work. There was a big commotion with Joe, the owner. He didn't want no part of it. I got mad, said a few choice words and broke a window. I went to jail but it worked out because the law sent Slim and Scamp to the hospital. Never saw either of them again. Both went off east to recuperate with family, or so I thought. I was in jail a while."

"So, that was the big thing between you and Smidgeon's father?"

"Yep. I tried to pay him for the window when I got out, but he banned me from the café forever. I sort of believed him."

Sam laughed. "She still holds onto that grudge and she doesn't even know why."

"Your daddy tells you something, it sticks with you."

Sam laughed again. "So what about this foreman? Lance, I think his name was."

"Yeah, Lance. He didn't outright say it, but I gleaned it from his questions. Sam, he knows something about the mine, or at least the notion of it. Slim and Scamp went out together all the time. Risky in those days, for a white fella to hang around with a black man. It was one thing to do ranching work, but hanging around, well, it was like getting friendly. Probably half of the reason they was beaten so badly. Sam, I've never told you this but...it was on the MacGregg place."

Sam stood up. "What? No, you never told me that."

"I just never much thought about it. Foggy details, all in the past."

"So you think Lance knows the clues?"

"Don't rightly know, but it might make sense. I mean, I never much wanted to go traipsing off in the hills like them two, I preferred to drink, but I figure Slim woulda likely told Scamp at least part of it. If he did, you can bet that old coot told his grandson, same as Slim told you. You know, I was mighty suspicious when he said he knew Tim MacGregg in college. The MacGreggs warn't too inclined to socialize with coloreds in my experience."

"Yeah, and Tim MacGregg told me Lance had always wanted to come see the ranch."

"You just need to watch your back out there, son. This kid knows something and he's smart. I can tell. He's going to be poking around."

"Yeah, I've been getting a little sloppy the last few trips. It's a rough and remote section of the ranch, so old man MacGregg didn't seem to be much interested in it, but if this Lance guy is looking for something and he knows the same clues Slim gave me, he might just stumble across it the same way I did."

"What about this weekend?"

Sam sighed. "I guess we'll do the same as before. I'll get Smidgeon to drop me off late Friday night. I'll meet you at the culvert early Monday morning."

"Gotcha. I'll be there, buddy."

Loot fussed a bit when Sam made him open the bag and pull out the food. He wasn't much hungry but he obliged the young man by eating a few fries and taking a bite out of the burger.

After Sam left, Loot put the food to the side and sat back in his recliner. The television was on but he left the sound turned down. He thought about the events of the evening and his head began to bob.

"Got a funny feeling about things...wish I could do more to help, but I'm so tired all the time..." he muttered to himself as he nodded off.

Eight

Dawn was rising as he approached the shadowy outlines of Diablo Rim and his thoughts turned to a vision of Slim on the jail floor, rasping with a fading breath. 'Follow the devil and look for the table," Slim had said. He replayed the scene in his head almost every time he went out there.

"Slim, Slim, Slim... what did you get me into?" he muttered as he tripped and caught himself.

The "table" had been a subtle hint and he had spent years looking for something big so he didn't even notice the significance of the small outcrop the first time he stumbled across it.

"Now, it jumps out at me, even from a distance."

He dropped his pack and surveyed the blocked opening on the opposite wall. The flat rock had stood the test of time and it still served to conceal the opening well. Sam sighed.

"Let's get to it," he said, as he looked up the cut scanning for a suitable piece of brush to block the opening. The scraggly bushes he needed were getting scarce after nearly two years of steady work and the old ones always disappeared between trips. He walked several hundred yards up the cut and found something suitable and broke it off. He returned and slipped on his work gloves and began to loosen the flat rock by rocking it back and forth until he managed to tilt it down flat to reveal the opening.

"Whew." Sam panted from the exertion. "Seems heavier every time. Maybe it is part of the curse, like Loretta and her mom said," he chuckled.

He peered into the hole. "Well, it *is* foreboding," he said.

He sighed deeply. The entire encounter with Loretta still stung, even though over two years had passed. Their paths had crossed briefly, a simple coincidence, then a brief, intense relationship until she discovered Slim's other secret by accident and, just like that, it was over. Who could have imagined Slim was her grandfather? And the mine?

"Cursed," her mother had said the last time he had tried to call Loretta. She told him they wanted no part of Slim, Sam, the mine, *or* the curse.

"I should have tried to contact her again, but then... she never contacted me either." Sam shook his head and added, "Of course, how could she after I left Austin?"

He shook off those thoughts of gloom and doom and began unloading his pack. He always brought twice as many batteries as he needed so he could stockpile them. It was the same with water and food. Anything extra he could stash in the hole helped him later. Long ago he realized he could sleep in the mine, so some things, like his sleeping bag and electric lanterns became permanent fixtures, along with stockpiles of food and water.

"What I need is wood...shoring material," he muttered.

Over time, he had also managed to carry in and stash most of the tools he needed, but lumber was the most difficult thing to transport. Still, carrying in what he could, over time he had managed to shore up the entrance and once he got a little farther in, he found an area where a past cave-in had opened up what he called the anteroom.

Once he'd cleared it out, he found he could almost stand up in there. It served as his warehouse and his living quarters, but he had painstakingly shored it up as well. The extended tunnel, where he was currently working, veered off and trended down from there. He assumed old Ben Sublett had likely found most of his gold farther down the tunnel, but it was unstable and cluttered.

The work seemed endless. He often had to nudge large rocks toward the opening, a few inches at a time. He also spent a lot of time scooping smaller debris into old, burlap potato sacks with his hands. He had scrounged a stockpile of sacks from The Mossback, and he needed a lot of them, because dragging the bags across the tunnel floor quickly wore them out. He always seemed to dislodge more debris as he struggled with the bags.

"One step forward, two steps back," he said, "and the bad thing is, I have to scatter everything I haul out."

Sam scanned the area around the cut, remembering his hundreds of trips distributing rubble in a random fashion so it would look like a part of the general landscape. He remembered the old movie *The Great Escape* as he thought about this. They had called it *dispersal* and it was one of the primary problems of digging an escape tunnel. He had the same problem, but the prisoners were disposing of dirt. He sometimes had boulders weighing a hundred pounds or more.

Inside the mine he was hidden from the outside world and protected from the weather. His lanterns lived on batteries and he augmented those with candles, but they used oxygen, or so Loot had warned him.

"Sam, the deeper you go, the more anything burning will eat up your air. At some point, fresh air won't be able to get back down there quick enough for you to breathe," the old man had said.

He wasn't deep enough, yet, so the opening still provided the air he needed, but he had no idea how far he might have to go to find a pay streak.

He pulled a small flashlight from one of the pockets on his pack and pushed the pack ahead of him as he clambered into the mine, pulling the piece of scrub behind him to block the opening. He crawled to the anteroom and scanned it with the flashlight, finding everything just as he had left it. He placed the pack against a side wall and located his hoard of water, food, and tools, all of which were stashed around the outer walls. He tested a small electric lantern and the dim light indicated failing batteries, so he changed them and used its light to find the rest of his lanterns and the small handmade candleholders. He had fashioned them out of old cans by cutting an oval out of one side. They even had makeshift reflectors with pieces of shiny aluminum foil covering the back side.

Once he had unloaded his new batch of supplies, he grabbed his tools and started down the opening on the far wall to begin the day's operations. The tools were primitive...a small shovel and a small sledge and an ancient old iron chisel Loot had found in his house after an exhaustive search. He inched his way down the shaft, pushing the tools with one hand and carrying a candle lantern with the other, all the while taking care not to touch the ceiling. He remembered the fear of his last close call.

"Gotta get a helmet," he grumbled. He also thought again about the walkie-talkies. "Still not sure those would work very far from way down here."

About seven or eight feet in, he reached his first obstruction of the day, a small boulder about a foot across. He put the lantern to the side, tested the rock and it moved readily, so he shoved his tools out of the way and grasped it as best as he could and by a combination of dragging and rolling he encouraged it backwards as he inched his way backward to the anteroom. He was soon drenched in sweat. Although the mine wasn't hot, the air was always damp. He panted from the exertion as he crouched in the bigger room and the two candles he had left burning danced crazy shadows across the walls. He muscled the rock to the outer opening and slowly moved it to the outside, pushing this time.

Of course the entrance was blocked by the bush he had placed there and just beyond, he could see the flat rock, also partially blocking the aperture. He shoved the bush out of the way and inched the boulder until it nudged past the flat rock. There was just enough room for Sam to scramble around his boulder.

Once outside, he stretched, relishing the fresh air as he caught his breath. He carefully glanced around, knowing this was when he was most vulnerable. He spotted a place on the opposite wall and looked down and assessed the weight of the rock. Although it was heavy he could just barely pick it up by crouching and using his legs to dead lift. He managed to carry it several feet before dropping it.

He had to rest after the exertion and used the time to examine the rock for any flecks of gold. He didn't see any on top so he rolled it a bit to reveal the other side.

"Nothing, but it doesn't pay to not look," he said.

He continued nudging it closer to the opposite wall by a combination of pushing, pulling, and lifting. Finally it was close enough for him to call the operation complete. The dampness of the rock made it seem somewhat darker than its surroundings, but experience had taught him the sun and dry air would quickly transform it.

Back in the mine, he reached behind him to retrieve the bush and pulled it to block the opening. Sam started back down the hole to do it all again. It was hard work and each operation could take several hours. By mid-afternoon he was exhausted. Some of the rocks were too big to move, and had to be broken into smaller pieces inside the shaft, using the chisel and small sledge. Eventually, he always found a weak spot.

Late in the afternoon he was working with his chisel on a particularly large obstruction. He had been working his way down to this boulder for many months. It almost completely blocked his view and he had long hoped it might be the key to getting farther down the mine.

"This baby is going to take a while," he whispered.

The rock was too big and heavy to haul down the passage, so it was imperative he break it into pieces. So far he had only managed to dislodge a few pebbles. As he chipped away at it, he knew all of the smaller pieces would have to be dealt with as well. He winced with every hit, because the metallic clang of hammer-on-chisel was deafening in the confined space.

When he connected, there was always a spray of shattered fragments, some of which peppered his face, so he always squinted and turned his head as he hit. Sometimes this served to spoil his aim and more than once he wasted the effort or worse, hit his hand.

"I really need safety goggles," he said after one shower of particles, "but it's so humid down here, they'd probably fog up."

He made scant progress against the boulder. He had connected, whack after whack, for what seemed like an hour and had barely made a dent in the thing.

Loot had told him long ago he might need to use explosives at some point.

"Explosives?" Sam had said.

"Some rocks ain't gonna break," Loot explained.

"But how can I expect to use explosives? I'm trying to do this in secret!"

"Don't rightly know, Sam, but one day you might just need to cross that bridge."

At the time, Sam hoped this was a skill he would never have to master, but as he hammered in vain he began to think maybe this one rock would need the extra effort. He examined it closely with his flashlight, looking for evidence of a depression or crack he could take advantage of.

Sam was exhausted, even though he had scrambled outside several times to get water and fresh air. He was at that point again, about ready for a break.

"I might just knock off for the day," he said to himself, then added, "after a couple of more good hits."

He spied what he thought might be another likely spot, not far from the top, and wrenched his body to get a maximum swing from his small hammer. The impact of hammer and chisel against rock rang a little different this time.

"Is that it?" he murmured.

He had encountered such a change before and it usually meant he had finally managed to start the fracture he needed. Of course he didn't expect the boulder to just suddenly cleave itself in two. He would have to capitalize on a series of small successes to eventually get the job done. He placed the chisel again and twisted his body against the tunnel wall and prepared to swing with as much force as he could.

"Watch it." The faint, gravelly whisper came from nowhere.

Then, things happened quickly. The hammer clipped the top of the shaft as it bounced off the chisel and the last thing he remembered when the top of the mine came down on him was what he thought might be the beginnings of a crack in the boulder. He was in no position to quickly back his way out of the tunnel because he was on his left side with his arms stretched out. He dropped the hammer and chisel and immediately tried to cover his face but only managed to cover his nose and mouth with his left hand as he cowered against the muffled crescendo of falling rubble. Then everything went black.

Sam came to and cautiously opened his eyes. It was dark...his candle had been snuffed in the rush of air from the collapse. He began to wonder how long he had been unconscious, then he coughed and gagged hard against the still settling powdery cloud of debris.

He felt a brief wave of relief when he realized he probably hadn't been out very long if dust was still in the air. But the relief faded quickly... being trapped in this hole was his worst nightmare and even as he wheezed dirt out of his lungs, he tried to assess his situation.

He was gratified to realize there was at least *some* light, most likely a reflection from the anteroom, where he had left a couple of candles burning. As near as he could tell, about three-quarters of his torso was buried. Sam tried to carefully move his body and legs. Any motion was slight but he didn't try too hard because he was wary of causing another cave-in.

"Nothing seems broken," he rasped, still coughing up dust. He tried to draw his right hand down from the area of the boulder but it was blocked by debris.

"Okay, could be worse," he said. "I think."

His lungs ached from coughing, but finally as the air cleared, he managed to slow his breathing.

"It's bad, but I can't panic." His voice was hoarse.

He moved his left hand past his head, trying to work material away from his outstretched right hand. Handfuls of loose rocks somehow found an escape route as he worked. A few larger rocks had no place to go but eventually, with a lot of effort he managed to free his right hand. He was elated when he was able to pull the hand down closer to his face. The effort had left him exhausted and he was drenched in sweat. Slowly, he began to work material away from his body in whatever direction it would go.

His legs seemed to be almost free and he tried some lurching motions with them in an attempt to jostle his body in a snakelike fashion to see if he could slither his way out. Any progress seemed inconsequential.

"Going to need more room around my hands and arms," he gasped.

He wondered if he could go forward more easily than backwards.

"No, I need to get out, not get myself farther in."

For some reason, he again thought about the idea of a walkie-talkie.

"I should have looked into it when I was back east," he grumbled to himself, trying to calm himself with random banter. "But it doesn't matter; it wouldn't work way down here, anyway."

Once again, he tried to slither backwards, this time trying to push debris away from his upper body with both hands. After long minutes of exertion, he thought he had made some progress.

"It's not much, maybe an inch or two, but I think it's working," he said, almost croaking because of the dirt caked in his throat.

His efforts required numerous breaks. He had been tired before the rocks had fallen, but these exertions were exhausting him. After each stop, he forced himself to continue working.

"Wish I had brought a canteen down with me," he said, "but I have to make so many trips out with rocks, getting water was never a problem." He shook his head. "Can't give up... I just have to keep trying."

He continued working, making slow but steady progress. Occasional smatterings of pebbles still sprinkled down on him, usually if he tried to be too aggressive. The space vacated by his body became a ready repository for the newly shifted material.

The reward for each exertion seemed to be measured in fractions of an inch, followed by another rest period of uncertain duration. Sweat caked dirt to his clothes and skin. After each pause, he renewed his efforts as minutes ticked into hours. He wondered how long the candles he had left burning in the large room would continue to give him light. He didn't even think about the precious oxygen they were consuming.

Eventually he managed to turn almost face down, which allowed him to start pushing armfuls of debris toward the far end of the void. This more determined effort had a swift reward when he suddenly realized he was free.

He worked himself up to all fours to crawl the rest of the way out and then paused for a moment and gently sobbed, "I thought for sure I was done."

Sam slowly backed into the bigger room and grabbed one of his jugs and gulped deep mouthfuls of water before he collapsed in a heap on the floor.

One candle was feebly trying to maintain itself in a flickering show of shadows on the anteroom walls when he woke up. His head hurt and his body felt as if it had been pummeled in a street fight. He cautiously felt around and found several tender spots on his head. He hadn't realized he had been hit in the rock fall.

"I was lucky I was wedged against the wall when I swung the hammer," he said.

He found several more tenders spots on his arms, especially his right arm, and there was another large painful spot on his side. His upper thigh and hip were bruised as well.

"Haven't been this beat up since MacGregg's goons found me," he laughed to himself. One particularly tender spot on his head throbbed even more when he laughed.

"I guess Smidgeon was right."

She had argued with him about using a helmet. "Miners *always* wear one," she had said.

Sam had balked at the expense and at the space it would take up in the tight confines of the lower shaft. Now it seemed like a good idea.

"Man, if a really *big* rock had hit my head..."

He sat and quietly and pondered the realities he might face, hidden, badly hurt, and buried in that the deep hole.

"I've made sure nobody has more than a vague idea of where I am."

The entrance was camouflaged but only from a distance. If someone found the right cut along Diablo Rim, they might figure it out, but he knew finding the mine would be unlikely unless someone was actually looking for it.

He made his way to the entrance and pushed the bush away from the hole. Outside, the light of a quarter moon illuminated the landscape and the early spring air was cool. Sam relished the freedom of being out of the mine, and almost gulped the sweet desert air.

"I needed that," he said, almost coughing again.

The mine was dank and smelled of dust after the cave-in. He leaned against the small ledge across from the "Y" and wondered how deep he would have to go before fresh air became a real problem, and considered the problem.

"Ben Sublett did it," he said. "So it can't be too deep."

Sam shook the notion out of his mind.

"I wish I could just go home now and rest... and think." He sat in the dark and wondered what he would tell Smidgeon.

"She won't like this... no, not one bit," he muttered. "Then she'll balk at me coming back, I know it. I need to rethink everything, think about what I can tell her."

As he returned to the mine, he picked up a rock and spun and threw it at the opposite wall. It made a loud noise but it was followed by another noise, a slight ruffle and another sound of smaller rocks tinkling down the slope much closer to him. It was only then he heard a slight distinctive panting sound. There was another shifting of material. Something was moving.

A word silently shouted an alarm through Sam's mind, "COUGAR!"

He dove into the mine opening and scurried down the hole to the larger room. He heard a muffled "clump" outside the entrance and heard more deep pants, followed by a guttural hiss.

"HO! CAT!" Sam shouted, "HO!" He followed this with his own take on a deep growl. He grabbed his knife and unsheathed it and picked up the closest excuse for a weapon he had, a nearby full jug of water.

"GO ON! GET OUT!" he shouted again, following it with another throaty growl. He was doing his best to sound big and mean but he was scared to death.

He could barely make out the contours of the big cat silhouetted in the moonlight. It was crouched in the opening, staring down the hole like it couldn't decide what to do. Sam put down the water jug and grabbed a baseball sized rock from the floor and squinted.

"I don't believe it," he whispered under his breath. "This day keeps getting better and better...he's actually *purring!*"

It sounded like a big housecat as it proceeded to recline in the entrance. Sam knew what was going on...it had him trapped and didn't have a worry in the world. He looked around until he found three more rocks, all debris from his recent brush with death. He stacked them in the entrance like he was getting ready for a snowball fight.

From what he had read about cougars, it probably would stay there until it got hungry enough to pursue him. When that happened, he had no place else to go so he'd have to make a stand.

As he peered down the passageway, he remembered his college days at the University of Houston, where the mascot had been a live cougar. Her name was Shasta and sometimes Sam used to sit outside the live mascot's enclosure and she would lounge on her concrete throne and stare at him, totally jaded.

He shook his head to dispatch the memory and decided he had to go on the offense.

"Cat!!!! GO HOME!"

Yelling seemed to have no effect, so he considered his angle of attack. The passage was low in relation to the anteroom, and not perfectly straight, so throwing a rock was going to be difficult. He'd have to do it on his knees so he knelt facing the exit and considered the angle. He could just make out the profile of the big cat. It looked smaller than his mental image of Shasta, so he hoped it might be an adolescent.

"Might work to my favor. I still might be able to scare it off."

It was monitoring him by sound, the way a house cat might, looking away in apparent disinterest but with one ear cocked toward him. When he first started coming out to west Texas, he had studied about the local wildlife and remembered reading cougars were more closely related to housecats than true lions. They generally hunted by stalking, usually attacking from behind.

"He must have been tracking me out there," he whispered, "I guess I attracted it when I tossed the rock. I've already been lucky twice today, let's hope my luck holds!"

He rotated his shoulder in its socket to loosen it up a little against the aches he had already suffered and took aim down the passage. When he heaved the rock, it bounced off the left side of the passage close to the end and clipped the big cat's ear. The startled cat jumped and glared down the passage just as Sam let another rock fly. He caught the puma right on the snout.

It released another terrifying guttural hiss, sounding like a cross between a cat hacking up a fur ball and a grating meow. A third rock hit it in the chest and the big cat gave a final deep hiss and jumped away.

"GO! CAT! GET OUT OF HERE!"

Sam listened intently and squinted down the tunnel, brandishing the fourth rock. All was quiet. The entrance seemed clear. He crouched and ate some snack crackers and took another swallow of water while he waited, which helped to clear his head. He silently wished he could just pack up and head out, but knew it would be another full day before Loot would pick him up. He lit a fresh candle and sat in the dim light.

"Cat's gone."

The whisper had the resonance of an almost familiar, gravelly voice, and it sent a chill down his spine. He squinted around the dimly lit space where vague shadows danced against the backdrop of boards and ragged rock. He could not help but conjure a mental visage of Slim, steadfastly watching over him.

Sam answered with a nervous chuckle, "I hope so."

He sat alone in the dim light for the better part of an hour thinking random thoughts. He thanked his luck, then remembered his talisman, missing since he went to help Moll. He was still looking for it. Then he rekindled memories of Slim, and finally, he tenderly wished he was cuddling with Smidgeon, stroking her long dark hair as she hugged him tight.

He took a deep breath and decided to cautiously move down the shaft to the opening. He saw the dried bush he used as a cover just an arm's reach outside. He hoped the cat had moved on to easier prey because he needed to grab his bush before he went to sleep. He took a deep breath and slowly reached out, grabbed one of the thicker branches and pulled the bush to fit firmly in the opening. Sam listened, hearing nothing but the normal sounds of the desert night. He retreated backward down the pathway and proceeded to bed down.

He woke up later than he had expected. His bruises hurt, his head hurt, and he was demoralized. Although Saturday had been a bad day all around, he knew he had to endure another full day out there. Sam crawled down to the entrance of the mine and peered through the dried branches of the bush. It was quite cloudy but the sun was up.

"The cat better be long gone," he muttered as he pushed the bush aside and emerged from the hole.

He quickly surveyed the area. All he saw were rocks and brush. From what he had glimpsed in the dark, he thought the puma was not quite full-grown. Sam sighed. An older, more experienced cat might not have been so easily scared away.

He walked around, stretching his legs as he tried to focus his mind on what he needed to do. He looked down at the mine entrance and felt dread at the thought of going back in, but he knew he really had no other choice. Even if he didn't start clearing out the debris from the cave-in, he'd at least have to spend most of the day using the mine as shelter and protection.

"Somebody might be out hunting," Sam said, then added, "Guess I've got nothing else to do, so I better do what I can."

Sam worked steadily through the day and managed to clear out a fair portion of the new rubble. He slowly filled crumbles of rock and pebbles into his burlap sacks, then dragged the bags to the entrance. Once outside, he distributed what he had collected, always examining each load by the handful before he scattered it. On one trip he even found one small sliver of a nugget about the size of a cut toenail.

"One bright moment in a dreary day," he quipped as he stashed the yellow rock in the watch pocket of his jeans.

He didn't want to go too far into the tunnel without a helmet and more shoring, so he stopped working early. He was battered and bruised and more than a little wary of the unstable walls and ceiling.

"Smidgeon was right," he said as he peered into the lower opening with a light. "Maybe Loot has something I could use."

The old man had managed to extract most of Sam's working tools from the bowels of his junkyard of a house. He actually had a good general idea of the treasures he had gathered, but finding something specific was usually a bit of an ordeal.

Sam turned in early and all too soon he snapped awake at the sound of his digital watch echoing in the anteroom. He sighed and stared in the dark for a few minutes before beginning his practiced routine. He had prepared the pack the night before, so all he had to do was hydrate and eat a bite, then scuttle down the entry shaft. He struggled to pivot the big rock back in place and once he had sealed the opening again, he headed off toward the highway. With the overcast it was darker than usual. He had made this hike so many times he wasn't worried about the distance or the direction, but he did turn around to listen a few times to make sure he wasn't being stalked by his new friend.

"A big cat wants easy prey," he said. "Hopefully I inflicted enough surprise and pain on him...maybe he won't think I'm a trouble-free meal."

As he walked, he deliberated the next inevitable conversation with Smidgeon. He also thought about the situation with the mine itself.

"Gotta get more lumber out here, but how?" he mumbled to himself as he walked.

His thoughts meandered while he walked, like they always did, so he again spent a bit of time wondering about his missing good luck piece. Then another thought popped into his head: he wondered if *that* was the reason for this apparent turn of bad luck, but he quickly shook off the thought.

"I'll go crazy thinking like that," he said. "But I *did* have the thing when I drove east."

He tried to recount his stops, but the trip for Godson's funeral was a blur of emotions and events and he had a hard time piecing together the timeline. Then he thought about Moll's sudden "bolder move." It was totally out of character for someone he considered a trusted old friend.

"She was drunk and grieving...it had to have been a combination," he mused.

He lost his course in the dark and hit the highway at a spot he guessed was about a half mile north of his usual spot. It wasn't the first time he had missed his mark in the dark. He had just lost concentration as he approached. Now he hoped no vehicles would come along while he hiked the short distance down to the protection of the culvert. He glanced at his watch after he dropped his pack at the base of the culvert.

"Right on time," he said. Dawn was just beginning to light up the sky.

Soon a vehicle drove past and he heard the familiar toot of the old Jeep's horn. He got up to the roadway and flashed his flashlight and threw his pack in the back when the truck returned and lumbered to a stop.

"What the heck happened to you!" the old man said, "you've got blood caked down the side of your head."

"What?"

"You're all bloody!"

Sam got in and turned the rear view mirror and used his flashlight to examine his head. He could see a dirt-caked bloody smear down the right side of his head.

"Oh, man," he said. "I think it looks worse than it really is but I've got to wash it off, hold on."

"Got a full jug of water in the back," the old man answered as Sam got out of the truck.

He splashed handfuls of water against the side of his head several times before getting back in the truck. Loot tossed Sam a wad of paper towels he had scrounged from the floorboards, put the truck in gear and eased it down the highway.

Sam dabbed the wad of towels to dry the side of his head. "Any better?"

"Maybe a little. What happened?"

"Cave-in," Sam answered. "I guess I caught a good one on my head. I had no idea I was bleeding."

"Maybe it was a slow leak...you okay?"

"Yeah. It shook me up pretty good, but I'm okay. Feels like another bunch of ranch hands have beaten me up though."

"A knock on the noggin ain't good. Need a hard hat down there."

"Yeah, Smidgeon has mentioned it more than once."

"Smart gal. I've probably got something you could use, somewhere. I'll poke around."

"Thanks, Loot."

"Mess up the mine?"

"It's not too bad, I guess, it's been pretty easy to clear out. Had a big boulder I was trying to break. Guess I clipped the ceiling with the hammer."

"Need shoring, Sam."

"I know. It's almost all I thought about on the hike. I'm going to have to make a lot of short trips carrying in loads of wood before I do much more with the deeper tunnel."

"Two could carry twice as much."

"Be twice as visible, too. There isn't much room down there, either...there's not really much room for two in the mine and it's not a safe place to camp outside."

"Well, we'll figure out something," the old man said.

The ancient truck rattled into town just as the sun was peeking up in the east. At the house, Sam cleaned up and examined his forehead. The cut was just under the hairline on the right side of his forehead, and was ringed with a bruise. It had looked a lot worse with the combination of caked-on blood and dirt.

"It should be easy to explain away to most people, but Smidgeon is not going to like it," he said,

As he started toward the front door, he felt a wave of dizziness and sat in the living room for a few minutes.

"Probably just hungry. I hardly ate out there," he said to himself.

While he rested, a thought popped into his mind. He picked up the phone and dialed Moll's number.

"I haven't checked on her since I got back. Besides, I want to ask her if she maybe found the box with my little good luck piece." There was no answer.

"Strange, she's usually up by now, but shouldn't be gone to work yet," he mused as he hung up and headed out the door.

Nine

Sam eased in the back door of the cafe just as the morning rush was beginning. He could tell, because the parking lot was full. He always seemed to run a little late after a weekend at the mine because he was tired and dirty and it took time to stow his gear and get cleaned up.

He immediately started washing the pile of dishes in the kitchen because he noticed the sink was already full. While he worked, Chuy brought him a cup of coffee and a chorizo and egg taco.

"Breakfast for you, *señor* Sam," he said, smiling to reveal the gold crown on one of his incisors. "Say, whachu got there?" He pointed to the side of Sam's forehead.

"Oh," Sam laughed, "yeah, I got a little bump."

"You okay? You don't look so good."

"I'm fine," he said as he gobbled down the taco and took a sip of coffee. He purposefully downplayed the injury, but he knew that if Chuy noticed so quickly, Smidgeon would notice. After another sip, he returned to the dishes. As he worked at the sink, Smidgeon came in with an order.

"Sam!" she said. "Thank heavens you finally got here!" She came over and he leaned over to offer her a cheek because he was up to his elbows in dishwater. As he bent over, he realized too late he was presenting her with the wound on his head.

She kissed his cheek, then her smile turned to a look of concern.

"What's this?"

Sam whispered, "Nothing. A rock hit me and cut me a little."

"A little? Are you okay?"

"I think so. Just one of those things."

She reached out and affectionately squeezed his upper arm gently but happened to touch one of the bruises he had sustained in the rock fall. He winced in pain.

"There too? What in the world happened out there?" she whispered.

"You know we can't talk here."

"Oh, we'll talk," she said as she gently stroked the spot on his arm before she headed back out into the dining room.

Smidgeon didn't mention it again throughout the breakfast and lunch shifts, but she could tell he was off his game. She gave him his space, but continued to glare at him with glowing eyes. It was accompanied by a deviously sweet smile and Sam knew he was in for some big trouble. He tried to keep up, but could feel his pace gradually slowing down the entire day. After the lunch rush, she walked over to him as he was busing tables; the café was empty.

"Sam, I'll take the evening shift tonight... you go home and get some rest."

"You've been up since before dawn," he said. "I'm okay."

"Yeah, right. Who are you kidding? You've been up even longer. Look, I'll talk to you about all this later. I've been watching you. I'm pretty sure you got hit harder than you're saying so I'll say it again... you go home right now and take it easy. If you push back on me about this, I'll close the café right now and take you to the doctor. Do you want that?"

"No," he replied sheepishly. "But I'm fine."

"Maybe you are, but I'm the boss here and I'm telling you to go home."

"The boss of the restaurant or the boss of me?"

"Right this minute, I'm both," she said with her hands on her hips. She was trying to look stern and businesslike, but her body language almost made him laugh out loud. "Now, take that tub in the back and go home!"

"Yes, ma'am," he said, bending down to give her a kiss.

When he got to the house, another wave of dizziness swept over him as he walked in the door. MamaKat curled around his legs and he stood there for a minute to let his head clear.

"Whew, dizzy," he said, "Maybe she was right, MamaKat."

"Rowrr," came the reply.

Sam went into the little front bedroom where he stowed most of his gear. His pack was on a small divan by the window. He shoved it aside, stretched out and fell asleep almost immediately.

~ * ~

"Baby, wake up. Honey?"

It was as if an angel were talking to him, a voice on high, interrupting whatever mundane dream-thing he was doing. He opened his eyes.

"Wha...?" A figure crouched in the dark by the side of the divan. It was Smidgeon.

"I was wondering if you were going to wake up; I've been shaking you and talking. How long you been asleep? Since you got home?"

Sam nodded.

"Well, get up and wash your hands. I brought us some burgers from The Mossback. We better eat them before they turn on us." Her laugh came with a wonderful Smidgeon smile.

Sam stood a little too quickly and he hoped she didn't see him stagger with another wave of dizziness, but he should have known better.

She spun around and helped steady him. "Hey, sweetie, you okay?"

"Just stood up too fast. I'm okay. Slept too hard."

"I'm hoping that's what it is. You come in here and eat; then we're going to talk."

Sam thought he knew what was coming and did not want to talk about it but he was resigned to his fate.

The burgers were lukewarm and the fries were limp, but he hadn't eaten much at all in the previous thirty-six hours, so he began to eat quickly while Smidgeon politely nibbled and watched him until he realized he needed to slow down.

They chatted about the café and Smidgeon shared some local gossip. These were regular conversations since the café encompassed most of their daily lives. He was grateful she was deferring the inevitable and, even with the small talk, he was trying to formulate what he wanted to say to her. When the meal was over, she cleared the table, took Sam by the hand and led him to the living room. She sat on the couch, playfully patted the seat spot to her and Sam sat down. She took his hand in hers and turned to him.

"So, Sam… sweetie… now… why don't you just cut the bull and tell me what the hell happened to you out there?"

He hesitated at first, then meekly responded, "Cave-in."

She swallowed hard and stared at him for just a moment before repeating the phrase. "Cave-in?"

He nodded. "Yeah. It was a pretty bad one."

"So, that's how you got hit on the head?"

He nodded again. "I was almost buried. I was on my side, trying to break a boulder too big to haul out. I guess I clipped the roof. I wish the rock had broken as easily as the tunnel did."

"Are you okay, I mean, I guess your head doesn't look too bad but what about the rest of you?"

"I didn't even realize I had been cut until Loot told me this morning. I'm bruised up pretty good. The worst thing is, I've lost months of work. This made even more work."

"Sam, maybe it's time to just let this thing go. I mean, you've given this a good shot. We have a thriving business and I've grown so dependent on your help it's a hassle when you take off to go out there. I mean, I know I signed up for this in the first place, but...honey, I'm not going to lose you out there."

"You know I can't let this go. I just can't." He lifted the back of her hand to his lips and kissed it. "I love you, baby, but I can't do it."

"I love you too, but you have to listen to me, Sam. Nobody even knows where it is. Sure, you got out this time, but you get buried again, I mean, get trapped...there's no way I can find you. You understand that? I can't bear the thought of you being buried in a pile of rubble at the bottom of some hole, slowly dying because you were too stubborn to listen to common sense."

"I know. I need to rethink how I'm going about this."

"And your head," she said. "You just might have a concussion. I really should take you in to the doctor."

"I'm okay," he said, gingerly touching the sore spot on his forehead. "But I've changed my mind about the whole hardhat thing. You were right."

"Wait, what's that? Are you saying I was *right*?" She laughed. "Finally, you're saying something sensible."

Sam smirked as he continued, "Loot thinks he's got something I can use."

"I'm not sure it's enough. I really don't. How can I let you go out there again? I mean, if you were overdue, missing, I'd have to just head out there and look for you and I don't have a clue of where you are. At the very least you need to show me, or somebody, where it is."

"You can't leave the restaurant and Loot's too old and I don't think he's well. Godson might have been a good bet, but he's dead. Who else do we have?"

"My cousin, Hezekiah. He could do it."

"Hezekiah?"

"He was a big help when you went back east. He's young and he's strong and I'm sure he can keep his mouth shut."

"I'll think about it. Don't worry right now, though. I need to shore up what I've got and that means hauling lumber. On foot, it will take quite a while to stockpile what I need. Those will be a lot of short overnight trips. You know, like I did early on when I worked on the front portions."

Smidgeon put two fingers on Sam's chin and nudged his head over so she could kiss him, then gently caressed the side of his face, looked him in the eyes and kissed him again.

"You need to know something, Sam Milton. I'd kill you if you up and died on me out there."

"I know," he laughed.

She stood, took him by the hand again and led him to the bedroom.

"Now, why don't you show me those bruises," she said softly, "so I can kiss them and make them all better?"

~ * ~

The next week was a blur. Sam's head still ached from time to time but he never went to the doctor. He opted out of a hike to the mine the following weekend because the weather was iffy. He still didn't feel right about Smidgeon's suggestion to enlist the aid of her cousin, but he knew it was an argument he would not be able to win.

At Smidgeon's urging, Hezekiah came to visit Sam at closing time one night and they talked for a while in the darkened restaurant. When Smidgeon had first made the suggestion, Sam remembered her mentioning Hezekiah helping her in the café when he left after Godson's death but he couldn't quite recall the face. But when he arrived, Sam recognized him from one of the church functions they had attended. He was young, about twenty, and roughly Sam's height but with a stouter build. Sandy hair and blue eyes were framed by scraggly attempts at growing a beard along his jaw line. His handshake was strong and he had calloused hands, showing the boy was no stranger to hard work.

"So, Hezekiah. You're Smidgeon's cousin?"

"Yeah, I reckon I am," he said. "Everybody but her calls me Hez," he laughed.

"Well, that figures," Sam said. "Can I call you Hez?"

"Sure thing. So, what's this all about...she just said you needed my help. I think the world of Smidgeon and would do anything to help her. Some in our family don't care much for your living arrangement, but I figure it's her business, hers and yours, so as far as I'm concerned if she loves you, you're family, just the same as her."

"You ever heard of Ben Sublett?"

The young man raised fingers to his chin and stroked sparse whiskers as he thought about his answer. "Hear'd something a while back. Legend, I think. Something about gold."

"That's right. It's said he had a gold mine back in the eighteen hundreds."

"Up in the Guadalupes."

"Maybe a little closer," Sam said, smiling.

"Wait, you mean...?"

"Maybe. Who can know for sure," Sam started, then related a short version of the jail story. The young man listened intently, then sat silently for a long time, staring at his hands clasped in front of him.

Finally he looked up. "It's the kind of stuff kids dream about," Hez said, smiling broadly. "What do you need from me?"

"I've been digging out there, but it's unstable. I've, well, been a little hesitant about bringing anybody else in there. You know, the MacGreggs would likely string me up if they caught me out there."

"No doubt."

"But by myself, I can't bring in enough lumber to shore it up right. One man, hiking miles in, can only bring in so much."

"Wood is heavy," Hez nodded, "two can carry twice as much, maybe more."

"I've got supplies out there, hadn't figured on feeding two, but I'm looking at a bunch of quick trips just carrying wood. I had a bad cave-in last weekend, almost buried me."

"Two would be safer, with one in the hole...the other could dig him out."

"Yeah, that's the other part of this idea. I've had cave-ins but I've been lucky. Smidgeon is worried because nobody else knows where it is. But anybody I bring in has to keep quiet. You already know a lot...I'm hoping I can I trust you."

Hez stood up and faced Sam, extending his hand. "I told you how I feel about my cousin, and about you. If you need my help, you've got it. Your secret is safe."

They shook hands and Hezekiah added one more question, "So, when we going?"

Sam laughed, "Maybe a week out, on a Friday night if the weather allows. Quick in and out."

~ * ~

Hezekiah proved to be a valuable helper. He could carry half again as much of a load Sam could and he was quite ingenious. He devised a rig he made specifically for the purpose of carrying a bigger load of wood.

"I seen something like this in some *National Geographic* magazine. Some natives somewhere had a rig like this to carry firewood. I gots a good memory for stuff," he told Sam.

After the first trip, Hez usually lead the way, and rarely consulted the compass, which alarmed Sam, who would insist they check their bearings in the dark, but the young man seemed to have an innate ability to keep on track. After four such short trips, Sam felt they had enough wood stockpiled to begin shoring up the fragile tunnel and on the next trip they began to work on the mine itself. As Sam had promised Smidgeon, Loot had scrounged him an ancient round hardhat and Hez brought his own.

They followed the same routines on the return trip, with Hezekiah riding in the back of Loot's truck. Sam was worried it might look suspicious, but Loot assured him it just looked like they were going out either hunting or working. "I'm just glad you have somebody along to make it safer for you, Sam."

"I have to admit," Sam told the younger man one day, as they worked on the deeper shaft, "you have been a godsend. I can't imagine trying to do this alone. It would have taken me half a year to get this much lumber out here." As he said that, he remembered how long it had taken him to shore up the outer tunnel and anteroom.

The shoring work was especially tiresome alone, as each plank had to be retrieved. They took turns in the tunnel, the second man feeding the other planks from the stockpile.

"Shucks, Sam," young Hez said. "I love it. This is an adventure. I don't even care if we don't never finds no gold."

Sam smiled. Deep down, he shared the same sentiment. Getting rich wasn't the important thing, but he *did* need to see what was at the end of the hole.

Ten

Sunday was his day off, but to Lance it seemed pretty much like any other day. He saddled up his favorite MacGregg horse, Pinto, then he headed off into the backlands of the ranch. He found it relaxing and it allowed him to get a better feel for the land. He sometimes took his dog Prewash with him, but this particular Sunday the dog had stayed home because he knew the area he wanted to explore was rugged and he didn't want to worry about the old pup.

He guided Pinto down a lonely jeep trail for quite a while, then veered off onto what looked like a wildlife trail. Eventually he approached a steep drop-off, where he paused to scan the area below. It was mid-morning and with the sun beating down, he was already starting to sweat. A slight glint below the ridge caught his eye.

"What's that, Pinto?" The horse ignored the question.

Lance dismounted and moved closer to the edge of the slight cliff to get a better view.

"Definitely saw a flicker of light off of something. What the heck would be out here?"

He secured the reins to a nearby mesquite tree and meandered his way down to the base of the ridge. He tried to remember where he had seen the reflection and poked around the general location until he finally found what he was looking for.

"Hah. Small pot, like for camping," he mumbled to himself. "Looks old. Probably been here a while. Just dumb luck the sun caught it just right."

He walked around the general area again, poking among the rocks and brush until he found a rusted can with holes cut in it. He turned it around in his hands.

"Tin can stove, I guess. Must go with the pot."

He looked toward the open end of the gully, then looked back up at Pinto, standing patiently at the top of the rim.

"Weird," he said, dropping the remnant of the can next to the small pot.

He made his way back up to the rim, thinking about his finds and who might have left them.

"Lost illegals, maybe," he said. "Bad place. Ain't nothing around here but the ranch and, I guess, the highway way over there," he said, glancing into the distance.

Once remounted, he pulled the reins and moved away from the ridge.

"Keep an eye out for bones, Pinto," he joked. "If anybody got lost out this way...well, they likely died."

He rode along for another hour or so, sometimes returning to the broken down jeep trail, sometimes revisiting the rim for another look, comparing what he saw to his memory of the maps he had studied.

He bent and gently stroked the horse's neck. "Ain't seen nothing, Pinto. There's one more cut I want to see, then we'll head back."

They approached the edge of the ridge again and a deep cut into the rim fanned out below. Barren landscape dotted with boulders and sparse vegetation stretched toward a distant plain. Unlike the spot where he found the pot, this part of the rim wasn't quite as steep. Lance spied a vague trail close by.

"What you think, girl? Think we can make it down this little trail? Somebody or something managed to do it."

The horse snorted and shook its head.

"Maybe you're right." Lance laughed and patted Pinto's neck again as he dismounted. "I'll leave you up top again."

Once he secured Pinto, Lance made his way down the rough trail.

"Animal trail," he muttered. "Glad I didn't push the horse. She knew."

At the base of the trail, the cut extended to his right, gradually widening, but in places the walls were quite steep.

"Almost a little canyon. Looks like a good place," he said, making his way through rocks and boulders and scratchy brush. Overhead a hawk kept a wary eye on his progress, soaring in wide circles. Lance also never stopped scanning in all directions, especially behind him.

"Good place for a big cat to stalk and ambush," he murmured. "Hope the horse is okay up there."

To Lance, this cut looked exactly like all the others. Erosion had slowly eaten away at the slopes of the rim, cutting a deep "V" into the mountain. He had a general idea of what he was looking for, but he didn't see it. He struggled to remember the stories his grandfather had told him.

"Follow the devil," he muttered. "That's what grandpa Thad had said." He looked back at the top of the rim. "Diablo Rim...the devil, right?"

He looked down the cut. "Ain't nothing like no table, though."

He had wracked his brains for years, trying to figure out the table reference. He again scanned the horizon, hoping he might see a mesa-topped mountain in the distance.

"*Nada*," he said. "Then there was the other thing grandpa said. Something about the 'why of it', but I think it probably hinges on finding the danged table, whatever it is."

Another hundred yards or so down the cut, Lance stopped in his tracks and stared. A small slab of limestone had fallen on a boulder and was wedged against the canyon wall. To the young foreman the piece of rock looked like...

"A table!"

Lance ran to the rock and put his palm against the flat surface, as if testing it to see if it was real. Then he remembered the final clue his grandpa Thad had uttered those many years ago and turned around. He stared in disbelief as he saw two ancient fault lines, cracks in the limestone of the wall, one intersecting the other.

"A 'Y'!"

At the tail of the Y there was an oddly placed bush and in front of it another slab, flat on the ground. The scraggly plant seemed unnatural and almost as soon as he focused on it, the plant suddenly rolled away, as if pushed. Then he could clearly see the hole and a figure moving, struggling out of the hole. Lance reached down toward the small gun he kept in a special sling in the top of his boot, but he froze in surprise as the figure took shape... it was a man in a round hard hat dragging a heavy burlap sack. The man stood and removed the hat to wipe his brow. At this point he noticed Lance and dropped the hard hat with a dull clang. They both stood, for several tense seconds, not saying a word. Lance had immediately recognized the face. He assumed the other man had done likewise.

Lance straightened up. "Sam?"

Sam looked completely crestfallen and lowered his head as he gave a brief nod. Lance took a step forward and Sam suddenly looked up again and took a step back toward the hole.

"Hold on, Sam. Hold on."

Sam's face flushed and his eyes widened and looked as if he were about to spring like a bobcat, but Lance didn't know if he was the target or the hole was the target. He felt a wave of alarm because had no way of knowing what weapons Sam might have down in the hole. Then he remembered the offhand statement Loot had made about Sam and he realized the enormity of the apparent *faux pas*. This was no coincidence and the old man obviously knew a lot more than he had said.

Lance put up both hands, palms facing out.

"Hold on, Sam, let's talk. I think I know what's going on. It ain't as bad as you think."

~ * ~

When Sam emerged from the mine and saw Lance, his brain flushed with shock and alarm. Hezekiah had stayed home this trip to tend to his sick mother, so Sam was working alone and it had already been a long day. He had grown dependent on the young workhorse's help and he struggled to lug the heavy bags of debris out of the mine by himself. Now, his worst fear was realized in the form of the solitary figure facing him. He immediately recognized the foreman.

His first impulse was to rush Lance, but in a split second he reassessed the notion and considered jumping back into the hole, but that also seemed to be a foolish option. Lance raised his hands, palms out. He wanted to talk.

Sam's mind was reeling, but he managed to stifle his shock and reassessed his options. He remembered Loot mentioning the night Lance visited him and the suspicions he had raised about the foreman were obviously true. Slim *had* to have shared clues with the grandfather. The fact Lance was standing here proved the point. He must have been 'following the devil' and recognized the significance of the table-like rock. Then Sam realized something else. If Lance had indeed been searching for the mine, the secret was still probably safe.

"Okay. I guess we talk."

"Look, Sam, I'm as surprised to see you as you are to see me."

"Well, I guess it makes sense. You mentioned the mine to Loot. He figured you knew something. Didn't expect anything like this to happen this soon, though."

"Can we walk up the arroyo a ways? I need to check on my horse."

"Your horse? You don't have anybody else waiting, do you?"

"Naw, just the horse. Pinto's up at the top of the rim. I've been gone a lot longer than I expected. We can talk while we walk back there."

Sam picked up the bush. "Let me shove this back in the hole and cover it up."

Lance nodded and Sam did as he had said.

"Not much of a cover," Lance chuckled.

"Well, I don't, well...didn't...much expect anyone to be coming up this cut. It's more to cover it from a distance, to just sort of blend in." He kicked the flat rock. "This is the real cover."

Lance chuckled, then extended his hand.

"First, I want you to know I'm not here to blow your gig. Okay? I've been out looking most every Sunday since I got here."

"Loot said you showed up and asked some questions, mentioned Slim *and* the mine. We both figured you knew something."

As Sam shook his hand, Lance said, "I thought there was something strange when he blurted out your name...it was something about not telling you about my granddad being with Slim when they was beaten up."

"Yeah, he told me Slim had been beaten once, but he sorta missed that one detail."

"So you knew Slim?"

Sam nodded. "He told me about the mine before he died."

"Oh, man." Lance looked down and lightly shook his head.

"We were in jail. He was in on a drunk charge and I was in on...well, it doesn't matter. He'd been hit, but I think wasn't well anyway. Alcohol had pretty much broken him. The clip to the throat the cops gave him was just the straw that broke the camel's back, you know?"

Lance nodded. "Slim and Grandpa Thad was partners. These old timers all put a lot of stock in trust and friendship. Once you started helping him, I reckon you had forged that kind of connection with him. I guess he told you the same things he told grandpa...like 'follow the devil'..."

Sam added, "Until you see the table..."

Lance finished, "...then turn around and you'll see the why of it."

They both stopped, stared at each other and laughed out loud.

Then Sam sighed deeply and shook his head. "You figured it out a lot quicker than I did. I spent almost ten years before I noticed Diablo Rim on the maps."

"Well, Grandpa told me he was on MacGregg land when he was beat up...when I met Tim in college it seemed almost like fate. I always figured the last place they ended up would be a good place to start. But Tim never would let me come out here, well, at least until his daddy passed."

They were at the base of the rim. A horse snorted nervously above them. Lance moved deftly up the faint wildlife trail. Sam squinted up and saw him talking to the horse, patting the nose and stroking the mane. Then he came back down and they started back out the cut.

"Horse looks okay," Lance said. "Too rough to risk him, I mean, bring him down such a rickety trail, you know? But I was mostly worried about something like a big cat getting him."

"Yeah, one was stalking me out here not too long ago. I had to scramble into the hole to wait him out."

"No kidding. So, the hole you found, you reckon it's the mine?

"Fits the clues."

"You find anything?"

Sam shook his head. "Couple of flakes. Haven't been down to the end yet. Been abandoned for years...most of it was collapsed.

I've slowly been digging it out...had a bad cave-in not too long ago, almost killed me. Still cleaning up from that."

"So, you work in the little café for your grubstake and come out here on weekends?"

"Depends on the weather." Sam stopped and looked Lance straight in the eye. "So what do you want?"

"Sam, I don't know what I want. This is...well, you know, it's been gnawing at the back of my head since I was a little kid."

They started walking again.

"Believe me, I know the feeling. Been a part of most of my life. I called it 'the fever' for a long time."

"Good name for it. I think I have it too. Can I take a look?"

Sam sighed again. "Don't see how I can refuse. Sure."

They were soon back at the mine entrance where Sam retrieved his hard hat and removed the bush from the entrance. "Got another one you can use inside."

"Safety regulations?"

"Got knocked silly in the last cave-in, so it seems like a good idea. I resisted the notion for a long time."

Lance laughed. "Yeah, literally got some sense knocked into you."

Sam tugged at the burlap sack he had dropped, dragged it out of the hole and left it outside.

"Usually spread this stuff around...don't want to leave the sack sitting too long. Somebody might see."

"Not likely. Nothing scheduled out this way." Lance laughed again. "I reckon I can keep that schedule up for a long time."

Sam smiled. For the first time since this encounter began, it seemed as if this might work out okay.

~ * ~

Lance was about three inches taller than Sam and after carefully placing his weathered hat on the ground, he struggled to follow the shorter man through the mine entrance.

"This is tight, Sam. This how you found it?"

Sam laughed. "Shored it up a bit, but yeah. There's more room up here," he said, nodding ahead.

Lance moved into the anteroom and could tell there was more headroom. He raised his head to stand.

"Hold on, low ceiling," Sam said, "but you can crouch or maybe stand on your knees."

Candlelight danced on the sides of the room.

"Past cave-ins left this cavity," Sam explained. "First part I cleared. Did find a couple of tiny nuggets clearing it out, but the tunnel extends down this way," he said, pointing.

Lance nodded toward the sleeping bag and various assortments of tools and supplies and asked, "You stay down here?"

"Can't sleep out in the open… too visible. It's cool down here all year long. When I was first searching, I never came out when it was hot or cold, but there's not much temperature variation in here."

Lance scurried over to the far tunnel. "And this is the money pit?"

Sam guffawed. "Hah! Hasn't been, at least so far. But it's what I would call the real mine. Was almost my tomb."

Lance sat and rubbed the dust off his palms.

Sam sat as well. "So where does this leave us, Lance?'

"Up 'til now, this was just a notion for me, like a dream. I reckon you probably felt the same way. A big part of me never thought I'd ever find a damn thing, yet here it is. I'm still processing it, Sam."

"You're right, I did feel that way."

"And you've done a ton of work on this thing."

"Probably several tons," Sam chuckled.

Lance put his hand on Sam's shoulder, "Sam, just to be clear, your secret is safe. I know, it seems like I'm part of the ranch, but this is different. I've got no stake in turning it over. I mean, you're trespassing and all, but then again, if I turn you in, I get nothing. Nobody gets nothing."

"That's true." Sam brushed a tickle from his nose.

"You found it fair and square and I guess I've got no right to intrude, but I want you to think about something. Slim and Scamp were partners, you know? I really think we've each inherited part of their legacy. If you'll have me, I'd really like to partner up."

"Partners," Sam's voice lost a little tone at the end of the word. "Didn't plan on any partners. Already got too many people involved."

"Loot, I figure, and you said something about the café owner's cousin helping you. Means she's probably in on it too. Anybody else?"

Sam nodded. "You're smart, Lance. Yeah, that's about it, except a couple of friends back in Austin who I told about it. Still, nobody but Hezekiah knows where it is...and now you."

"Not even Loot?"

"Nope. He usually picks me up, so he knows where I come out, but he's never been all the way out here."

"Bit long in the tooth to go tramping cross country."

"Pretty much, although sometimes I wonder if he might surprise us. He's a pretty strong guy."

"Don't look well, not to me anyway. I watched my Grandpa Thad slowly dwindle. I think Loot's started to go the same way."

"Aw, I hope not, Lance. He's been a good and loyal friend."

Lance shook his head. "Who the heck can know for sure? Anyway," he extended his hand. "Partners?"

Sam hesitated. Flickering candlelight flashed crazy shadows across his face as he pondered the question.

"Look, it must be awful man-hauling timber and stuff," he said, pointing to the small pile of boards and tools stashed along one wall. "I can cache supplies for you. I've got a *reason* to be out here...you don't. I can get away with a heck of a lot more than you can, get things closer. I bring a lot to the...well, to the table." Lance tried to suppress a giggle.

Sam laughed at the pun and extended his hand and Lance shook it. "Okay, partners." He sighed. "Like you said, I guess we have a joint legacy to fulfill."

"I best be getting back. Hope Pinto isn't cougar meat by now."

"Yeah, I have work to do, too. Didn't plan on such a long break and I still have a bag of crap to spread around."

"Don't know much about no gold mining, but shouldn't it be sluiced?"

"Ideally, but how in the world am I going to run a sluice out here? Just going for the big stuff right now. I want to get to the bottom of the deep shaft. *That's* where old Ben must have been working."

They both scurried out of the hole and stood near the entrance. The late spring warmth was a welcome relief after the cool dampness of the mine.

"So, how long you going to be here?"

"Through tonight. I usually start hiking out to the highway about midnight," Sam said.

Lance whistled. "Quite a hike."

"Did much worse when I was searching blindly."

"I got nothing to write with or I'd give you my number," Lance said, putting his hat back on.

"I close the café most nights. Drop by at closing time and we can talk. I've got a white Volkswagen—easy to spot." He laughed. "That's how I met Loot—he spotted my car parked on the side of the road several times and figured out what I was up to."

"Crafty old coot," Lance said, adding, "I better get out of here, Sam. See you soon."

They exchanged a final wave as Lance swiftly walked toward the top of Diablo Rim.

Eleven

Sam managed to clear only one more bag of debris from the mine after Lance left.

"My heart just isn't in it," he said as he finally dropped an empty sack in the anteroom. "I feel like the wind has been knocked out of me." He sat on top of his rolled sleeping bag, gulped water from one of his jugs and considered his new situation.

Things had been improving, especially with Hezekiah's help. The mine was safer and with the additional shoring they had added, he was making steady progress on the lower shaft. The arrival of Lance Norton was something he could never have anticipated and he thought long and hard about the implications.

"I don't know," he said to himself while mindlessly rearranging his tools, "but I have a gut feeling. I think I can trust him." Then he added, "What else can I do?"

He ate a Spartan dinner of Vienna sausages and crackers, and turned in early, only to suffer through a fitful sleep before his alarm woke him about midnight. He swore under his breath when he thought he heard a muffled rumbling, then quickly scrambled down the tunnel. As he approached the exit, he could hear the rain and the tunnel was briefly illuminated by a flash of lightning. This was followed by another rumble of thunder.

"Just bloody great."

Every foray was based on a good weather forecast and he had been lucky in the past, but the weatherman had failed him this time. Drizzle and light rain didn't bother him, but this was a major storm and he knew it made navigation difficult and the lightning made it dangerous.

"Nothing to do but put on my poncho and head out."

Pivoting the wet entrance stone was more difficult as the rain pelted his face and he struggled to keep his grip, but he finally managed to get it into place. He looked up the cut toward the rim, worried about a flash flood but reasoned that if flooding were a problem in this gully, the mine would have been revealed long ago. Still, he thought to himself, flooding was always a concern in this country. He squinted in the dark, thankful there didn't seem to be much runoff so far.

Sam hiked to the east, maintaining his bearings as best as he could. One particularly bright flash of lightning gave him a glimpse of one of his regular landmarks, so he was fairly certain he was right on track. The weather alternated between light rain and periods of torrential downpour. Some of the dry streambeds he regularly crossed had standing water, but he had no trouble crossing them. He lowered his head against the driving rain as he moved on. Lightning was his worst fear because on the flatlands between the small outcrop of mountains and the highway, he was often the high point on the land and he couldn't help but imagine himself to be a human lightning rod.

"Most miserable hike of my life," he mumbled to himself, and for some reason he remembered the parting words of Loretta's mother as the word "curse" filtered through his mind while he stumbled through the rain.

Then his thoughts again turned to his missing good-luck piece, the small cross-shaped rock. It was such a small thing, one tiny detail in a mountain of thoughts, but he searched his memory, trying to remember when he last saw it.

"The trip when Godson died," he whispered. "I had it then."

As he was leaving, he had almost forgotten it, but had pointedly gone back to retrieve it. It had always been a part of his travel kit since the ice storm and he recalled the odd feeling it gave him as he followed the instructions of the old woman to hold it tight for several miles so the power would bind to him. He remembered the time he first told Godson and Moll about it, right after he had found the mine.

"I know this rock, a fairy stone," Godson had said.

"That's right," a surprised Sam had said. A trucker told him the same thing when he had first met Loretta and showed it to her at the truck stop where they had taken refuge.

"Where'd you get this little case?" Moll had asked.

"Loretta," he had said, "she gave me the case."

Loretta had been quite impressed with the story of the old *bruja*, but Godson and Moll scoffed at the supernatural qualities of the rock and the implied power of the old Mexican witch-woman.

His heart raced as he thought more about it, but the preoccupation was a welcome diversion from his misery.

"Where the heck could it be?"

Smidgeon had lived in the southwest all her life and knew the reputation of *brujos* and *brujas* so she was a bit intimidated by the object and the story behind it. As a rule, she wasn't openly superstitious, but she always made Sam keep it hidden.

"Surely if she had seen it, she would have told me to put it away," he reasoned. "She didn't even like to touch it, so I doubt she would have stashed it anywhere herself."

A sudden wave of hard rain thrashed him in the face as he continued his wretched hike.

"I'm glad I'm hiking out, not in," he said, and his resolve to continue was fueled by thoughts of warmth and dry clothes.

He kept moving steadily east, trying to squint through the raindrops pelting him, scanning between lightning flashes, searching for scant outlines of his landmarks while he walked. His boots and pant legs were soaked but his pack was still dry under his poncho.

Finally, he got close enough to see headlights and taillights in the distance, shimmering through splatters of rain. Seeing a few souls braving the highway in the storm renewed his hope Loot would be there meet him.

It was still pitch black when he stumbled onto the highway. Sam didn't know if the storm had delayed the first hints of dawn or if it had caused him to hasten his pace. He also didn't know where he was in relation to the culvert. In the past, whenever he had gone off course he had trended toward the north, so he decided to turn right to head south.

"Worst I can do is hit Van Horn," he tried to joke to himself. He didn't laugh.

Headlights appeared on the horizon but he didn't care. He had no place to hide so he just trudged on and hoped they wouldn't notice him. It was raining so hard he could barely see, but the headlights sped toward him and splashed past him at highway speed.

Sam trudged on. More headlights appeared.

"Middle of nowhere rush hour," he mumbled. It was a misery-driven attempt to keep his spirits up.

This time the vehicle slowed slightly but still moved past him. He kept walking but was soon surprised by an old pickup easing alongside him. It was Loot.

Sam struggled with the straps of his pack under the poncho before dropping his burden in the truck bed. He knew everything was going to get soaked and he didn't care, but old Loot got out and threw a small tarp to him.

"Figured we'd need this," he yelled through the downpour.

Sam tucked it around the pack and got in the cab.

"Sorry, gonna get your seat wet," he said.

"No problem, this old girl's seen worse," Loot said, patting the dashboard. "You're maybe a mile south of the culvert. I barely noticed ya in this rain. You give up on me and start hiking to town?" He laughed.

"Usually I tend north. So I headed south when I hit the road. It was impossible to get a bearing in this," Sam said, nudging his head toward the side window.

"I wondered if you'd even try it. Dangerous. Lightning will reckon you're an easy target."

"I know, but...well, I just never figured on this mess...forecast was great last Friday."

"Darned weatherman don't know nothing. If you weren't here I'd just figure on tomorrow."

After a mile or so, another car came up behind them on the highway. As it passed them with a splash, Sam blurted out, "That new MacGregg foreman found me."

Loot had been intent on the passing car but Sam's comment gave him such a start he almost drove off the road.

"What?" He struggled to maintain control of the old truck, then when he got the truck stable he stared intently at his passenger.

"I was dragging a bag of rocks and there he was, just standing there looking at me. You were right, Loot. He not only knew something, he *knew the clues*, word for word...he was following them. His granddaddy Scamp was in on it...he got the clues fair and square just like I did." Sam laughed, "Took me ten years to figure out Diablo Rim, but he focused right on it."

"So, we done then?"

"Not sure. He just wants in. It's funny...he's a lot like me in a way. He's had this riddle working on him all his life, the same way it did with me."

"He's got the fever," Loot chuckled.

"Yeah, I think he does. Anyway, he's going to come to the café one night so we can talk. He said he can likely help and you know, he's in a position to do it, like bring a lot of supplies close in. I'm hoping we can trust him. What do you think?"

"Tricky stuff," the old man said as the truck rattled and splashed south toward town. Then he added, "But, like as not, I guess we're stuck with him. For what it's worth, I kinda like the guy. Liked his granddaddy too."

~ * ~

It was raining hard as Sam walked up to the porch with his pack. He heard the phone ringing as he fumbled with his keys but by the time he opened the door, it had stopped. MamaKat chastised him for his tardiness as he unloaded his backpack. The pack itself was quite wet but it had protected most of the contents. When he finished emptying it, he hung it on a hook in the laundry room to dry.

"Still can't find it," he muttered to himself, thinking of the small jewelry box.

He rummaged through the drawers of his dresser, knocking a few random items to the floor but again came up empty-handed. He looked over shelves and even under the divan in the small room. Then the phone rang again.

"Hello?"

"Sam! I've been worried sick ever since they changed the forecast."

"Aw, you didn't have to worry. Just a little rain, that's all."

"A LOT of rain. And lightning. It doesn't take a direct hit to get you, you know."

"Yeah, I know."

"So, you're okay?"

"Yeah, just got in. Soaked to the skin, but I'm fine."

"You take a hot shower and see how you feel. I'd rather you take a day off than get sick because you tried to do too much, you know?"

"You're sweet, you know that? I think I'm fine. I was just looking for something. I'll get cleaned up and come on in."

As he put the handset into the cradle he added privately, "No need to tell you the other news quite yet." He knew the revelation of Lance Norton's involvement wouldn't sit well with her.

~ * ~

Business was slower than usual at The Mossback but there were enough customers to keep the routine busy. Late in the day, Smidgeon almost insisted he go home, but he convinced her he was fine. Toward closing time he saw a truck pulling into the parking lot.

"He didn't take much time," Sam said under his breath.

The rain had stopped but Lance Norton scraped any remnants of the storm off his boots before he entered the restaurant.

"Hey, Lance, you want something to eat? It's been dead, so I think Chuy's shut down part of the kitchen already, but we could probably rustle you up a burger."

"If you can add some fries, I'll take it," Lance said, removing his hat.

Sam gave Chuy the order and joined Lance in the dining room.

"So you made it out okay," Lance started.

"Yeah. Not my favorite hiking weather, but it wasn't the first time. I was more worried about lightning than anything."

"Worse on a horse, you really *are* the highest point a lot of times."

Sam laughed, "Not sure it matters much out on that open plain."

"Yeah, a close hit will get both you and the horse."

They both got silent as Chuy brought out the food.

"Mister Sam, it's eight. Okay if I leave? Everything is done except for a little bit."

"Fine, Chuy, I'll get it; you go ahead and take off."

Chuy nodded to Lance and headed back through the kitchen and they heard the back door slam shut.

"Now we're alone," Sam said as he locked the front door and flipped the placard to the 'closed' position.

"Good burger," Lance said when he returned.

"Thanks. I think we do a pretty good job here. You know, I always liked this place. In the early days it was one of my regular stops. I'd hike out of the hills and stop to get a bite. It was kind of a tradition for me. It was a long drive back home to Austin, so a good breakfast was a priority."

"So you've always hiked all night like that?"

"Yeah, there wasn't really any other way to do it."

Lance whistled through his two front teeth. "Wow, Austin is a long trip from here. Now I understand why you moved out here. I mean, at least I came out to work in my field, but you, I just couldn't figure it. Educated city boy and you came *here*? Now it makes more sense. Don't get me wrong, she's a sweet gal and all and love will make a man do some strange things but … gold, well it's a whole different story."

Sam nodded, and interrupted the small talk. "So, how are we going to handle this? Taking on another partner was never part of my plan, but I guess I don't have much choice."

Lance took another bite out of his burger, and chewed it slowly as he put it down on the plate, looking Sam in the eye the entire time.

He swallowed his mouthful and said, "Here's how I see it. You found it first, but it's pretty obvious I would have eventually found it too. Heck, I *did* find it. We both had the same information from the same source, the same clues, right? I know it's a tough nut to swallow but it's just me, well, me and my dog. You said just a couple of people you know are in on it, right?"

Sam nodded. "Nobody else is directly involved. And only you and the cousin know where it is."

"Listen, there is one big advantage to taking me in…you told me about the cave-ins. You let me know when you go out and somebody can call me if you don't show up."

"I'd probably be dead by the time anybody knew I was in trouble."

"Maybe, maybe not. I could get out there in a hurry if I knew something was up.

"You really should get a radio or walkie-talkies or something."

Sam laughed. "We've talked about it, but I doubt I'd be able to get a signal through the rocks all the way to the highway."

"We use some on the ranch…they have pretty good range. Maybe you could just use a CB radio."

"There's no power down there to run anything like that."

"I could bring in an old car battery, Sam. We could get a couple from the junk yard and swap out charged ones when we need to. Remember, I belong there. I can drive up to within a mile of the place, seriously. There's an old jeep trail not too far from the rim up where I left my horse."

"I don't know, Lance. Can I trust you?"

"Sam, who am I gonna tell? I'm the same as you. I've had a story rattling around in my brain for years. What did you call it? The Fever?" Lance chuckled. "I've had *the fever* for years. Just couldn't do nothing about it until I got the call from Tim. Since then, believe me, I've been prowling Diablo Rim every Sunday and have even managed to do a little looking on work days too. It was just pure, dumb luck I happened on you yesterday."

"I get so squirrelly down there, I didn't know what to think when I saw you."

"I hoped you didn't have a gun."

"No, I've tended away from guns, figured they were too risky. I assumed I'd probably get shot first if I had an encounter."

"Jose woulda probably shot you."

"He had his chance, but see? I didn't have a gun so he didn't."

"What?"

Sam related the incident on the ridge when the three hands had found him and tossed him down the small cliff, leaving him for dead.

"You know, I think I know that place. I found an old pot and what looked like a rusted tin can stove not long before I found you."

Sam blinked in disbelief. "Tin can stove? I had one of those in my pack...stuff scattered all over the place when they threw my pack down. I looked all around for it."

They both shared a good laugh.

"I guess I was in a bit of a hurry, afraid they'd come back, so I rushed, picking up what I could find and got away from there. I skirted around several outcrops and back up the arroyo and found the table rock. I saw MacGregg's plane flying circles later so I know they were looking for me. I guess they had no idea where I had gone and then some weather started moving in and I was able to use it as a cover to get out. I was lucky."

Lance slapped the table and gave a whoop. "Man, that's how it goes sometimes, isn't it? Get beat up, left for dead, and then turn around and find a treasure."

Some lights pulled into the parking lot as they were talking. Sam looked out the window and saw it was a patrol car. Lance noticed too.

"Clay Dodge," Sam said. "Local cop."

"Here we go," Lance said.

"What do you mean?"

"You'll see."

The officer walked up to the door as Sam unlocked and opened it.

"Hey, Clay, what's up?"

"Just checking things, Sam." He nodded toward Lance, "Everything okay here?"

Sam glanced in the direction of the nod then returned his gaze to Clay.

"Not sure what you mean. Lance and I are just talking. He came in late and wasn't finished eating, so I sent Chuy on and we've just been...well, like I said, just talking. Everything's fine."

Clay's eyes darted around the dining room a couple of times, then he said, "Just seemed a might out of the ordinary for The Mossback, you know? Miss Smidgeon know about this?"

"Clay," Sam laughed, "we're just talking. We're both Houston boys, you know? Just catching up on news from back home. Lance is my friend."

"Well, okay then," he said. "Everything looks okay here, I guess. Have a nice evening." He glanced at Lance again, "Probably time for you to lock up and head home, don't you think?"

"Yeah, Sam," Lance interrupted, "I've got to head back. Ranching starts before dawn, you know. We'll finish dissecting the Astro's chances later."

Sam laughed. "Yeah, I still say they'll have a time of it this year."

"Naw, they're better than you think..."

Clay shook his head and walked back to his patrol car as Sam locked the door.

"It never ends," Lance said.

"What?"

"You ever work late in here?"

"All the time," Sam answered.

"He ever stop and check on you before?"

Sam thought for a minute. "No, he hasn't."

"But you sit in here with a black guy and he stops in to check on you."

"I see what you mean. It *was* kinda odd."

"Just par for the course, my man, par for the course. Means we need to be a little more discreet."

"Yeah, I guess so."

"But I do need to be getting along, because I really do have to get up early. That part was true," Lance said, stifling a yawn.

"Me too," Sam said. "She always punishes me with long days after I get a 'weekend off' as she says."

"She thinks scratching at the rocks and hiking miles in the dark is downtime?"

"I guess so. Now I have to figure out how to tell her about you."

"You think you have to? I mean, can't we keep this between us?"

"She's a good woman, Lance. I'm not going to start keeping secrets from her, you know?"

"Besides, her cousin will rat you out."

"Right."

Lance laughed deep and long as Sam unlocked the door and let him out. Headlight shadows shifted across the walls as he scooped up the plate and wrappers from the table. He washed the last of the dishes before he eased out the rear door.

Smidgeon was waiting for him in the living room when he got home.

"You're late," she said. "I hear you were entertaining that foreman from the MacGregg place."

"Clay called you?"

"Yeah, I guess he thought I should know. What's going on?"

"A couple of things. For one thing, Lance just came in late and got a burger...but the main reason he dropped by was because we needed to talk."

Sam locked on Smidgeon's questioning gaze as he sat down to continue.

"Smidgeon, he found me out there."

"What do you mean?"

"He knows about the mine."

A wave of shock flashed across her face and she blinked in disbelief.

"What? How could he, I mean..." she stumbled for words.

"His granddaddy worked out here in the old days. They called him Scamp, and he knew both Slim and Loot. Slim told him the same things he told me and I guess Scamp told Lance. He had the same clues, Smidgeon. He's been out looking since he started working for MacGregg."

"So, I guess, like the old movies say, the jig is up."

"Not really. He knows MacGregg would just take over. Knock down the mountain. You even said the same thing the first time I told you about it."

"Yeah, Tim would probably be worse than the old man. No respect for the land, he'd just go for all the gold the easiest way he could."

"Lance knows that. And he has the same kind of motivation I have...he's wanted to find this his whole life. Believe me, he wants to work together."

"He has the same, what do you call it...fever? Just like you," she said.

"Exactly. Plus he's in a position to help. He can get supplies in closer, shoring and stuff. He can sneak it around.'

"Oh, right. He's the foreman. He's supposed to be there."

"Right. This is the kind of stuff we were talking about."

"Well, I don't think you should be plotting your schemes in my restaurant at night. I mean, me? You know I don't care but generally speaking, out here whites and blacks consorting together can draw attention, you know? It's why Clay stopped in and why he called me."

"Yeah, we talked about that after Clay left."

"I just pretended I already knew about it. But I was already waiting for you. I *did* want to ask you something else."

"What?"

"What was going on this morning? Your room was a mess," she said. "I straightened it up a little but what were you doing?"

"Looking for something. That little rock I got a while back, you know, looks like a cross?"

"Oh, your magic good luck piece from the old Mexican witch woman? Ugh. Good riddance."

"Yeah. Not sure what happened to it. I had it when I went east, when Godson died."

"You usually keep it hidden. Maybe you dropped it, like at the motel or something"

"Well, I didn't even unpack at the motel in Sonora and in Austin I stayed at Godson and Moll's. I don't remember seeing it there, either."

"You stayed with her?" Smidgeon blinked rapidly as she continued, "You didn't tell me that."

"She needed someone there, Smidgeon. She's one of my oldest friends."

"Why didn't you tell me?"

"I-I, guess I just didn't think about it. She's like a sister, you know?"

"She was under a lot of strain...losing a husband can do strange things to a woman."

Sam knew that fact very well but chose to avoid further confrontation. "She *was* upset...I don't think I left it there, Smidgeon," Sam said. He grabbed her clasped hands and raised them to kiss the, but she pulled them back.

"I just wish you had told me," she said as she got up and left the room.

~ * ~

Smidgeon watched Sam snore softly next to her and realized she hadn't worried herself awake like this in a long time. She silently slid out of bed, put on her robe and tiptoed into the living room with MamaKat following her. When she sat on the couch, the cat immediately jumped to her lap and went back to sleep. She ran the evening's events through her mind as she stroked the soft fur.

"He stayed there alone with *that woman*," she whispered in the dark. "I just can't get the notion out of my head. I don't know, I have a funny feeling about it. What was he thinking?"

The cat rolled in her lap and squinted at her, its head upside down.

Incessant purring punctuated the blackness and Smidgeon continued, "...and now we have to deal with this new guy, this Lance. I don't like it."

The cat rubbed its head against Smidgeon's hand as if to sympathize with her.

"I know, baby, you don't like it either, do you?" she whispered.

She thought long and hard about these things. "Sam is," she started, then reconsidered her thoughts, "well, I mean, we're not married or anything, but I love him. I really do. I wish I could have gone with him, I mean, it was his best friend. But I can't afford to just close the restaurant and, well, it's even tough when he goes off into the hills. I need him there. And, I need him *here*, too." She sniffed, trying to hold back the sobs she knew were coming.

The cat chirped a faint meow as she purred and rubbed hard against Smidgeon's hand.

"Yeah, you need him too, don't you? Of course you do. He's a sweet man. But all this stuff is like staring down a double-barreled shotgun. I can't bear to think of him leaving me or even worse, getting hurt or killed by making a bad mistake out in that stupid gold mine. I've got troubles coming and going." Tears dribbled down both cheeks. "I don't understand...why didn't he tell me?"

She got up, walked to the kitchen and started cleaning. It was what she always did when she was upset and couldn't sleep.

"Kitchen don't need cleaning," she whispered, "but I'm wiping down the countertops anyway." The cat rubbed lazily against her legs as she walked around.

"Smidgeon, what's going on?" Sam was in the doorway, staring at her with groggy eyes.

"Couldn't sleep, so I'm puttering around. Did I wake you up?"

"Who you talking to?"

"Just yakking to the cat, means I'm talking to myself I guess. I'm sorry if I woke you up."

"Is something bothering you, I mean, do you want to talk or anything?"

She dropped her rag and walked over to Sam and hugged him hard.

"You'd tell me if anything was going on, wouldn't you?"

He hugged her and ran his hands up and down her back.

"I'm not sure what you mean, sweetie. I tell you everything."

She pulled back and penetrated him with her dark eyes.

"I'm worried about a couple of things, and both bother me a lot."

"Both?" Sam looked at her as if he didn't understand. "You mean Lance?"

She nodded and added, "And...her, that woman in Austin. Why would you stay at her house and not tell me?"

He put his hands on her shoulder. "Look, the Lance deal, well, I don't know what to expect there except for one plain and simple fact...he found the mine. What else can I do besides just take him in and go along with it? He hasn't turned me in or anything. I think I can trust him but I don't know. I could be sitting in jail right now or worse, you know?"

Smidgeon nodded as her eyes brimmed with tears.

"We'll have to see how it all plays out. It's a gut feeling, but I like Lance. I think I can trust him. And Moll? She's one of my oldest friends. Where else was I going to stay? I didn't grab enough cash to stay in a motel for too many days. It isn't like here; it costs a lot. And she'd just lost her husband, my best friend. She needed somebody there. Smidgeon, she's like my sister...there just wasn't any other way. Okay?"

He pulled her to him and held her tight. She hugged him back and pressed her cheek against his shoulder, leaving a wet spot. It sounded believable, but she still held a glimmer of jealousy in her heart as she squeezed him as hard as she could.

"Sweetie, I love you," he said. "I'm here *now*, here with *you*. You have to trust me. She's a friend, nothing more. It was a bad time for her; I couldn't just leave her alone. Hey, I left you here with all those macho cowboys, right?"

She laughed, wiping her moist cheeks. "You know I ain't hobnobbing with no cowboys."

"Right. Of course you're not. Now, let's go on back to bed."

She followed Sam back into the bedroom and snuggled into his shoulder in the dark. Despite his reassurances, she was still awake and she spooned with him, listening to him snore for what seemed like hours until she finally settled into an uneasy sleep.

The next morning she eased through her regular daily routine despite her fatigue. The normalcy of her work seemed to relax her and she slid back into her practiced role of Smidgeon, the restaurant owner, again. When she could, she peeked across the cafe, watching Sam as he worked and realized she liked the way Sam had fit himself into her world. Most locals had accepted him, and more important to her, he seemed to have accepted them. She also realized she didn't want to ever risk losing him.

Twelve

Loot was in his recliner watching television when he heard a knock on the door. He teetered a little as he navigated the remnants of his life in the cluttered den and hall. It was late afternoon and he wasn't expecting visitors. He reached for his shotgun but decided to take a chance this one time and opened the door without it. It was a woman wearing sunglasses, dressed in dark clothes. She didn't look threatening, but even without his shotgun, Loot was not in a trusting mood so his one word comment was brusque and punctuated by furtive glances around the yard and street.

"Yes?"

"Mr. Meldings? Loot Meldings?"

Loot managed a feeble nod. The only vehicle he had seen was an unfamiliar, dark, four wheel drive parked down the road from his place.

"I'm a friend of Sam's. May I come in?"

"Sam sent you?"

"Well, not really, but he's mentioned you to me countless times. I really need to talk to you, Mr. Meldings. It has a lot to do with Sam and I'm hoping you can help. May I come in?"

This introduction took him a little off guard, but it intrigued him that she so casually mentioned his friend. She seemed harmless, so he stifled his suspicions and opened the door.

"Sorry the place is such a mess."

"It's all right, Mr. Meldings. Sam told me about your house, but I have to admit it is quite remarkable to see it in person," she said with a chuckle.

"Any friend of Sam's can call me Loot," he said.

In the den, Loot cleared away a layer of newspapers from the small couch next to his recliner.

"Have a seat, young lady."

"You have a bit of a gruff look about you, but you are quite the gentleman," she said, removing her sunglasses to reveal piercing blue eyes.

Loot plopped down in his chair and let it swing back. "Sorry to be so informal but this feels better on my back. Afraid I've got a touch of old age coming on," he said with his distinctive cackle. "So, you're a friend of Sam's, miss...I didn't catch your name."

"Oh, I'm sorry," she said. "My name is Monee Grivois." She extended her hand and he gently shook it, then she added, "Sam doesn't know I'm here."

"Oh? Well, what can I do for you?"

"I'll get right to the point. I know about The Sublett Mine. I need to know exactly where it is." She paused to let her statement sink in.

Loot's bloodshot eyes narrowed on the young woman. She was pretty and had a nice voice, but her comment seemed to carry a certain edge to it. His heart began to pound and he fought past another wave of dizziness as he stared at her while he struggled for a response. He did not want to let the woman know she had affected him. But he did know one thing: very few people knew about the mine and Loot knew a bit about most of them, but this woman seemed to be a total stranger.

"I—I'm not sure what you mean..."

His mind was working. She said she was a friend of Sam's, but he had never heard Sam mention a Monee Grivois. He searched his memory for clues. He began to wonder if this might be some trick associated with the MacGregg foreman, but his thoughts were interrupted by her response.

"Don't be silly, Loot. I know you and Sam are as thick as thieves. You probably know as much about it as he does. I just need the *exact* location."

"Listen, little lady, I don't know nothing you can use."

"But you do know there is a mine, right? I followed you last Monday morning and I know you picked him up north of town. It was raining that morning."

His gaze narrowed at her, "I remember a car out there...thought it was a bit strange. That road is usually deserted that time of morning."

A sly smile broke across the woman's face. "See, I already know quite a lot."

Loot's heart raced as he tried to make some sense of the situation. There was something about this woman that just did not add up.

"Calm down, Loot. I won't hurt you..." she reached out and gently touched his arm, "*unless* you don't tell me what I want to know."

It was only then Loot noticed the smallish gun in her other hand. In his youth he might have been ready and just slapped the gun out of her hand, but he had let his guard down and sitting back in his chair he was not in a position to react.

"No need to pull no gun on me. I can tell you what I know but it ain't much. Yeah," he said, "Sam's thinks he's found something up in them hills, but I've never been up there, don't know where it is. Figure it is west of where I usually pick him up. That's as good as I've got."

"Then someone else must know. Tell me."

Loot only knew of three people who knew the location, but he wasn't about to share that information with this interloper, gun or no gun.

"You ain't acting like no friend of Sam's. If'n you were, you could ask him directly."

"Oh, Sam and I have a long and intimate association. I've known about this thing long before he ever met you." She slipped the gun into her coat pocket and Loot felt a slight relief.

This statement seemed to turn the tumblers of his mind just right. The realization of her identity must have shown in his eyes or face, because he almost immediately felt a slight pinch on his arm. She had pulled something else from her pocket and had moved too quickly for him to react.

"Sam's taken a lot from me, and I'm going to start taking from him," she said as she faded from his view.

~ * ~

Loot felt like he was opening his eyes out of a dream.

"He's coming out of it..."

The voice was familiar.

"Yeah, it took longer than I expected."

The second voice sounded familiar to him too.

He looked around. The television was off but there was a glow in the room.

"It always does. Come on, buddy."

Loot twisted his neck as if to pop it but there was no popping sound like there usually was. The woman who had been there was gone, but he squinted at the two figures looming near him in a glowing haze. He reached for the recliner handle but he was fumbling with air.

"Loot! Welcome back, buddy!"

He knew *that* voice...and the other one too.

"Slim?"

"Yeah. Come on..."

He squinted at the other figure. "Scamp? Scamp Norton?"

"The same, you old cuss."

"How?" Loot started to say, then he stopped. A sudden awareness dawned on him. As he rose, he looked down at the disheveled body below him.

"Don't be a feared of nothing, buddy, it's all good." Slim was reaching out as if to pat him on the back but he didn't feel anything. "It don't hurt or nothing, just takes a while to get used to."

~ * ~

Sam was working with Chuy in the kitchen when Smidgeon pushed the door open.

"Sam, Gil from the feed store is here asking for you."

Gillet Osmond was not quite as old as Loot, but his wire-rimmed glasses framed eyes that were wrinkled reminders of the harsh west Texas climate. His mottled moustache still had more hints of brown than the mixtures of white, gray, and brown on his head. Gil and Sam shared a mutual friendship with Loot and when Sam still lived in Austin, Gill had served as a go-between for them. He was standing alone by the door as Sam approached and extended his hand.

"Afternoon, Sam," Gil said, as their hands clasped.

Sam shook the hand but immediately felt a wave of foreboding. "Hi, Gil. What's up?" Gil Osmond ate regularly at The Mossback but he had never just dropped by to visit Sam before.

"Can we step outside?"

Sam nodded and they stepped into the relative privacy of the parking lot and walked toward the edge of the building.

"Bad news, I'm afraid, Sam. Loot is dead."

Sam stared back, speechless, his mouth open.

"I was dropping some food off there, leftovers the missus sent over to him. We'd been worried he wasn't eating enough. The door was ajar and I found him sitting back in his recliner, cold as ice."

Enough shock eased from Sam's brain to allow a minimal response. "I-I-I just can't believe it. I mean, lately he'd been complaining a bit about being tired, but...well, he seemed okay. I'd bring him food too. I know he wasn't eating enough."

"I thought it strange the door was unlatched, though. Didn't see his shotgun by the door either. Sheriff and I looked around a bit for it, but, well, you know his place."

"Yeah. He'd been talking about cleaning it out."

Gil smiled. "Old coot's been saying that for as long as I've known him. He was old, Sam. Just his time, I reckon."

Sam shook his head. "I am still having a hard time...well, it is just hard to hear."

"I know you were close, Sam. Loot talked about you almost like, well, I ain't seen him pal around with anybody as much since old Slim was around. When Loot was working more, I'd see him at the feed store a bunch, but he had a taste for liquor back then and got in some trouble with it. Don't know if you knew this about him, but he had a snatch of time in prison back then. After he got out, me and the missus sort of adopted him. We'd have him over for dinner and such. We both had alcoholic daddies and did our best to steer him away from the stuff. He had it bad for a while. Alcohol ages a person something terrible too, Sam. Like I said, it was probably just his time."

Sam shook his head. "It just doesn't seem right."

"Well, I got another reason to come here, Sam. You need to go see that lawyer fella up town, Mr. Bertram. A few months ago Loot got me and the missus to meet him there. Sam, we witnessed a will for him. I gotta tell you, he left you most everything. The truck, the house, everything. There's one box of mementos he left to somebody else, but the rest is yours."

Sam shook his head again. "Why would he leave me anything?"

"Don't rightly know, but like I said, he liked you, Sam, almost like a son."

Smidgeon opened the door and stuck her head out. "Everything okay?"

Sam told her the news. "Loot is dead."

She scooted out the door, gently closing it behind her and embraced Sam. "Oh, honey, I'm so sorry."

"I know you didn't care much for him, but thanks."

"I'll never speak ill of the dead, Sam. He was your friend and I'm sorry for your loss." She hugged him again.

Gillet Osmond gently placed a hand on Sam's shoulder. "I best be heading out, Sam. Take care. Let me know if you need anything. You go up and see Mr. Bertram in a few days."

Sam shook Gil's hand and finished by embracing it with both of his hands. "Hey, I'm so sorry, Gil...I know you were close too. Thank you so much for coming out and telling me in person."

"Seemed only right."

Sam and Smidgeon waved at Gil as he drove off.

"Bertram? The lawyer?" she asked.

"Yeah. Loot apparently has a will."

"Did Gil say what happened to him?"

"Said he just found him there this morning, dead in his house."

After they returned to the dining room, Smidgeon said, "Sam, you want to take the rest of the day off?"

"Naw, I'm pretty numb, but I think I'll feel better if I just keep busy."

"Two friends in just a couple of months...that's a lot to take in."

"I know," Sam said, shaking his head, "I know."

Sam decided to keep to a normal routine and stayed on after five. It was a slow night, and about six Clay, the deputy, dropped by.

"Got a minute, Sam?"

"Sure. This about Loot?"

"Yes, sir. Just tying up some details. Gil told us you were basically his heir and we verified the information with Mr. Bertram."

"Gil told me that as well. It was news to me."

"Old Doc Williams serves as medical examiner for the county. He's doing a report now. Everything appears normal so far. Just procedure. Loot was a tough old cuss, but it was probably just his time."

Sam nodded. "I'm still sort of processing it."

"How'd you two become friends?"

"Just sort of hit it off. It was tough coming here and I don't know, just started talking to him one day in a parking lot. He mentioned needing help setting and checking traps, so I started tagging along because I love hiking around in the back country. He'd joke he wasn't as young as he used to be. It was fun. Good male bonding." It was their standard cover story.

Clay laughed. "Yeah, never had any professional dealings with him, but the old-timers say he had a wild side in the old days. I heard he even did a little time. Well, you go see Mr. Bertram in a few days...I'm sure this whole thing can be settled up pretty quickly."

"Thanks, Clay," Sam said as the deputy headed out the door.

Thirteen

Several days later, both Sam and Smidgeon were summoned to the law offices of Sidney L. Bertram, attorney at law. Although Smidgeon knew Mr. Bertram just like she seemed to know everyone in town, this was Sam's first official introduction. He immediately recognized the short, stout man as an occasional customer at the café. The red suspenders under his suit coat were not easy to forget.

"Miss Smidgeon, it is always a pleasure."

"Oh, Sid, you know there is no need for that Miss Smidgeon stuff," she giggled.

The lawyer chuckled, then turned to Sam. "Glad to meet you, Mr. Milton. Can I call you Sam?"

"Sure," Sam said, with a tinge of nervousness. Law offices, police stations, and principal's offices all seemed to instill similar states of apprehension and it did not seem to depend on the situation.

They sat in a small office and Mr. Bertram nervously arranged neat stacks of papers that needed no straightening while Sam and Smidgeon settled into their seats.

"Sam, as you may or may not know, Kelvin Earnest, better known as Loot, Meldings named you as the primary heir to his estate."

"I wasn't aware Loot even had a will. The first time I heard anything about it was when I was informed of Loot's death and Gil Osmond told me about it. Loot never mentioned any of this to me."

"I see. Now, going on, his death has been determined to have been from natural causes so everything is just a matter of routine. He paid for my services up-front and asked me to serve as executor of his estate."

"He paid?"

"Yes, sir. In cash. He said he didn't want anyone to be burdened with anything relating to his eventual death. He requested no memorial service and specified his body be cremated. He prepaid for that as well."

"Yeah, I was a bit surprised there was no service or anything."

"Those were his wishes, Sam. As for his estate, he left you his house and all of the contents, including his 1956 Jeep truck. The house and land were totally paid for. Almost an acre. Smidgeon, he left you something too."

"Me? Why would he leave me anything?"

Bertram pushed an envelope across the table. "He said it was unresolved business between him and your father."

She opened the envelope and found five crisp hundred dollar bills.

"What's this for?" she asked, then she saw a handwritten note in the envelope. The handwriting was shaky and hard to read but she managed to make out:

"Payment in full to Joseph Toll for one broken plate glass window at The Mossback, 1963, plus interest."

Smidgeon wiped a tear from her eye.

Sam took her hand and said in a scratchy voice, "He only recently told me the story about the window. He had been drunk and there was an argument between him and your dad. It ended with Loot somehow breaking a window. Your dad would never accept payment."

"I represented Loot in that case," Bertram said. "He served nine months in the county facility."

"Okay," she sniffed. "Better late than never, I guess." She dabbed a tissue to her eyes then blew her nose.

Bertram continued with the business at hand and began to pass Sam papers to review.

Sam signed and initialed page after page of the diverse legal mumbo jumbo and at the end, Bertram packaged one set of papers in a thick envelope and gave it to Sam, officially turning over ownership of Loot's estate.

Sid Bertram pointed to a small, weathered suitcase in the corner. "That's the only other thing left. A case of mementos left to one Loretta Longo Smythe of San Antonio."

The name startled Sam. "Loretta?"

Smidgeon's face flushed. "Isn't she the girl you told me about? The one from the truck stop?"

"Yeah, she's the one," he said as Smidgeon glared at him.

Mr. Bertram interrupted. "You know her?"

"Knew her a couple of years ago," Sam said.

"At a truck stop?" Mr. Bertram glanced at Smidgeon as he said this.

"Yes, met her at a truck stop and knew her later in Austin." Sam squirmed uncomfortably adding, "What's in the case?"

"I have no idea," the lawyer said, and he began idly shuffling papers again. "And, of course, it is of no concern of yours."

With their business concluded, Bertram expressed additional stiff condolences and led them to the door. Smidgeon carried her envelope and Sam grasped the key to the shack on Tesoro Road along with his own envelope of papers.

The mood in the car was somber as Smidgeon drove them toward The Mossback and Sam silently examined the key, turning it over in his hands as if it held some secret.

Along the way, she finally broke the impasse. "You thinking about her?"

"Who?"

"That woman."

"What? No, not at all. Why would you say that?"

"She'll be coming out here to collect whatever it is."

"Maybe. Who knows? I suppose she might not."

"You never told me he knew her too. This stinks, Sam, this really stinks."

"What does?"

"Everything."

"Smidgeon, what are you talking about? Loretta? She doesn't even know where I am. What's the matter?"

"First I find out you stayed with Moll and now this other floozy from your past crops up. What am I supposed to think? What the hell is going on?"

"Smidgeon, I need to ask you the same question, what the hell is going on?"

She did a quick U-turn in the middle of the road, and a pickup behind her sounded its horn. "I'm dropping you at the house. You've got another place to stay now; why don't you just move your stuff over there today?"

"Smidgeon, don't be silly."

"Silly? Look, Sam, I think I need some time to think about all of this."

"What about the restaurant?"

"I'll handle it. I always have."

They pulled in the driveway of her house. "You're serious?"

"I'm serious. I can't abide you two-timing me."

"Nobody has two-timed you."

"I don't know that. I-I...I just need some time to think. You have a place to go now, so go."

"What about The Mossback? You need me there."

Smidgeon looked down as she thought for a moment. "You go get started on what you need to do over there at Loot's place. You told me it was pretty awful. Like I said, I need time to think...we *both* need time to think. We'll talk about everything in a few days, okay? I'll get by in the meantime. I get by when you go gallivanting off into the hills, don't I?"

Sam got out of the car and leaned in the window. "I don't know where this is coming from, but I'll go. I love you, Smidgeon."

She shot him a menacing glare that softened a bit as their eyes met. "I hope so. I think I love you too, but I...I need time to just think things over, okay?"

"Fine," he said, turning abruptly toward the house.

MamaKat curled against his legs as he surveyed his little room. The reality of Loot's house was not something he was prepared to confront on such short notice. He doubted he would have room in The Clunker to carry much of the debris out of the place, for one thing, then he thought about Loot's ancient truck and decided one of the first things he'd need to do is find the key. He flipped through the papers he had brought from the lawyer's office and found the title to the old truck, already signed over to him. It had been one of the papers he had mindlessly signed in Bertram's office. Sam shook his head.

"Old Loot had been anticipating his death," he muttered. "In spite of the mess over there, he obviously had most of his business well covered." A tear ran down Sam's cheek.

A short time later, with his car stuffed to the brim, Sam pulled up behind the rusty truck in the driveway at the battered shack on Tesoro Road. He glanced at the old garage beyond the truck and remembered pulling into it the first time Loot had taken him out to Diablo Rim.

Once inside the house, he looked at the piles of mess with new eyes.

"This is no longer Loot's mess," he mused, "it is *my* mess."

He realized he had never even seen any other part of the small house, so he explored for a few minutes. There was a trail heading down a hall where he found a bathroom.

"The bathroom needs cleaning but it actually is not too bad," he muttered.

Another trail lead to a bedroom where he had to assume there was a bed hidden beneath the piles of debris.

"Another mess," he said. "I guess he slept in the recliner."

Sam continued exploring and found a second bedroom in the same state as the rest of the house, with one exception: a narrow path through stacks of stuff lead to a closet door. Curiously, the area around the door was clear enough to allow the door to swing fully open. Sam returned to the little den and then went into the kitchen. It was pretty bad but like the bathroom, it was at least minimally functional.

"I'll need cleaning supplies," he said to himself as he scanned the dirty pots on the stove and a small pile of dishes in the sink. Then he shook his head.

"I don't have much cash," he said. He thought about Smidgeon and the restaurant. Both had supplied all his living requirements for over two years. "Maybe she'll cut me some slack and give me a little money." He sighed. "I'll see what I can find first, though."

He carefully rooted around the kitchen and under the sink. There *were* a few things he could use. He located some dish soap and he actually found an unopened package of sponges, along with some other cleaning supplies. Searching the small table and the counters turned up various packages of garbage bags.

He looked over the other piles of debris in the kitchen and wondered to himself, "maybe Loot will provide for me, I just need to do a little prospecting."

He chuckled at the word. "Hah! This really *is* pretty much like working the mine!" Then he reassessed the metaphor. "Come to think of it, I better be careful, I could get buried here too."

~ * ~

While he was rummaging in the kitchen Sam made one of his first important discoveries.

"The truck keys!" Sam was elated. He *needed* that truck. "Hopefully it will start. I'm going to need to haul a lot of trash."

The truck keys were on a single ring attached to an enormous ring of other keys hanging in the kitchen. He conjured memories of Loot fiddling with all those keys and smiled. It was another reflection of Loot's life, like the house— a few useful things in a mountain of clutter. After removing the small ring, he returned the huge ring to the hook.

"I'll probably need it again before this is all over," he prophesized.

He found there was already a lot of bagged trash in the kitchen. In fact, there were several bags of trash in the den as well. After moving these outside, the kitchen seemed almost manageable. The den already looked better too. There was so much to do, he found he could jump back and forth between projects for some variety. After cleaning all the pots, pans, and dishes he could find, he moved to the den and concentrated on the small couch. Once the protective cover of random debris was removed, it seemed surprisingly fresh. By the side of the couch he uncovered a box fan and he positioned it in a window. After he managed to open a few windows in other areas of the house, he switched it on, pointed to blow air out the window. He had grown used to the persistent background odors of the house but the resulting steady flow of fresh air through the house definitely made a difference.

In the evening, after hours of steady work, Sam went back into the kitchen because he was hungry. In one cabinet he found an assortment of canned goods, mostly soups but there were a couple of cans of Wolf Brand Chili as well. All were dusty. One can of peaches had obviously gone bad because the top was puffed up. He tossed it in the one of the trash bags.

The freezer held a couple of packaged dinners and the old trapper even had a couple of cheap frozen pizzas. He considered his options and chose one of the pizzas. The thought of a frozen pizza didn't much appeal to him, but he had another idea. He started the oven and found a cookie sheet he had washed earlier. He greased this with an unwrapped stick of margarine he had found in the refrigerator. He examined it before using it, and thought it was of questionable age, but decided he had no other choice.

"Hopefully such a small amount won't kill me if it's bad," he quipped.

When the pizza was unwrapped and in the oven, he checked his watch and after a couple of minutes he folded the pizza in half and pressed the edges lightly. After a few more minutes in the oven, he gingerly flipped it to brown the other side.

When he judged it was ready, he moved his meal to a plate and let it cool another minute before he tried a bite.

"Not bad," he said, "not bad at all...poor man's calzone, just like in college!"

He settled on the couch and ate his creation, then decided to turn in. He had retrieved his belongings from The Clunker and unzipped his sleeping bag all the way and spent his first night curled up on the couch. Strange sounds permeated the night and for him it eerily mimicked the feeling of sleeping out in the hills. He missed the warmth and softness of Smidgeon snuggling next to him. He even missed the inevitable presence of the cat, who at some point most nights would nestle between them.

Thoughts of Smidgeon turned to concern about her sudden change of attitude.

"I can't believe she is suddenly so obsessed with Moll and Loretta," he said to himself.

He had never told her about Moll's advances that night in Austin, but he contemplated an uneasy notion. "Her woman's intuition must suspect something."

He shook his head. "And Loretta? It's been over a long time," he said. "I doubt she'll even come get that case and even if she comes, she doesn't know I'm here."

Still, he had to wonder about the coincidence. Loot had never mentioned Loretta. Sam thought about it and mused out loud, "Then again, I never mentioned her by name to him either...all these blasted coincidences."

As he tried to drift off, he thought of Loot's passing and for some reason the voice of Loretta's mother echoed in his mind, intoning the word *curse* over and over as he fell into a fitful sleep.

~ * ~

A new truck sped down a graded road kicking up massive clouds of dust.

Lance pushed himself deep in the passenger seat when his boss, Tim MacGregg, pushed harder on the accelerator as the truck slid through a curve. Soon they were on the paved road and Tim drove even faster toward Van Horn.

"Want to get a bite of lunch?" Tim asked.

"Sure, boss, what do you feel like?"

"How about The Mossback, I haven't been there since I hit town right after daddy died."

Lance squirmed internally. He didn't relish the thought of interacting with Sam in front of his boss.

When they walked in the door, Lance detected a slight lull in the background chatter as he surveyed the place. It was subtle, he decided, but it was there. He glanced at Tim and realized from the smirk on the boss's face, that he was enjoying the moment.

"Hey, Tim." Smidgeon Toll had appeared almost out of nowhere and added, "And...I forget your name."

"Lance."

"Right, Lance Norton, I remember now. You two just sit anywhere and I'll be right with you."

"Thank you, ma'am," Lance said. He had his hat in his hands but Tim never removed his.

When they sat, Tim made a side remark, "I always liked her," he said, tilting his head toward Smidgeon. "But she was one of the few girls around here I couldn't get my hands on."

"And she's with that other dude now, so you should just forget that stuff," Lance joked.

"She's a couple of years older than me, but she still looks good. A little plump but... man, I bet she's..."

"Shush... stop it," Lance said. "You clear on what we need to order at the feed store when we're finished eating?"

"Yeah, yeah, but I'm counting on you to have it clear. You make the order and I'll write the check."

Smidgeon approached the table with two cups of steaming coffee.

"Morning, Miss Smidgeon," Lance said.

"Ain't you the gentleman," she said.

"My mama threatened the gentleman into me. I'm hungry...what you got that will fill up a working man?"

"You might like our Especial," she said, pointing to the boxed item on the menu.

"Looks like it has everything but the kitchen sink," he said.

"If you want a big meal, it's your best bet," she said.

"Sounds good to me," Lance said, folding up the menu.

"Just a burger and fries," Tim said. "Where's your beau? I don't see him."

Her response was curt. "Not here today," she said, turning quickly, her long ponytail trailing behind her.

"Oh, my, there must be trouble in paradise," Tim chuckled.

"Knock it off, Tim," Lance said.

Lance's eyes widened when the plate of food arrived.

"Dang, you should have brought that dog of yours along," Tim said.

"Yeah, I guess so. Prewash would have a field day with this."

After they ate, Tim retired to the restroom, leaving Lance a wad of bills for the check.

While paying he asked, "So where is Sam?"

Smidgeon seemed forlorn in her response. "Loot left him his house, so I guess he's over there."

"Everything okay?'

"We're fine, but I guess you might say we're just experiencing a little bump in the road, you know?"

"Yes, ma'am. Sam's a good guy. Whatever it is, I know he thinks the world of you, so just take it easy. Things will work out. But just so you know, you better watch out for old Tim."

"Oh, he's wanted me to be another notch in his belt for years, I've got his number. Don't worry."

"Ha, ha, well, just wanted to give you a fair warning. He's really pretty much an a-hole in my opinion. I can work for the guy and not like him."

"Seems to be the MacGregg family trait."

Lance smiled at the joke. "You think Sam would mind if I dropped by?"

"I have no idea. I imagine he's up to his earlobes in that mess over there. I heard it was full to the brim with unmitigated crap. Dubious gift, if you ask me."

"Oh, right. I've been there. I'll drop by tonight and see if I can give him a hand."

"Lance, would you mind letting me know how he's doing?"

"Sure will, Miss Smidgeon."

~ * ~

It was a slow afternoon and Smidgeon took advantage of an empty dining room to sit and nurse a cup of coffee. The brief conversation with Lance had stirred her emotions.

"Lordy, I miss Sam," she whispered as she stared into the swirls of vapor rising from her cup. "Wonder if he'd mind if I brought him some food, maybe an Especial."

She smiled as she remembered the first time he'd ordered it. That was the moment she realized she was attracted to him.

"I told you it was big," she had said when his eyes widened as she set it down. Lance's similar reaction had reminded her of

Sam's and now she couldn't get the thought of Sam out of her mind.

"I don't know why I reacted so horribly to Loretta's name. I regretted it almost the second I said it but, I am just afraid of losing him, so what did I do? I send him away? I must be losing my mind."

The door to the café opened and a woman dressed mostly in black came in. Sunglasses covered her eyes and a dark scarf covered most of her head, but a few tufts of red hair stuck out. After looking around, the woman saw Smidgeon sitting alone. She came over and sat across from her.

Smidgeon picked up her order pad but the woman waved her off. "I don't want to order anything. I just wanted to tell you something."

"Do I know you?"

"No, not really. I'm a...well, this is about Sam. Gossip around town is that he's moved out of your house."

"Not sure this is any of your business."

"Rest assured, I'm making it my business, and, well, just keep away from him."

"Who are you?"

"Never mind who I am. Just stay away from him. If he's out of your life, you have nothing to worry about."

Smidgeon had never been one to have some other woman tell her what to do and she felt her face flush. "Now you just listen here..." she started, then she saw the woman show the handgrip of a small pistol in her purse and she abruptly stopped talking, her mouth gaping.

"I mean it. Stay away from him."

"You think I'm afraid of you? I know every sheriff and deputy around here for several counties. Come in my place and show me a gun?" Smidgeon stood and glared at the intruder.

The woman closed her purse as she stood up and faced Smidgeon. "I mean it. As for the gun, I'm just a helpless woman passing through. So I have a gun. Who cares? It's my word against yours. I haven't done anything. But you had better *remember-what-I-said.*" The emphasis was unmistakable.

The woman darted out the door. Smidgeon had been so stunned by the encounter, especially after seeing the gun, she stood there for a moment transfixed, then realized she should get a license number or something but by the time she got to the door, the speeding vehicle was obscured by a cloud of dust.

"I really need to get that parking lot paved!"

A wave of relief swept across Smidgeon and she leaned against the wall to steady herself momentarily. She wracked her brain trying to figure out what had just happened. The woman's identity was a mystery.

"I'm sure it was nobody from around here. I know everybody. It was probably that Loretta woman, come here to collect the stuff Loot left her. She sounded like a bit of a flake, leaving Sam and all. But how could she have driven out here so soon? It doesn't seem possible; it's a long trip."

She thought about Sam. She'd have to ask him, despite the warning. It would give her a chance to break the ice and see how he was doing. Then a thought popped into her head. What if the woman was watching Sam too? She discounted the notion.

"Some bimbo with a gun ain't gonna scare me away."

She also made a mental note to mention the encounter to the first deputy who might drop by for a meal.

~ * ~

"I hope it doesn't rain," Sam said as he added another item to one of the piles he had made in the front yard.

His cleaning plan had evolved over the previous couple of days and he had decided on the pile method. One pile was definite trash. To save time, he located that pile in the back of the rusty Jeep pickup. Another pile was composed of things he thought he might be able to sell.

"Gonna have one heck of a yard sale," he said to himself every time he added another tidbit.

The remark about rain sparked Sam to look at the cloudless sky. He was drenched in sweat. It was hot but it was a bit cooler inside. He had discovered Loot had an old evaporating cooler in one window in the den and it worked surprisingly well in the dry Van Horn air. He surveyed his two piles and started to revise his plan yet again. He spied the small garage. He hadn't even looked in there yet. Loot had "cleaned it out" to conceal The Clunker on his first Diablo Rim trip two years earlier.

"I should probably switch to the garage, but I guess I need to see what clearing I might need to do there, then maybe I can use it as a staging area," he muttered.

He opened the double doors.

"Not too bad," he mused. "I doubt Loot even opened it again after I pulled The Clunker out."

Cleaning it out at the time had obviously meant just relocating junk to the yard. The yard had been one of the first big chores. Luckily most of that stuff had been metal and he found a local guy who would pick up scrap metal for nothing.

A battered pickup pulled up about five-thirty. Sam had been busy relocating the "keep" pile to the garage for several hours and he emerged from the garage when he heard the truck rattle up and park. It was Lance.

Lance said, "Howdy, stranger," as he approached.

"Hey, Lance, what brings you out here?"

"Was asking about you at The Mossback. Sounded like there might be a little tension going on between you and Miss Smidgeon."

"A little. Loot's death has been a strain on me and I guess it extended out a bit too far. Got sparked up a bit when he mentioned another woman I had some history with in his will."

"Oh, I see," Lance smiled. "Jealousy will tend to stir up the burned bits from the bottom of the pot."

"Right. Anyway, Loot left his place to me, so I've just been clearing it out."

"Some gifts are not really gifts at all."

"Yeah, but this won't be a bad little house once it's cleaned up."

"This the trash pile?" Lance asked, touching one of the items gingerly with his boot.

"No, this is the 'sell' pile," Sam laughed, then pointed to back of Loot's truck. "That's the trash pile."

"Ah, I see the distinction now. Well, you'll be able to have a heck of a yard sale. Do they have those here?"

"I guess they do. I'll find out. Decided to move my piles to the garage, in case it rains."

Lance looked at the sky. "Don't seem to be much chance of rain, Sam, not for a while, anyway."

"You never know around here."

"Hah, maybe so. Well, let me help you, then we can talk."

With Lance's help, the second pile was relocated fairly quickly. Back inside the house, Sam made them cups of instant coffee. Lance was amazed at the condition of the interior.

"Wow, this is...well, you've done an amazing amount of work. He actually had *furniture* in here!"

"Yeah. Some of it is still in pretty good shape. A lot of the top layers were more trash. I lost count of the number of trips I've made to the dump."

"I can only imagine." Lance sat and changed the subject. "So what about the mine?"

"Been so busy with this I haven't had a chance to think about it. Plus, I depended on Loot for rides...and Smidgeon. I guess I may be back to using the old broken-down-car routine, which isn't good because a lot of people know my car now."

"Well, maybe I could help you out. I might even be able to get you closer, you know? Cut down on your hiking time. You could even camp in my spare room if need be."

"Won't Tim get suspicious?"

"Naw, I rarely see him. Might have to figure out something with the hands, though. There's a lot of work to be done on a ranch, but I can't always be running out the jeep trails with no reason. I'll think on it."

Suddenly Sam jumped up. "I totally forgot! Wait a minute," he said and he ran into the small living room and returned with a snapshot. "Is this your grandpa?"

The picture was of a younger Loot and two other men, one of them a short black man.

"Oh, wow. Grandpa Thad!"

"Yeah, I figured," Sam said, then he pointed to the other figure, "because that's Slim."

"So, the three *vaqueros*," Lance laughed.

Sam smiled, "Yeah, I thought the same thing."

"Look at them three, all piss and vinegar."

"All gone now," Sam said. "Loot was the last, I guess."

"End of an era," Lance said, then he extended a hand. "Well, maybe not *totally* the end."

Sam shook the hand and they both chuckled.

"Well, let me know what you wanna do."

Sam said, "It might work out. I'm still hoping Smidgeon will calm down."

"Hey, man, it's been a tough time and I know hard times, believe me. Things will work out. I put in a good word for you and I thought I detected a slight softening up on her end. She wanted me to report back on how you were doing."

"She did?"

"Yes, she did. Believe me, that's a good sign." Lance waved as he walked back to his truck.

Sam busied himself with the coffee cups as he heard the truck drive off. A short time later, he was puttering in the bedroom when he thought he heard a knock on the door. He wondered if Lance had returned.

"Dang, busy day," he quietly mumbled to himself as he began to open the door. A short figure with a familiar face peered back at him, holding a paper sack.

"Smidgeon!"

"Hey, sweetie. I bought you some food," she said, handing Sam the sack.

He sniffed at the bag, "Especial?"

"Yeah, Lance ordered one when he came in today and it made me think of you. I thought you could use a good feed."

"Come in, you want to split it?"

"Naw, I ate earlier. But, Sam, I *do* want to talk."

Once inside she remarked, "Either you've done a lot of work or this place wasn't as bad as you always made out."

"Oh, it was worse, lots worse. I've lost count of how many loads of trash I've hauled out of here."

Smidgeon surprised Sam by suddenly reaching out and pulling his body to hers and she held him tight.

"Sam, I'm sorry!"

The embrace lasted for a long minute. "Me too," he whispered.

He broke the hug and led her into the den. "Let's sit down and talk about it."

"So you've set up quite a little nest for yourself over here," she said.

"I thought I had no other choice."

"I guess not, but before we go too far, first I need to tell you something."

"What?"

"A woman came in and warned me to stay away from you. Sam, she had a gun!"

"Baby, you okay?"

"I'm fine; you know I don't scare so easy, but I have to admit...maybe she succeeded, just a little. I'm worried about you too."

He took her hand, "So, this woman, what did she look like?"

"I couldn't tell, not really. She was dressed in black and wore sunglasses. I think she had red hair. She took me off guard with all of this and I didn't follow her to the door right away, and when she sped off she kicked up so much dust I couldn't get a good look at her car. Do you think she could be that Loretta girl?"

"I don't know. The only person who's been out here besides you is Lance and he just left not long before you got here. I guess we could ask the lawyer if she's picked up the case. Otherwise, I have no clue. I will tell you one thing, though."

"What?"

"Loretta doesn't have red hair. Nobody I know has red hair."

"Asking the lawyer is a good idea. Still, why would anybody warn me away from you?"

"Smidgeon, I really have no idea. Baby, there is no one else in my life besides you."

She smiled and took his hand. "Sam, I want you to come back. I miss you something terrible. You've... you've, well, you're just *needed*, you know?"

Sam hugged her again. "I miss you too, Smidgeon. Maybe let's just go a little slow, ease back together." He waved his arm. "For one thing, now I've started cleaning out this place, I'm afraid I've gotten myself a bit obsessed with it. There is still a hall full of stuff and two more bedrooms to go through, and uh," Sam looked down at his feet, then embraced her. "Well...I want to come back, too."

She leaned up and kissed him. "Does that include sleeping together?"

"Of course, and does it mean I'm back to working at The Mossback?"

"We're struggling without you. You're my best worker."

"What a relief. I'm practically broke."

"Oh, sweetie, I'm sorry, I should have known you'd need some cash. Seriously, you always work so hard, you've earned it."

"I know, but I didn't want to beg. Actually, I've done all right with what I've found here. Not everything in the house was trash, and luckily both the truck and car had gas."

"Don't be silly. It's just that we have always so informal about money, I mean, because we were like always together, you know?"

"I know."

"Well, do you want to come on over and...well, you know."

"What about the food?"

"Oh, dear, I forgot about the food."

Sam opened the sack. "Smells good, and I'm starving."

"Go ahead and eat," she said.

"You sure you don't want some?"

"Maybe just a bite."

Sam cleared a few items off the little table and he set a new record for eating an Especial, pausing every now and then to pass Smidgeon a forkful.

"Don't eat so fast, honey."

"I told you I was starving."

The remains were deposited in one of the active garbage bags and they were ready to leave. Smidgeon was standing by the front door, her keys in her hand. Sam embraced her again, and said, "I don't know who this woman is, but we'll face whatever we have to face together."

"Sam, I'm sorry...you just make me so crazy sometimes."

The door locked, they got in their separate cars and dove off. He smiled as he followed her tail lights in The Clunker. It drove almost if it knew the way and was heading home.

Fourteen

Sam was back at work at The Mossback the next day. It was just like he'd never left except they had agreed on a new schedule. They would alternate evenings during the week, which would allow him time to complete his work at the Tesoro Road house. There was one other order of business to complete. Sam needed to visit Mr. Bertram to check on the case Loot had left for Loretta.

The waiting room was empty and Sam thought to himself, "one good thing about a small town, you can usually see an attorney pretty quickly."

"Sam! To what do I owe this pleasure? How is the house working out?"

"It's coming along. I mean, I always knew it was a mess. He was such a pack-rat."

"So I gathered. Everything okay?"

"Yeah, I'm making headway. It is at least livable now. Mr. Bertram, I wanted to ask you something."

"Sure, Sam."

"Has the woman picked up that case Loot left her?"

"There's a coincidence for you. I'm expecting her this afternoon. An associate of mine in San Antonio found her. She contacted me a few days ago and said she was planning on driving down here today."

"But you haven't seen her yet."

"No, Sam, the case is still in my office."

"Thanks, Mr. Bertram. I was just curious."

Back at the café, Sam gave Smidgeon the news.

"So it probably wasn't her."

"I guess not."

"Well, who could it be? Sam, you've got to be honest with me."

"I am. I hadn't dated anybody for ages before her, and then I was with you."

"What about that woman you worked with?"

"Sally?"

"Yes. Sam, you need to understand something about women. They can sometimes develop a crush on a guy, you know, even get obsessed, but keep it a secret. It eats at them the same way the mine ate at you all those years. It can make them do strange things."

"Not Sally, no way. Not her."

"Can you call her? At least make sure she's in Austin?"

"Well, I know she changed jobs and I don't have that number, so I'll have to call her at home tonight."

"Will you?"

"Yes, Smidgeon, I'll call her, but it's not her."

"What about Moll? Have you checked in with her lately?"

"Tried to call a few weeks ago. No answer."

"Call her too. Okay?'

"Will do. It's not her either, though. I seriously don't see Moll with a gun. Maybe it's a customer or someone else from around here."

"I would have recognized her. I know everybody around here."

"Maybe so, maybe not. From what you said, she was sure trying to conceal her identity. Like you said, it could be some secret crush, although I don't see that happening, with me."

She hugged him. "You underestimate yourself, sweetie."

After work, Sam left The Mossback and retired to the Tesoro Road house to sort through more of Loot's debris, but his first order of business was to make some calls. Loot hadn't had a phone but Sam had one installed soon after he moved in. He called Sally first.

"Sally?"

"Sam! This is a surprise!"

"Yeah, I've been really bad about calling."

"Tell me about it."

"How's the new job?"

"It's a job, you know? How's your life?"

"Some ups, some downs. You remember the old guy who was helping me?"

"Oh, the one from the parking lot?"

"Yeah, Loot. He died and left me his house and all of his stuff."

"Oh, I'm so sorry to hear that, Sam. Wait, didn't you tell me his place was full of junk?"

"Yeah, and it was even worse than I imagined, but I'm getting a handle on it. Say, you and Robert haven't been through here recently, have you?"

"Lordy no. We went to Toronto a few months ago... well, he went for a job but I just tagged along. Loved it..."

Sam interrupted, "But nothing driving out this way, like going west."

"No, why?"

"Just some weird stuff going on out here. Smidgeon said somebody came in and threatened her to stay away from me."

"What? Who'd do that? You got another girlfriend out there or something? I mean, I know you're not the type to cat around, but...

"No, seriously. To be honest, we did hit a bumpy patch recently but in the meantime I've just been hunkered down cleaning out the old man's place. It's only been a couple of weeks anyway."

"So who could it be? Someone from your past?"

"I doubt it...you know I really hadn't dated in years."

"Seriously. Except that one woman, what was her name?"

"Loretta. I doubt it could be her. I don't see her doing something like this, and anywathe timing doesn't work out because we know she's been in San Antonio. Coincidentally, she was due to come out here today. Loot left her some mysterious case of mementos or something. But Smidgeon was threatened yesterday and the case was still at the lawyer's. I asked about it today."

"Well, there's got to be an answer somewhere. Didn't you date another woman? You know, before we worked together."

"Sheesh, long gone. Haven't seen her in years. The only other woman I know is Moll, you know, Godson's wife, well, widow."

"Oh, I wonder how she's doing. What an awful time she's had."

"It was. I have had a hard time getting ahold of her...going to try again right now, and I better get to it. I've still got at least two trash bags to fill before I call it a night."

"Sam, you be careful. I know I'm always telling you that, but listen this time...be careful. You know the old saying about a woman scorned; some woman might have an interest in you, someone you hardly even know. Watch your back. Wait, is this why you called? You thought it was me?"

"Smidgeon's theory."

From the sound of her laugh, Sam could almost imagine Sally doubling over. "Oh, I see. Well, you know I care a lot about you, Sam, but not to the point of stalking and making threats."

"I know, I know, but I gotta keep her happy, right?"

"I guess. Hey, don't be such a stranger. Come back and visit once in a while, okay?"

"Will do. Take care."

Sam hung up. "So it wasn't Sally," he said to himself. "I *knew* it wasn't Sally."

He dialed Godson and Moll's number. Besides checking up on her, he also wanted to ask Moll about his good luck piece. A nice phone company recording told him the number was disconnected. His heart raced a little.

"It's not like her to let the phone go," he mused, then added, "or maybe she moved? I would think she'd have let me know."

He sat and thought further back in his past, mainly because Sally had mentioned the previous girlfriend. Her name was Anne and they were dating when he moved to Austin. He didn't know where she was.

"I doubt it could be her. I mean, she broke up with me, and anyway, it was a long time ago. She wouldn't even know I was out here. No, it's got to be someone out here, somebody I've run across. This is nuts."

Sam returned to the back bedroom. The ratio of trash to any sort of usable or sellable items was much higher in this room. It only took him about a minute to fill another trash bag.

In the distance, he heard a knock on the door.

"Coming," he yelled, as he tried to dislodge himself from a precarious spot without causing an avalanche.

He opened the door and his jaw dropped.

"Loretta?"

"Hi, Sam."

"I have to say, this is quite...well, I'm surprised to see you here."

"The lawyer in town mentioned you...it surprised me too. He gave me the address when I picked up the case the old man left to me. What a waste of a trip. Can I come in?"

Sam instinctively glanced around the yard, "Sure...place is still a mess."

"I remember your old place in Austin, Sam," she laughed, "You won't shock me with your lousy housekeeping."

"No, it's not that. This was *his* place. Professional packrat. I'm an amateur compared to him."

Sam led her into the little den and they sat down.

"This isn't that bad; you must have done a lot of work."

He chuckled, "Yeah, hey, can I get you some coffee or something?"

Loretta shook her head. "No, I need to get back to the motel. I have a long drive back home in the morning." She dropped her eyes momentarily, then fixed them on him again. "Sam, I need to tell you. I wanted to say I'm sorry about everything, you know, back in Austin. It just, well, I wasn't prepared for what I found."

"I know. I had no idea. Who could have imagined? Slim being your grandfather and all. To be honest, it kind of weirded me out too."

"But, well, you didn't even try to call me or anything."

"What? Wait, I *did* call. Your mother never told you?"

"No. When?"

"The day after Christmas. I was planning the big trip out west, remember? You helped me, a lot. I was on my way, drove straight through from Houston and stopped in San Antonio. That is when I called. She said you didn't want anything to do with me. She told me the mine had cursed her father and now I was cursed too."

"Sam, I had no idea. But I can see her doing that. The whole notion of the mine had long been a blight to her life. And I guess to my life as well. You know, helping you, well, it reminded me of stories of my grandfather, but I never imagined for a minute you were working on *his* information. I guess my feelings for you just blinded me to the reality. I was quite shocked when the lawyer told me you were out here, but then again, I guess maybe I'm not so surprised after all."

"Well..."

"Just so you know, I did try to drop by to see you about a year ago. I couldn't stand it, that you had never even tried to contact me...well, I mean, I didn't think you had. But they said you had moved, didn't know where. I figured you had moved on with your life."

"I guess I did. I had to, Loretta. The phone call with your mom left me pretty upset and confused, but I continued on with the trip. I had to. There was trouble and a lot of stuff has happened since then. I've almost died a couple of times and, well, I met someone new."

"Really? You're with someone? Out here?"

"Yeah."

Loretta looked down again. "I guess it was too much to expect you might still be available."

"Available?"

"My life hasn't been so good, Sam. I've had a couple of flings. After you never, well, after I thought you were gone forever, I got back with my old boyfriend for a while, you know, the one from the ranch near Ozona. *That* didn't go well at all. I have a protection order against him now. Nothing has seemed to work out. Maybe there *is* a curse, you know?"

"Don't be silly," he said, patting her hands. "Or I'd be cursed, right?'

"You sure you're not? You said you almost died."

"But...well, I'm doing dangerous things..."

"I think that's how the whole curse thing works, Sam."

"So what's the connection between you and Loot?"

"Loot? Oh, Mr. Meldings. I honestly have no idea. It was the mystery of it that brought me here. I didn't know who he was and getting contacted about inheriting something, well, I had to come. Curiosity, you know? All for a suitcase with pictures and tidbits. I guess they were friends, Loot and my grandfather, I mean. It was certainly nothing worth driving across the state to pick up. Part of the curse, right?"

"Aw, come on, stop it. Loot had been getting more sentimental lately. A grandson of Scamp, another old friend of Loot's, showed up in town recently. Loot and Slim and Scamp all ran together out here."

"Scamp... I know that name too. He's mentioned in some of the stuff in the case."

"Could I look through what he left you? I mean, it isn't too personal, is it?"

"I didn't even know the man, Sam. The lawyer said Mr. Meldings gave him extra money to help find me, so yes, you can see it; you can have it if you want."

Loretta reached out and touched Sam's shoulder as she said this. "It's over in my motel room. We could go over there and get it."

Sam's heart rate spiked, causing him to stammer, "I, uh, uh, no, probably not a good idea, Loretta."

"I see, I guess you are afraid I'd seduce you or something. We had something good back then, Sam. I miss you."

"Loretta...I, uh, well things have changed. I'd, uh, why don't you bring the case to the restaurant tomorrow?"

"Restaurant?"

"More like a little café. The woman I'm involved with owns it. The Mossback Cafe."

"I saw that place...looked like a greasy spoon."

Sam winced slightly. "People seem to like it. We're fixing it up."

Loretta sighed. "Okay, the greasy spoon it is. I need to head back pretty early. It's a long drive."

"Yeah, I know."

"Oh, I forgot, you know the trip well. I don't know how you ever managed doing it so many times." Loretta stood up. "I guess that's it. Sam, I'm sorry. I've regretted what I did to you almost from the moment I left. I wanted to come back a thousand times, but, well, you never, I mean, I guess you did, but..."

"Loretta, it's all water under the bridge, as they say. What's done is done."

Sam opened the front door, flooding the yard with light and as she kissed him on the cheek Sam could see their two figures silhouetted on the mottled ground.

"You're awesome, Sam. You really are. I hope this woman knows how lucky she is."

"See you tomorrow. I get there early, but if I'm in the back just ask for me."

A tear rolled down Loretta's cheek. "You sure you can't just come over to the motel for a while?"

Sam swallowed hard. "I-I really don't think that's a good idea."

Loretta reached up and touched his cheek, then turned and left. Sam could hear her sobs as she walked to her car.

As she drove off, Sam thought about their brief time together, but his thoughts were punctuated by the final encounter with Loretta's mother over the phone. Smidgeon's brown eyes bubbled up in his mind and he thought out loud, "It doesn't matter, I know who I love."

He decided to call it a night and locked up the house, then on the way to Smidgeon's place, Sam recounted the evening's conversations in his mind.

Smidgeon met him at the door and kissed him.

"Welcome home, stranger," she said, and she led him toward the bedroom.

"Wait, right now? What about dinner."

"Later. First, well, we still have a lot of catching up to do."

~ * ~

A bit later, Smidgeon asked him if he had called Sally and Moll.

"I talked to Sally," he said. "She and Robert haven't left Austin in months. There is no way she came out here. She'd never threaten you, anyway."

"Okay, but what about Moll?"

"Couldn't get through. Number disconnected."

Smidgeon cast Sam a quick glance. "Disconnected? That's weird."

"Maybe she moved back home or something. She likes to travel; it could be she just decided to take a long trip. She always wanted to travel."

"I hope she's okay," Smidgeon said.

He didn't mention the encounter with Loretta, but since she was supposed to drop by, he figured Smidgeon would be able to see nothing was going on.

The next morning at the café everything seemed normal, with the usual regular customers dropping in to get their daily fix of coffee and a hearty breakfast before they dealt with the business of the new day. As he watched Smidgeon interact with them, Sam wondered, as he often did, if they came in as much for her friendly banter as they did for the food.

About nine, Clay from the sheriff's office came in and ordered a cup of coffee.

Sam happened to be at the register. "Hey, Clay, how are things this morning?"

"Trouble at the Dolings Motel. Body found in the parking lot."

"No way."

"Yep. Apparently she was jumped. Her room was open. We're still investigating."

"You said 'she,' so it was a woman?"

"Trying to notify next of kin now. Apparently she was from San Antonio."

Sam's heart skipped a beat as a grim uneasiness flooded his brain.

"San Antonio?"

"Yeah, guess she was passing through."

Smidgeon came up, "Hey, Clay!"

"'Morning, Jo. Was just telling Sam here about the body that was discovered over at Dolings."

"Dolings! I hope Marcy is okay."

"She's fine. She found the woman. Look, Sam, you fill her in, I need to run back there…"

"Clay… the woman. Was her last name Smyth?"

Deputy Clay almost dropped his coffee. "How could you know that?"

"Acquaintance. Loot left her something in his will and she met with Sid Bertram yesterday to pick it up. I knew her a few years ago back east. She was the granddaughter of an old friend of Loot's. Another thing. She came by the house on Tesoro Road last night."

Both Clay and Smidgeon were staring at Sam in amazement.

"That could likely mean you were the last person to see her alive…" Clay began.

Sam finished the statement, "…except for the killer."

"Sam you didn't tell…"

Sam interrupted her. "I know. She was going to come by here today to show me the suitcase Loot left her. She wanted me to go there to get it last night but…well, I didn't. It wouldn't have been right, you know?" Then he dropped his head. "But I guess she might still be alive if I had gone with her to get that case."

"Jo, I'm going to need Sam to come with me for a few more questions in a more official setting."

Sam could tell Smidgeon was flustered by all of this new information. "Go, Sam, do what you need to do."

In the patrol car, Clay asked a few more questions. "So, why exactly did she come by the house on Tesoro?"

"Like I said, we had history. I told Bertram when the estate was settled because I was surprised when he mentioned her name. I guess he told her where I might be." Sam chuckled nervously, "Better she came by there than the other house."

Clay cracked a sly smile at that and continued, "And you didn't mention this meeting with Jo?"

"Sore spot. She gets jealous. You know, this kind of stuff is hard to talk about with women. Either way it seems like you will get in trouble."

"Well, it's trouble now. So there is supposed to be a suitcase with Loot's belongings in the motel?"

"That's what she told me. A bunch of junk, she said. She was a bit miffed she drove all the way from San Antonio to get it. She was going to let me look through it."

"Why would you care? I mean, you got the house, right, and the truck? What do you care about a suitcase?"

"I knew Loot. Thought maybe I could help her figure out what why Loot thought she'd be interested in those things."

"What else can you tell me about this woman?"

"I met her about two years ago in Ozona. We rode out a storm together at a truck stop. After she came to Austin we had a brief fling. It was only a couple of weeks. I guess it was just one of those things. She has been out of my life since then, at least until the lawyer mentioned the suitcase when we were settling Loot's estate. Then last night I was cleaning at Loot's like I do most nights and she just showed up. I think she was curious, for one thing. Our breakup had been sudden...she left me. I'd tried to contact her, but her mother wouldn't ever put me through so things just stopped there. I think she wanted to clear the air. I don't know, maybe she wanted to try to get back together. She asked me to go with her to the motel but, well, I didn't. Told her that wasn't a good idea. Suggested she come here with the case before she headed back east. The last time I saw her, she was driving off."

Clay picked up his radio microphone. "Sarah, this is Clay, unit six, over."

"Go ahead. Over." The response crackled with static.

"Get ahold of Sid Bertram and have him meet me over at Dolings. Over."

"Ten-four."

"So, the last you saw her she was driving off. Nobody else was at your house?"

"Nope."

"Still, if you was…"

"What?" Sam asked.

"Well, if you had, let's say, evil intentions regarding this woman, I don't see you waiting until she got all the way to the motel to do anything to her. That's in your favor, Sam. You could have done her in out at Loot's old place. Much more secluded. Granted, Dolings is pretty dead right now, but there were a few guests. You didn't bear no grudge with her, did you?"

"It was over a long time ago, Clay. I wasn't interested in starting anything up, either. Smidgeon and I have a good thing."

"But you think *she* wanted you to come back?"

"I don't really know what she wanted. But she did ask me over and like I said, I told her it…well, I just told her I couldn't do it. We didn't fight or anything, back then or last night. The breakup was over some slight misunderstanding. I think she, well, she maybe regretted it but that's life, right? I made it clear I had moved on, which is why I told her to come by The Mossback, so we could be on the up and up."

"Right. I wouldn't feel too kindly to you if you hurt Jo… most everybody in town would feel the same. Well, here we are."

They drove into the Dolings Motel parking lot. Although it was a fixture in town and he drove by it all the time, Sam hadn't actually been on the property since Smidgeon had arranged a room for him after his encounter with the MacGregg hands. Emergency vehicles were blocking the way to the back lot, so Clay parked in front and they walked around. Sidney Bertram drove up and parked as they reached the far corner of the building. Clay motioned for him to follow and they continued around the side of the building.

The contours of a body were plainly visible under a motel blanket. This was near the sedan Sam had seen driving off the night before. A motel room door was open. Sam could see it was the room next door to the one he had occupied the last time he had been here and a sense of dramatic irony flushed his brain. His eyes flashed to the car and Sam briefly wondered what had happened to her classic '63 Chevy. Then he forgot the notion as another deputy approached.

"Hey, Clay."

"Wyatt. Anything else to report?"

"No trauma apparent. She just dropped in her tracks. I guess it might be natural, like maybe a heart attack?"

"Ain't likely in someone so young."

"Overdose maybe?"

"She probably would have done that in the room with the door closed, don't you think?"

Wyatt nodded, then added, "Marcy said she alternates rooms...front was half full so this one she put in back. Bad luck for her, I guess."

Sid Bertram joined the small group.

"Morning, Sid."

"Clay, what's this all about?"

"Sam here said you had a meeting with this young woman yesterday."

Clay crouched down and lifted a corner of the blanket revealing the face. Sam knew what to expect but was still shocked to see Loretta's pretty face reduced to a peaceful blank canvas outlined by the cold asphalt. She looked as if she might be sleeping.

"Oh, my," Sid said, visibly shocked. Clay returned the blanket.

"Loretta Longo Smythe, of San Antonio," Sid said.

"We know. Did she meet with you?"

"Yes, indeed. I gave her a case of belongings left specifically to her by Loot Meldings."

Clay looked at Sam. "Okay, good, it shows part of what you said is true." Then he turned back to Sid. "What did this case look like?"

"Worn, beige, like what you would call an overnight case about so big," he held up his hands about shoulder width to illustrate. "Older style, like from twenty or thirty years ago."

"You find anything like that, Wyatt?"

"Nope, not in the room, not in the car."

"Sam, can we search the Tesoro Road house? Not that I want to. I was there after Loot died. You could hide an elephant in there."

"I'm about three-fifths done clearing it out. But yes, you can search. I stayed at Smidgeon's place after I left there. She'd probably let you search her place too."

"I'll get up with her. Wyatt, I want the medical examiner on this. Quick. We might even need to send her down to El Paso for a more detailed report. This smells like murder to me. A first class mystery."

"Will do, Clay."

"Sam, you've told me enough for now. Don't leave town. Understand?"

Sam's thoughts turned to the mine, but he knew he could defer digging for a while. "Okay, Clay."

Fifteen

The search of the Tesoro Road house took the rest of the day. As deputies tromped through the house, Sam almost winced every time he watched one of them pull another armload of debris from an un-cleared section of the house, only to dump it into the hallway or living room. He knew it was necessary, but he didn't like seeing his hours of hard work spoiled. This flurry of events had left him little time to process the reality that Loretta was dead.

He knew he should stay and observe but he was more worried about Smidgeon. Their recent troubles weighed heavily on his mind and he wanted to explain the situation to her as best as he could.

"Why didn't I tell her?" he muttered under his breath.

"You say something, Sam?" Deputy Clay was walking by and had overheard.

"Oh, nothing, just mumbling to myself. Clay, I'm going to head over to the café for a minute. Need anything?"

"You sure you don't want to stay here?" he asked.

"You aren't going to find anything and I skipped breakfast. I'll just be a few minutes," Sam answered.

When he walked through the front door of The Mossback, Smidgeon motioned toward the kitchen with her chin, walked that way and he followed her past the prep tables and out the back door where she stopped, spun around, and put her hands on her hips.

"Why didn't you tell me she came by?"

"I don't know, after what we'd just been through, I don't know, I guess I was afraid to stir things up again. It was stupid, I know."

"Sam, you're an idiot, you know that?"

He nodded, sheepishly.

"But, well, you came home to me. It tells me a lot, both about you and about *us*. After this last tiff, I resolved myself to have faith in what we have, but I have to admit, I didn't expect I'd be needing to test it so soon. But the bottom line is, I know we have to share some trust if we're going to ever make this work."

Sam hugged her. "I'm sorry I'm such a dimwit. She caught me off guard when she dropped by. She said she was upset and confused I never tried to contact her."

"But you said you did and her mother told you to get lost, right?"

"Right. All water under the bridge. I told her about her mother and also told her I had moved on and she seemed okay with it. Still, it was hard seeing her body lying there. I mean, everything was over a long time ago, but," Sam's eyes welled up, "nobody needs to end up like that."

Smidgeon reached out and drew Sam's shoulder over to hers. "Clay told me they'd likely search my place too. I told him to go ahead. I even signed a waiver. You can just let them in. Ain't gonna find nothing, because there ain't nothing there to find."

"No. Should be faster, too. Your house is nothing like Tesoro Road."

"You should have followed them around with a trash bag," she quipped.

"Thought about it. They've been sifting through a lot of stuff out in the living room and den so I just told them to leave it. Right now it's starting to look almost as bad as it did before, but with the back rooms cleared out, they've probably done me more help than they realize."

Sam gave Smidgeon a peck on the cheek and the ever-faithful Chuy came out the door right on time and handed him a cup of coffee and a wrapped hamburger.

"Thanks," he said and Chuy responded with a flash of gold from his broad smile.

"Nobody needs to mess with no cops on an empty stomach, Mr. Sam."

~ * ~

Back at the house, he sat in Loot's old truck and munched the burger and sipped his coffee while he watched the searchers. They had run out of available room inside the house and were dumping armloads of Loot's junk in the yard.

"Back to square one out here too," he said.

Another weather-beaten truck approached and parked beyond the line of police cars littering the street in front of the house. Sam watched in the rear view mirror as Lance Norton sauntered up the gravel driveway.

"Sam, I just heard about all this. You okay?"

Sam sighed. "Yeah, but it's hard to watch. What a mess."

"You know, my offer still stands if you need a place to lay your head."

"Oh, I'm okay. Smidgeon and I have patched things up."

"Scuttlebutt around town is that you were somehow connected to the girl who got herself killed."

"We had a fling a couple of years ago." Sam thought carefully about what he was comfortable telling Lance. "She apparently had a connection to Loot I didn't know about. She came to collect a case Loot left her in his will, mementos or something, and she came to see me last night not long after you left. That means I was the last person to see her, well, except for whoever killed her. The suitcase she picked up at the lawyer's is missing."

"Oh, so they're looking for the case?"

Sam nodded and tipped the coffee cup to drain the last of the tepid contents.

"What's up with you?"

"Just in town for some business and after I heard the gossip, I figured if they were searching your place you'd be here."

"Thought you usually came to town with Tim."

"Not this trip. Oh, you'll like this. Tim is busy pursuing some new girl he met at a watering hole down the road in Sierra Blanca."

"He's ranging kinda far, isn't he?"

"Well, most of the women around here already know him too well. He brought her out to the ranch a few days ago. Nice looking girl, but a little too high fallutin' for him, I'd say."

"How so?"

"City girl. You can tell."

"What's a city girl doing in a dusty ranching town like Sierra Blanca?"

"Don't rightly know, Sam. Don't add up to me either, but he gave her the grand tour the other day, spent all day out driving the jeep trails over the whole ranch."

Sam shot Lance a glance.

"No, I don't think they nosed around anyplace...uh, special, but they were out quite a while."

"Rocks and cactus and mesquite...just the way to a girl's heart," Sam said, laughing.

Clay came over as Lance and Sam were talking. "Sam, we're about done here," he said, then he glanced at Lance. "I'm sorry, you're...?"

"We've met. I'm Lance Norton, foreman at the MacGregg place." Lance extended a hand but the deputy didn't shake it.

"Oh, yeah, I remember, from the café a while back. You got business here?"

"He's my friend, Clay. Remember? We're both from Houston, Astros fans."

"Oh, yeah. They ain't doing so hot this year."

Lance laughed, "No, not like that run two years ago."

"Yeah," Sam added, laughing, "but I guess we're used to it."

"Sam, we need to head over to Smidgeon's place now. You coming? I already got somebody to get her to sign a waiver permitting us to search."

"Yeah, she told me to let you in, so I'll go hang out over there a while. Should be an easier search."

"Yeah, this was a doozy. Glad you had already cleaned up a bit. We tried to be as kind as we could."

"It's all right, probably helped me in the long run."

"You can bag up the trash, Sam, but maybe leave it around until I tell you it's okay to take it to the dump, all right?"

"Sure."

Lance shook Sam's hand. "Take care, Sam; talk to you later."

"Right. Thanks," Sam said with half a wave.

Sam locked up and led the procession to Smidgeon's place. As promised, the search took only about an hour and Clay pronounced the results.

"Nothing here, Sam. We appreciate your cooperation."

"I understand, Clay. It needed to be done. I'm interested in finding the killer too."

"Too many people dying around here. Now this makes me wonder about Loot."

"I know, right? I mean, he was old, but he seemed to be holding his own."

"Bad thing about a town like Van Horn is there's always people passing through."

"Well, with Loot, the examiner didn't see anything, did he?"

"Well, to be honest, the local doc probably didn't do a very thorough exam. Loot was old and we really had no reason to suspect anything."

"Gil told me Loot's shotgun was missing. He always kept it by the front door."

"Yeah, we looked into that, but maybe he sold it. Heck, he might have took it out on one of his trapping runs and left it. There's a question there, but it's not like it's a suspicious sort of thing, you know? I mean, you haven't seen it, have you?"

Sam nodded. "Naw, and if I had, I would have told you about it before you started searching."

"Well, we'll see if we get anything more from El Paso. Her body should almost be there by now. Thank you for your cooperation, Sam. Remember what I said, don't leave town until we have this settled."

Sam again nodded and Clay left with the other officers. It was getting on eight PM, so he drove the rusty truck back to the café.

The door was locked, so Sam used his key. Smidgeon poked her head out the kitchen door. "Sam! I was hoping it was you. Everything okay?"

"Yeah, they didn't find anything. Big surprise."

"Why on earth would anybody kill that poor girl? When you talked, did she say anything at all about the suitcase?"

"Just said it had papers and pictures and a smattering of random junk. She was a bit miffed she had driven all this way for basically nothing."

"Yet she came to see you. I'm sorry, honey, but it still just bothers me she came over and you didn't tell me. I want to know what you talked about."

"Unresolved crap, really. The lawyer mentioned me to her. I guess it was my fault for saying I knew her when we were at the office. He told her where I might be, otherwise she had no reason to even suspect I was in town. She said she had tried to find me, wanted to find out why I had given up on her so easily."

"And, well nothing more, right?"

"Smidgeon, to be honest, I know she was curious about me. I heard it in her voice. I'm sure that's why she invited me to the motel. The regrets of the past are hard to accept sometimes."

Sam grabbed her hand and said, "Like I told you before, I made it very clear to her I had moved on. Heck, she said she'd had relationships too, so I think she understood. To be honest, she seemed kind of lost."

"The important thing to me is you didn't go over there."

"Might have saved her life if I had, but no, I didn't. I couldn't."

"Sam, there'd probably be two dead bodies in the morgue if you had."

"You would have killed me anyway."

"Yes, I would have," she laughed then stifled it. "I'm sorry, this ain't no laughing matter. A girl is dead and it don't seem like anybody will be safe until they figure this out."

"You didn't mention the threats to any of the deputies?"

"No, with all the excitement I just forgot."

"Forgot?"

"Seems separate, Sam. Probably a coincidence. But at least now we know for sure it wasn't her. Anyway, they might start to suspect me, just because I had thought it was her, you know? Let's just let it be for now."

Sam sighed. "I guess. Seems like a mistake to me."

"This is west Texas, Sam. We can take care of ourselves."

~ * ~

It was mid-afternoon the next day and the café was almost empty when the door opened and a short thin woman with graying hair entered. She looked around sternly and her eyes settled on Sam, who was in the corner filling salt shakers.

She screamed, "You!"

Two cowboys in the other corner jumped out of their seats and their hats fell to the floor. Smidgeon rushed out of the kitchen, two steaming plates of food in her hands. She set them down on the counter and said, "What is all this about? You can't come into my place yelling, scaring me and my customers!"

The woman ignored Smidgeon and stormed over to Sam. "The sheriff told me you worked here. You killed her, killed my baby!"

"What?"

Then it dawned on him who this was. He recognized the voice even though he had heard it only one time.

"Look, I didn't have anything to do with what happened to Loretta."

"You're here, aren't you? She came here and you're here and now this?" The woman started bawling.

Smidgeon approached the woman and at the same time, out of the corner of his eye Sam saw a patrol car pull up. It was Clay.

"Look, Mrs. Smythe?" Smidgeon started. The woman nodded, weeping loudly and Smidgeon put a hand on her shoulder.

Clay entered and immediately approached the woman too.

"Mrs. Smythe, you can't go around causin' a ruckus. Come back to the station."

She looked at Sam with tear-rimmed eyes. "It's you. You and that Loot Meldings. I should have known he'd drag his drunken, worthless carcass into our lives again. I'm surprised Scamp Norton isn't mixed up in this too! I told you, you are cursed! All of you! And now my baby is dead!"

Clay shared an exasperated look with both Sam and Smidgeon. "Mrs. Smythe, you have a right to be upset, but you can't cause a scene. Sam here, well, no matter what might have transpired between him and your daughter in the past, we've checked him out. There is no evidence whatsoever that he's done a darn thing here."

Smidgeon put her arm around Mrs. Smythe's shoulder and led her into the hall down toward the restrooms and was calmly whispering to her as the woman continued crying. Sam and Clay retreated into the kitchen.

"Let me guess," Sam said. "You mentioned my name to her."

"I was just explaining the investigation so far and when I mentioned you and also said you worked at The Mossback she stormed out before anybody could stop her. I got here just as fast as I could. What's this all about, Sam?"

"I knew her father back in Austin. His name was Slim Longo. He and Loot and that Scamp guy she mentioned were all ranch hands out here in the old days."

"Before my time, I reckon. And what was that about a curse? Don't make no sense."

Sam saw his opening and decided to work it. "Tell me about it. The dead girl, her daughter ... well, it's pretty obvious she didn't approve of our relationship. Only got worse when we found out, quite by accident, Slim was the dead girl's grandfather. Slim had died and left me a Bible and some letters and wanted me to find her, his granddaughter. Never could find her. Then it was weird, this huge weird coincidence. It spooked her, Clay, and she left. It was the last time I ever talked to her before last night. Tried to find her once, called her mom and she gave me that same BS about her father and some curse."

"Geez, Sam. I had no idea. I've seen grief do some pretty hard work on a person's mind, and somewhere in there somebody gets mad about something. You know anything else you can tell me?"

"Loot told me there was some kind of incident with him and Slim and Scamp here at the café. And it gets weirder too, because when I met Slim, he was a drunk, a wino. I'll be honest with you, Clay, I had some trouble back then and got arrested and I ended up helping the old guy in jail. He was sick and he was hurt. He died in my arms. I told Loretta about it and I guess she told her mother. Apparently Mrs. Smythe thought everything was due to this curse. She said it had ruined his life and it threatened to ruin theirs as well. She was convinced the coincidence, Loretta and me getting together, wasn't an accident but was part of the curse and now she seems to think the curse is attached to me. Crazy talk if you ask me, but I guess in her state of mind it all makes some kind of sense to her."

Clay nodded in agreement. "I'll see if I can calm her down," he said, "I mean, she's distraught, you know? Her daughter's dead and we have no suspect and she feels like she needs to blame somebody and here you are... again. I'd probably do the same thing."

"Yeah, I know. Look, and I'm sure Smidgeon will agree, we understand, there's no problem here, just some yelling. She's upset."

"You best stay back here, out of sight, out of mind."

"Fine," Sam said and after Clay left, he carefully peeked out the kitchen door's small window and saw that another deputy had arrived, who joined Clay as he escorted Loretta's mother out the door and back to her car where yet a third deputy was waiting. The second deputy drove Mrs. Smythe away in her car. Clay came into the kitchen again.

"Sam, she started jabbering on and on about a gold mine. Says that's what the curse is about. Something called the Sublett mine."

Sam was already expecting this and nodded. "Old Texas legend. Kinda like the Lost Dutchman Mine in Arizona. Supposed to be up in the Guadalupes, you know, in the National Park. Come to think of it, when Slim was delirious, he mentioned the same thing. I had no idea what he was talking about."

Clay nodded again. "Woman's distraught. I told her we're doing everything we can to find her daughter's killer, but so far you seem to be in the clear so she needed to leave you alone."

"That true?"

"For the most part, Sam. We still have to consider you as a person of interest, but, well, in my gut I think you're clean. Don't disappoint me."

"What about Mrs. Smythe?"

"We'll take her back to her motel room and see if we can console her. It is a tough thing for a mother to lose a child. Anger like this can be part of the grieving process. She probably had all kind of stuff building up in her all the way out here. That long drive down I-10 can make even the sanest person a little crazy sometimes."

Sam shook Clay's hand. "Thanks, Clay, for the quick response."

After he left, Smidgeon came over to Sam.

"Lordy, she sure knows how to empty a restaurant," she said. "So she's Loretta's mom?"

"Yeah. It was definitely worse than the last time she went off on me, when Loretta left. She said the curse was what killed Slim and told me now I was cursed too. At least it was on the phone that time."

"Yeah, she went on and on to me about it. To Clay too. And I guess you know she mentioned the mine too. Better steer clear of the MacGregg place for a while, Sam."

"Yeah, Clay told me. I explained to him what I knew about the Sublett Mine, what's in the books about Texas lore anyway."

"Sam, do you think that was a good idea?"

"Well, Clay didn't know, but if they're talking about it at the station, it's quite possible somebody might also know something about it. Hezekiah did."

"He did?"

"Yep. Anyway, I think they pretty much considered it to be the rantings of a crazy person... or at least someone in the throes of grief. Plus, nobody knows where it might be. I told Clay it was just a legend. Even if nobody down there knows about it, if anybody cares to look it up, the facts of the legend are well known. I told Clay the legend says the mine is supposed to be in the Guadalupes. I seriously doubt she knows anything more than that. But until they clear this up, well, there is still going to be a small target on my back."

"What do you mean? I thought Clay told her you were in the clear?"

"He was just calming her down, Smidgeon."

"But the searches..."

"Yeah, it's good for me, but I'm still the last person they know who saw her alive."

Smidgeon hugged Sam tight. "Sam Milton, what have you gotten me into?" Then she looked deep into his eyes. "Do you think there really is a curse?"

"I don't know, sweetie, I don't know."

~ * ~

That evening, at Tesoro Road, Sam was picking up after the searchers. Clay had told him he could clean up, but not to throw anything away, so he was bagging trash and stashing it in a corner of the little garage.

His "keep" and "sell" piles took up most of the room, but he managed to stack bags along the side wall. The far bedroom was the worst hit, but it had also been the worst room in the house. It still smelled musty and there was evidence of deep dust on the few visible surfaces.

"Loot must have rarely come in here," he mumbled to himself.

The door to the small closet was ajar and he made his way over there. He remembered there had been a distinct pathway through the junk leading to that closet, so he assumed Loot had accessed it more than anything else in the room. He opened the door and saw the same things he figured the searching officers had found: pretty much nothing. A few odd pieces of clothing hanging, including a woman's dress. It was wrapped in plastic but it looked like an old wedding dress. He also found what looked like an old military uniform.

"War vintage, I'd say," Sam said to himself.

There was a cigar box on the shelf. Inside he found what he recognized as a purple heart and another medal with a predominantly blue ribbon bordered with red and white. The medal depicted an eagle in front of a cross. There were other uniform insignia in the box along with a couple of pictures. In one, he recognized a much younger Loot, standing alongside some tracked, armored vehicle. There was another far shot of what he assumed was the same vehicle.

"Half-track," he said. "Loot never mentioned the war, but he was definitely the right age." It was not unusual, he thought to himself; most young men served in the military in some capacity during the war.

As he stepped forward to replace the box, the floorboard creaked oddly and he looked down. There was a flap of old carpet covering the entire floor area of the closet. Sam thought for a moment.

"There's a throw rug in the den and one in the living room, but there is no other carpet through the whole house. Why would he bother to carpet this closet?"

He stooped down, lifted the frayed remnant and removed it. It was late afternoon and sunlight was beating against the lone window in the room. Dusty curtains were not closed completely, and a shaft of light shot through the dirty window right into the closet, allowing Sam to see something the searchers had probably missed.

"It's a cut out!" he said as he picked at the edges of the cut wood with his fingernails. The entire floor was cut to match the bottom molding, right up to the corners.

It was a good job and fit in so tightly he could not get a good grip on the sides with his fingernails so he pulled out his keys, tried one of those, and finally managed to nudge the edge of the board up high enough for him to start working the boards up. When he finally got a good grip on it, the entire section came out in one piece. Underneath, there had been a depression chipped out of the concrete slab of the house. Sam could see the metal rebars had been cut away as well. A wooden box was nestled into the depression.

"Search missed this," Sam said. "Doesn't say much for the sheriff's department, I guess."

He pulled the box out, set it on the floor outside the closet. It was obviously handmade, designed to fit into the hole in the floor, and had hinges and a latch with a small lock.

Sam remembered Loot's huge key ring hanging in the kitchen. He had left it hanging as a makeshift memorial to the old trapper. He grabbed the box and carried it into the kitchen.

Sixteen

Sam placed the box on the small kitchen table and fumbled with Loot's huge ring of keys.

"I wonder if Loot even knew what most of these keys were for."

He thought he heard a laugh in the quiet solitude of the house, then he remembered he was alone and uneasily looked around. He had imagined odd snickering laughs in the past but this one seemed a little different from most of those. He shook his head at the peculiarity of his thoughts.

"All this crazy stuff is slowly driving me nuts," he muttered.

On the nineteenth try, he finally found the right key. Although it complained briefly, the lock popped open with some minor jiggling.

Sam had spent weeks dealing with the mess in Loot's house so he was accustomed to the musty smells of stacks of old paper, but this time the odor was more pronounced. A piece of what looked like old wallpaper was nestled just inside the box. He moved it and stood there with his mouth gaping.

"Money," he said, adding in a low whisper, "a *lot* of money."

Sam whistled under his breath as he touched the bills. He picked up a few of the bills and examined them, then he sniffed at one. He could tell they were old and took a closer look at several of them.

"Money has a different type of mustiness," he said. "Must be the paper or something."

Most were Series 1950 or 1950A, some were Series 1934 with various letter designations. Sam didn't know a lot about paper money, but it was easy to assume these bills had been hidden a long time. He pulled up a chair, sat down heavily and stared at the box and its contents.

"That old coot. He sometimes complained about money, but this... who knew?"

He remembered his surprise at hearing Loot had paid the attorney in cash and Bertram had said he had even paid for a private investigator to find Loretta. He picked through the box again, gingerly fingering the small stacks of green paper.

"Not an immense fortune, but it's got to be thousands of dollars."

~ * ~

Three vaporous figures hovered in the background of the kitchen watching Sam count stacks of green bills.

"You old fool! You were holding out on of us!"

"Slim... Scamp... don't be like that...it was, well it was just my business, not yours."

"No wonder you wuz never much interested in finding the Sublett mine."

"Now, Scamp, I just, well, I just didn't want to draw attention to myself is all."

"But you did time for protecting us."

"Yeah, and I'd do it again," he chuckled, "but you wuz my pals."

Slim hovered close to Loot. "You knew he'd find it, didn't you?"

"Yeah, he's a smart boy. I figured as much."

"I was a wondering why you kept trying to shoo them cops away from that closet."

"I couldn't have them finding it, could I, Scamp? I just wish we could actually *do* something, move stuff. Scare people. Ghosts in the movies can do it."

Slim and Scamp glanced at one another and laughed.

"There's a way but you gotta learn the knack of it," Slim said.

"The Indian knows."

"Who's the Indian, Scamp?"

"Hangs out south of here, sort of teaches us lost souls to do stuff. They say he's out in the desert somewhere. Spooky stuff," Scamp said as he feigned a poke at Slim and laughed again. "Get it?"

Slim fanned at the wisps of Scamp. "Cut it out, you goof-ball. I ain't never much wanted to find him, but if'n you want, we can try to focus real hard. He'll know and he'll maybe conjure us over to him. If'n that's what you want, Loot."

"I do. I have a feeling Sam's gonna need my help sometime."

~ * ~

Sam finished counting the money.

"Twenty-six thousand five hundred and forty bucks," he whispered. "I guess it's safe to say Loot came from old money," he chuckled, then stopped as a chill ran down his spine and the hair on the back of his neck stood on end. He rubbed at it.

He replaced the stacks of bills, closed the box and decided to put it back where he had found it, replacing the piece of carpet over the crude trap door. As an afterthought, he placed a couple of the trash bags over it and in front of the door.

"Just looks like more of the mess," he mumbled, still rubbing at the odd feeling on the back of his neck. "I'm running out of room in the garage anyway."

~ * ~

Several weeks later, Sam was summoned to the sheriff's office by a deputy who dropped by The Mossback about four in the afternoon.

"Go on, Sam," Smidgeon said.

"I was planning on going over to Loot's place tonight."

"I know, I've got it. You just go see what they want." Smidgeon reached out and hugged him. "Just tell me what's going on, okay?"

"I will, I promise."

It was a short drive and when he got there, Clay directed him to a small room, he guessed for more questions.

"So what's this about, Clay?"

"Got the autopsy results from El Paso."

"And?"

"It took them quite a while to narrow it down, had to do some pretty extensive testing before they discovered it. Cyanide."

"Geez. Cyanide?"

"Pretty serious stuff. Injected, they think. They found a needle mark on her neck."

"Wow. She didn't have a chance, did she?"

"Not the way it was done. Pretty unusual too... whoever did it mixed the cyanide with phenobarbital and a huge dose of something called diphenhydramine; they said it's the main ingredient in Benadryl. A cocktail is what the lab called it. They think the Benadryl was put in there to throw them off. It almost worked."

"I think phenobarbital is a barbiturate. An antihistamine would have worked with it to knock her out and let the cyanide do its job."

Clay sat forward in his chair and stared at Sam. "I'm kind of surprised you seem to have some knowledge of these drugs."

"I have allergies, Clay. Antihistamines make me sleepy but I have to take them when my sinuses are messed up. Phenobarbital is pretty well known, heck, it's what Marilyn Monroe overdosed on. Those are common enough I guess, but where the heck would anybody get cyanide?"

"Nobody knows for sure. So you've never worked with it?"

"No. I don't know anything about it."

"Still, you went back east recently, right? You know anybody there who might have experience with chemicals?"

Sam could see where the conversation was going and he knew he'd need to choose his words carefully.

"A friend, Godson Millet, died in an automobile accident near Sonora and I helped his wife Moll with the arrangements. Spent a few days in Austin and Houston helping her make arrangements and going to the funeral. I was mostly with her, but spent some time with my family in Houston as well."

Sam gave Clay a list of phone numbers but told him, "The last time I called Moll, the number was disconnected. She was having a pretty hard time with it all, so I don't know if she moved or is having financial problems."

"Okay, we'll check on it out. Sam, you can go but I want to remind you again, don't leave town."

He left the sheriff's office and headed over to Tesoro Road thinking about the box in the closet.

"All I need is another search."

He wondered where else he might be able hide it. He considered taking it to the mine but he didn't want to risk making a trip out there himself, and he didn't want to involve Lance or Hezekiah or even Smidgeon with the money. It wasn't greed; it was the uncertain origin of the cash.

"It's fishy, just doesn't feel right," he said to himself as he pulled up behind the old truck. "There's enough going on without adding more complications."

~ * ~

The three wisps hovered in the desert, huddling together near a clump of cactus.

"Kupita?" Loot asked.

"That's what they calls him," Scamp said.

"I think it's a Comanche word," Slim said, "Reckon he's an old Comanche spirit. They say, all he does is wander and teach."

"Nice country. Mexico?"

"Not exactly sure. Last I remember, we was spooking Sam and talking about conjuring up the Indian and then we all three just seemed to end up here. "

A misty stern-faced figure materialized next to the group.

"Kupita..." Scamp said.

The figure grunted and pointed at a rock and spoke in a language they did not understand. His words were augmented with dramatic gestures.

A glow appeared as he concentrated on the rock, then they all felt an energy release. The rock hopped about six inches.

Kupita pointed at Slim.

"Naw, not me, I'm already pretty content with what I can't do."

Slim pointed at Loot. "He's the one what wanted to learn."

Kupita pointed at Loot, then down at the rock, continuing to stare harshly at Loot. He loomed close and whispered things Loot could not understand, yet as the other spirit continued to hover, he began to comprehend. He approached the rock and focused on it. The presence of Kupita urged him, in a very primal way, to push out from deep within his soul. Loot narrowed his concentration on the rock until he could detect some kind of force growing. Kupita motioned with his ghostly forefinger and Loot stabbed sharply with his own finger, in the direction of the rock. There was no progressive glow, as had been the case with the ancient one, only a brief muted flash, but the rock moved about an inch.

"You done did it," Scamp said. "You done did it!"

Kupita pointed at Scamp, who replied as he drifted backwards away from the outstretched finger, "No, not me. I'm good."

Then Kupita nodded at Loot with a sly smile and waved a spectral arm, whisking them all up and away.

Just as their forms flew into the sky, Loot recognized the familiar outline of the distinctive Presidio county courthouse.

"Marfa," he whispered.

~ * ~

Sam had almost cleared up the mess from the search, but as he worked, his thoughts never strayed far from the hidden box.

"Can't leave it in the house; they're sure to find it if they search again, but where can I put it?"

He also wondered about the money.

"Old bills," he mused. "Probably not marked, or Loot spending them might have caused a ruckus." Then he had an idea.

"I could run my own test. One bill, maybe spend it at the truck stop, or I could slip it into our register, swap it out with another one. Then just wait and see. It seems plausible. Van Horn is a cross-roads town on a major east-west Interstate, so if it gets any attention, well, the bill could have come from anywhere."

Then he returned to his more pressing problem.

"Where can I put the box?"

After another few hours of steady work, he was ready to add a few more things to the growing piles in the small garage. The dim bulb barely illuminated the space, but in the shadowy light he could see just well enough to deposit the things he had carried out.

"Going to have one heck of a yard sale," he muttered.

As he turned to leave, he tripped over a crude handmade ladder on the ground standing at a slight angle lengthwise along one wall. It was just two parallel two by fours with a series of one by four slats nailed across it. He'd undoubtedly seen this ladder numerous times but tripping over it had focused his attention on it and made him wonder why it was even there. He instinctively looked up. There wasn't much up there but rafters, but Sam saw potential.

"Maybe I can stash it up there!"

He lifted the ladder and carefully leaned it against the wall between the first and second piles and climbed up to take a look. It was too dark to see anything, so he descended and retrieved a flashlight from The Clunker's trunk and returned to his vantage point. Then he could easily see a small ledge along both walls. A few tools and the remains of near-disintegrated boxes littered the ledge in places.

"Dirty it up, and stick it up there. Scatter some grimier trash around it. It might just do the job. Hide it in plain sight."

Sam retrieved two twenty dollar bills from different stacks of cash and took the box out to the garage and placed it in the little alcove he had found. He finished by removing the makeshift ladder outside and placing it against the side of the building.

In all of his past actions in the garage, he had taken care not to kick up dust, but this time he shook out a dusty tarp from one corner and dropped boards on the dirt floor, all in an effort to create clouds of dust. At one point he realized he had been too successful and he had to retreat from the garage, hacking and coughing. The whole idea was to create a new concealing layer of dust.

"That's a good night's work," he said, still coughing as he locked up the house and drove home.

Back at Smidgeon's, she noticed Sam's new layer of filth.

"What happened over there? You're filthy!"

"Garage is pretty dusty and some of Loot's more obvious trash is, well, it's pretty awful. Tripped and fell a couple of times too because the garage is getting full."

"I thought you were going to call me. The word around town is that Loretta was poisoned."

"Small towns," Sam said, shaking his head. "Sorry, Clay just told me the same thing. Poison. Asked me a few more questions about my trip back east too; still suspects I know more than I'm telling. So the word is out?"

"Yeah, news travels fast. I don't think anything will ever replace small town word-of-mouth for instant communication," she said.

Sam laughed, then continued, "Clay said the lab called it a poison cocktail."

"Cocktail?"

"Like a mixture of chemicals and drugs. Primarily cyanide, but some phenobarbital and oddly enough Benadryl."

"Like for allergies?"

"Right."

"What's feen-o-ba-bar...what was it?"

"Phenobarbital. It is a very powerful sedative. It will knock you out pretty effectively. When it was combined with the antihistamine, it probably worked quickly, allowing the cyanide enough time to work."

"Where would someone get stuff like that?"

"I have no idea, sweetie. It is a very serious business."

"Hey," Smidgeon said. "You think Loot could have been killed too?"

"The thought *has* crossed my mind, but he was old and I was starting to worry a little about his health, so I doubt it. Why would anybody kill Loot?" He reached up and rubbed the back of his neck.

"I was just thinking about all this curse business, you know, from Loretta's mother."

"It's been on my mind too. An awful lot of bad stuff seems to be happening."

He didn't say it, but his thoughts returned his lost talisman as well.

Seventeen

A customer left the café just after lunch, but he quickly returned and waved to Smidgeon from the door. She walked over to see what he wanted.

"Jo, honey, looks like you have a flat tire."

It had been a very busy day at The Mossback and she was tired. The news took a second to sink in, then she blurted out, "What?"

"You've got a flat. I thought you would want to know." The customer was a regular, someone she had known a long time.

She ran out to the parking lot and found her sedan sitting with a slight tilt, one wheel resting on the rim.

Another customer had overheard the conversation and summoned Sam from the back. In moments Sam was at her side. It was a hot day and Smidgeon had a bead of sweat dripping from her furrowed brow.

"Odd to get a flat just sitting there," Sam said. "I'll put your spare on."

"New tire, too," Smidgeon said, wiping the sweat from her face. "I guess I'll take it to Billy over at the garage."

The news from Billy was not good.

"Tire's ruined," he said. "Looks like someone shoved a knife right through the sidewall. I can fix you right up, though. I've got the same tire in stock."

"I should have thought to bring a check," she said.

"Oh, heck, Jo, just drop it off whenever. Somebody got it in for you?"

"I don't know, Billy."

When she returned to the café, Sam met her at the door.

"Somebody cut the tire, didn't they?" he asked.

"How did you know? Billy call you?"

"No, just a guess. I found this when I was clearing a table." He handed her a napkin with a note scrawled on it. "It was that table in the corner," he said, pointing.

It read, 'YOU WERE WARNED."

They exchanged looks of shock.

"Lordy, we were so busy today, I don't remember who was sitting there," she said, blowing a strand of hair from her nose.

"Smidgeon, you know how busy we were and there were a lot of strangers today too... summer traffic I guess. I figure it's gotta be the woman who threatened you."

"I think I would have recognized her."

"You only saw her once and, well, she could have changed her appearance."

"Wouldn't somebody have seen her, I mean, out slashing a tire?"

"Easy to fake tying a shoe or something, crouch down, jab a sharp knife in the tire, get up and drive away."

"Wouldn't it make a lot of noise?"

"Not really, especially if you wait for a couple of big trucks driving by or something."

"Lordy. Sam, this scares me."

"Scares me too, honey. Maybe we ought to call Clay?"

"What's he gonna do?"

"Nothing, probably, but maybe just mention it the next time he comes in, okay? Save that napkin."

~ * ~

Lance Norton was loading a battered ranch pickup with hay when he saw a young woman ride past him as Tim MacGregg walked toward him from the other side of the barn. The woman cracked a sly smile and nodded as she moved by. He noticed the horse was one of Tim's favorites. She was quickly off down one of the trails leading away from the compound by the time Tim approached.

"So, we're renting out horses now?" Lance took off his hat to fan himself. "Hot today," he said, "not good riding weather. Going to tucker out the horse."

"What can I say… she just wanted to go for a ride so I let her. I told her not to ride him too hard or too long."

"Who is she anyway?"

"That same gal I've been chasing, the one I met in Sierra Blanca."

"I figured you had already worn out your welcome out there," Lance said chuckling.

Tim removed his own hat and nervously dusted the brim. "She's a hard nut to crack. Ain't got nowhere near the prize yet; she's quite the tease. Likes coming out here, though, so it won't be too long I reckon."

"You're a piece of work, Tim, you know?"

Tim replaced his hat and said, "Aw, a guy's got to have a hobby."

"Just make sure she don't kill herself out there. It's a lawsuit waiting to happen, you know? Or worse, she could run the horse to death."

Tim laughed. "You're right, we don't need a lawsuit, but I think she'll be okay. She looked good in the saddle too, like she's ridden a lot. I told her not to go out too far."

"How come you didn't go with her?"

"And show her what a bad rider I am? You know those horses don't like me. Always trying to brush me off their backs. I've been scared of them since I was a kid."

Lance laughed. "Tim, I keep telling you, you just have to show them you're the one in charge. It's all about attitude. Theirs and yours. You just have to take control."

Tim laughed as he walked away. "Give me a good V-eight anytime."

After he finished loading the hay, Lance drove the pickup down one of the ramshackle roads intent on feeding some of the ranging cattle. At one of the designated spots, where his hungry customers were already waiting, he saw the young woman. She had dismounted and was standing under the sparse shade of a mesquite tree. He pulled over to her and stopped.

"Need any help?"

"No, I was just waiting for you. I saw the hungry steers milling around here and figured you'd be along. Hot, isn't it?"

"Well, it *is* Texas, you know?"

She laughed. He couldn't see her eyes because of the sunglasses.

"You're not really from around here, are you?"

"No, ma'am. Born in Houston. But my granddaddy worked most of his life out here, so I figured I'd give ranching a go. I like it...guess it's in my blood."

"I'm from Houston too. That's funny, isn't it?"

"Guy in town is too. Might be a trend starting up, or maybe we're all just refugees or something."

She laughed at the joke, almost too hard he thought, like she was forcing it. He knew when a woman was flirting with him.

"So you was waiting for me?"

"Tim told me about you. He said you really knew the ranch and what I really want to see is the back country. He doesn't like to ride and wanted me to stay close to the house but I want to go way out there." She was pointing up the trail.

"Yes'm, he's the businessman, I'm the foreman. I do the work around here."

She laughed again. She was up to something, he was sure of it.

"I also know enough not to mess with the boss's woman."

She giggled. "What was your name? Lance?"

He nodded.

"Lance, I'm not *anybody's* woman."

"I don't reckon you are, Miss... er, you have me at a disadvantage."

"*Grivois*," she said, emphasizing a French pronunciation and following it with another giggle. "Monee Grivois."

"Sounds French," he said. He wasn't convinced.

"I was wondering, could you take me out on a longer ride?"

"I thought he drove you around already."

"I mean on horseback, so I can really *feel* the landscape."

"Ma'am, I mean no disrespect, but I have work to do. Don't have no time to go gallivanting around the place, you know?"

"Surely you have a day off, don't you?"

"Yes'm, I do. Sundays, mostly."

"Then how about this Sunday?"

"I don't rightly know, Miss Grivois. I'd have to talk it over with the boss."

"You don't have to worry about that. I'll just tell him it's what I want to do. I know what he wants from me and as long as I keep putting him off, he'll agree to anything I ask."

"And what if I want the same thing?"

"Well, that's another matter entirely, isn't it?" She pretended to adjust the bridle and smiled with a sidelong glance.

Sweat had dampened her shirt, making it cling to her body, revealing more than he was comfortable seeing. He was thankful he was wearing sunglasses of his own.

"Look, I have cattle to feed; you best head back to the house or you'll heat stroke the horse."

She mounted and said, "Sunday?"

"Let me ask Tim."

"Don't worry about Tim.

"Okay, Sunday," he said.

She slowly guided the horse away, but stopped and watched him unload a couple of bales of hay from her vantage point before moving up the trail toward the house. After he started driving again, he watched her in his rear view mirror. "I've got to admit, whatever her end game is ... she's good," he said, "I wonder what she's up to?"

~ * ~

At the Tesoro Road house, Smidgeon was helping Sam sort through more of Loot's mess.

"She threatened me about *you*, Sam. You've got to know who it might be."

"I've wracked my brain...I don't know *anybody* who would make threats or slash tires, especially not a woman."

"A woman is capable of doing a lot of things if she sets her mind on something, believe me."

"But no one I know is like that."

"I'm still wondering about your friend Sally."

"I've talked to Sally. It's not her. She hasn't been here."

"Okay, what about your friend's wife? What's her name?"

"We going through this again? You know her name. Moll. It's not her. It's not like her."

"You said you couldn't find her."

"Yes, but that could be anything."

"How can you know for sure if you can't find her?"

"All I know is, her phone was disconnected the last time I tried to call. It doesn't mean she's out stalking."

"Okay, what about your other ex-girlfriend?"

"Ann? She broke up with me *years* ago. I don't think she'd suddenly be intent on dredging up old business."

"A woman can bear a grudge for a long time. You just don't know."

"I probably don't, but I don't think it's her. It's got to be somebody local. You know, maybe developed some kind of fixation, somebody mentally ill."

"I know everybody around here. I'd know, or somebody would figure something was up and tell me. I've lived here all my life. I'm still betting it is that Sally woman. You shared an office with her for a long time and have been gone for two years. If she was fixated on you, it is plenty of time for her to get desperate."

"She has a long term boyfriend."

"You don't know women the way I know women, Sam. Call her. We'll see if she's there."

"Okay, I'll call her," he said and went to the living room.

The phone ran three times and then a woman's voice came on the line. "Hello?"

"Sally, it's Sam." He cast a glance at Smidgeon. She looked down and shook her head.

"Sam! How weird. Robert and I were just talking about you. I was going to call tonight."

"You were? Why?"

"He has a two-week job in California, so I'm taking some vacation time and we're driving out there. We'll be going right past Van Horn so we were going to drop by."

"Really, you're coming here?"

"Yeah. What's that restaurant called?"

"The Mossback Café."

"I figure we'll stay there overnight. There are motels, right?"

"Sure are. So tomorrow? We'll be looking for you."

"So, why'd you call?"

"We must have been on similar wavelengths. For some reason you just sort of popped into my head."

"Weird, but we used to do that kind of psychic stuff in the office, remember?"

"I do. Well, look, you guys drive careful. Leave early, it's a long drive but this is a good place to stop on your way west. I'm usually at the café until about eight-thirty."

After giving Sally the various phone numbers where he could be reached, Sam hung up and turned to Smidgeon.

"See? She's there. I've driven between here and Austin enough times to tell you there is no way she slashed your tire here at lunch, and got back to Austin to answer the phone."

"Okay, it's not Sally. But, did I hear you say she's coming here tomorrow? That's a pretty strange coincidence."

"Yeah, it about blew me away. Her boyfriend works in the film industry and has a job in California so they're driving out, heading right down Interstate Ten."

"Okay, so I guess we go back to this Moll woman. Do you have a picture of her?"

"Probably, somewhere in my crap, but I'll have to look around." Sam sighed. "You sure it isn't some old enemy of yours, someone who might be mentioning me just to get into your head?"

"Well, that's an angle I hadn't thought of. It would have to be someone from way back, and, well, how would anyone I knew from years ago know about you?"

"It would be easy to find out. It's a small town; everybody knows everything."

"Exactly why the theory doesn't hold water, because I would have recognized them. I know just about everybody."

"What about Mrs. Smythe?"

"She wouldn't bother with me; she'd just go after you," Smidgeon laughed. "In fact she already has."

"Yeah, guess you're right. You consoled her and she seemed appreciative."

"Anyway, it wasn't her ... the woman was younger."

As they finished loading three more trash bags in the back of the truck, Sam felt an odd sensation along his spine.

"Did you feel that?"

"What?"

"I just had a strange feeling, like somebody watching me."

"Sam, I don't need any more scaring today."

The sun had just set and they both glanced around, squinting against the dusky haze of the early western evening.

"Almost darker now than it will be when it is full night," Smidgeon said.

"Yeah. Just my imagination, I guess," Sam said.

Then they both jumped as one of the bags shifted slightly in the truck bed.

"Let's head home, Sam, this is just too creepy," Smidgeon said.

~ * ~

Late the next day, Sally and Robert walked into the café just as Sam was dropping off a plate to the only customer in the place.

"Sam!"

"Wow, you guys made it!"

"What a long drive. We just got a room, and came right over. We're starved."

Smidgeon came out of the kitchen to see what the commotion was.

"Sam, these are your friends?"

"Yes, Smidgeon, this is Sally and Robert."

Smidgeon immediately glanced at Sam and shook her head almost imperceptibly. Sam knew Sally had passed the recognition test.

"So nice to finally meet you, Sally. I've heard so much about you."

"The feeling is mutual. I've always tried to imagine you. I mean, you're the woman who lured Sam out to the wilds of west Texas."

"Well, he had been coming out here for a while before we connected. But, well, I love him."

Sam feigned a small kiss and then turned back to Sally. 'You guys sit down and I'll get you a menu."

"Sam, you visit with your friends, I'll get the menus. What you guys want to drink?"

"Tea? Unless you have something stronger."

"No, tea is about the strongest thing we have," Sam chuckled.

At one of the tables, they ordered some food, then briefed Sam on the boring details of their trip.

"It took so long to get here! How did you ever make that trip all alone so many times?" Sally asked.

"Yeah, Sally said you used to come out here a lot. It is a long grind," Robert added.

"I guess I got used to it," Sam said. "I'd break it down to landmarks. Okay, got to Ozona, now got Sonora, here's Fort Stockton."

"Whew, my hat's off to you, Sam," Robert said.

"So, what's going on out here in old boring Van Horn?"

"Actually," Sam chuckled, "quite a lot. Remember the old guy I told you about?"

"Yeah, what was his name...?" she started.

"Loot. He died not too long ago. Passed away sitting in his chair."

"Yeah, Loot. He died? Seems kind of sudden, doesn't it? Had he been ill?"

"Well, he'd had a hard life and had definitely been slowing down."

"Didn't you tell me he was a real pack rat?"

"That's an understatement, Sally," he said after he laughed so loudly the other customer jumped in his seat and glanced over. Sam continued in a more subdued tone, "Sorry, but Loot actually left me his house. Clearing it out has been quite a chore."

"Oh, wow. So it was a lot of stuff?"

"Yeah, Garbage, mostly. They should probably name a whole section of the town dump after him."

They all laughed again. The customer across the café paid them no notice this time.

"Still, it's weird he'd just up and die. I guess it happens, but it must have hit you pretty hard."

"Yeah, he was a good friend," Sam said.

"But she seems real nice. So this is her place?"

"Yeah," Sam said, "it's been here for years. Used to be her father's."

"I did sort of feel like she was checking me out, though, when she first came out, I mean. You got a little jealousy thing going on?"

He chuckled more quietly this time. "Heh, no. It's something else. Some woman came in recently and warned her... something about staying away from me. Then, well, her tire was slashed yesterday, and we found another note afterwards saying she was warned."

Robert leaned in a little, "Got a little side action going on out here, Sam?"

Sam shook his head. "No, of course not. Heck, she knows *everybody,* so she'd probably know about something like that before I did." Then he added, "She actually thought maybe it was you, Sally."

Sally was shocked. "Me? Why would she think that? What have you been telling her?"

"Nothing. She was just trying to narrow down the suspects. She imagined maybe you had been bearing a torch for me all these years. It just illustrates how weird all of this is. Suspects are few. Oh, right... of course. Other stuff has happened too. Remember the woman who stayed with me a few years ago?"

"Oh, I remember. I never met her, but she called a few times. Loretta?"

"Yeah, Loretta."

"She just suddenly left you before Christmas?"

"Right. Well, Loot left her a suitcase filled some personal stuff, things relating to her grandfather."

"Oh," Sally said. She glanced around and lowered her tone. "I'd forgotten everybody was all connected like that. Did you see her?"

"Yeah. I was working over at Loot's house when she dropped by. We managed to clear the air a little about our breakup. We parted on good terms, but later at the motel she was, well, she was killed. Murdered."

"What?" Sally blinked, wide-eyed. Even the usually staid Robert sat forward a little at the word. "Murdered? What motel?"

"Dolings."

"Oh, thank heavens that's not where we are staying."

Sam noticed the one other customer get up to leave so he went to check him out at the register, just as Smidgeon brought Sally and Robert's food. When he returned they were already eating heartily.

"Man, this is a good burger," Robert said. Sally nodded, her mouth full.

"Yeah, it is," she finally managed to say.

"Well, we do try the best we can," Smidgeon said.

"So Loretta was killed?" Sally asked.

"The autopsy said she was poisoned," Sam said.

"Seriously? Do they know why?"

"Not really, but everything seemed to be centered on that suitcase. Nobody knows exactly what was in it, but it was the only thing missing. She was going to drop by here to show it to me before she headed back east but, well, of course it never happened. Since I was the last person to talk to her, they still have their eye on me."

"Oh, dear." Sally looked shocked and concerned.

"Yeah, it's all a big mess," Smidgeon added.

"You think it has anything to do with the threats against you, Smidgeon? And what about this Loot guy passing away so suddenly? They check him for poison?"

Sam and Smidgeon exchanged glances.

Robert chirped in, "Sally, you've been watching too many movies of the week."

"Maybe ...still, there seems to be a lot of stuff going on here," she said. "You guys should move to Austin where it's safer. Well, compared to this, anyway." Sally continued, "it's good to see you guys, but after this little chat, I think I'll be glad to be heading west in the morning, away from all this craziness."

They all shared a good laugh and the four of them continued with small talk past closing time, before they all hugged and parted ways in the parking lot.

Eighteen

Sam was at the register when Clay came into the café the next morning.

"Hey, Clay, need some coffee?"

"Yeah, sure."

Sam caught Smidgeon's eye across the café and motioned with his chin toward the coffee station as Clay continued, "...been out since early this morning, working a bad wreck out on the highway."

"Really? What happened?"

"Couple out on the interstate collided with an eighteen wheeler and went out of control. The trucker said it was like they couldn't stop. He blew his horn but they just kept coming and ran smack dab into him."

"Heading east-bound or west-bound?"

"West."

"A couple?"

"That's what I said."

"What kind of car?"

"Toyota... Cressida, I think. Kinda hard to tell at this point," he answered.

Sam's heart sank. He was sure Robert drove a Toyota Cressida.

"Clay... I, I, I... I think I might know them. Friends of mine from Austin. I mean, they were here last night, had dinner here. They were passing through on their way to California from Austin."

Clay's eyes widened. "Austin? This car was registered in Austin to a Robert Eckels."

Sam swallowed hard. "You said it was a bad wreck. Are they..."

"Dead. Both of them, Sam. I'm sorry."

Sam stood there with a blank look on his face.

"Look, Sam, I shouldn't have named any names, okay? Next of kin, that sort of thing. But, you know, a positive ID would be helpful. What were they doing here?"

"Just passing through, Clay. I used to work with the woman, Sally. Sally Beeman is her name. Robert is her boyfriend. He works in the film industry. He had a job coming up in LA so they were driving out there together, expecting to mix a little business with pleasure. They stopped on the way. They dropped by last night for dinner and so we could visit a little." Sam looked up, his face still blank. "So you mean you need somebody to identify them?"

Clay nodded.

Sam dropped his head. "Yeah, I guess." His mind flashed back to Sonora when he did the same thing for Godson. "I guess it's never easy..."

Clay put a hand on Sam's shoulder. "No, Sam, it never is."

Smidgeon came up with a hot Styrofoam cup of coffee in her hand, "Hey, Clay, here's your coffee. I fixed it just the way you like." Then she noticed the expression on Sam's face. "What's wrong?"

Sam blurted out. "Robert and Sally..."

Clay finished the thought, "Bad wreck killed a couple out on the highway this morning. I had no idea...apparently they were Sam's friends."

"My Lord, they were just in here last night."

"So he was saying."

Smidgeon was instantly just as pale as Sam. She rubbed his shoulder. "Sam, I-I'm sorry. I know you thought the world of Sally."

Sam's eyes were brimming with tears. "Clay wants me to ID the bodies."

"You go, Sam, I've got things here. You go on."

Sam was silent as he rode with Clay to the scene of the wreck. The car had obviously flipped but landed upright. Clay spoke with one of the other deputies and then came back to the patrol car.

"Sam, they've already got the bodies in the ambulance. Come on, we can get this over quickly and I'll get you back to the café."

Sam walked with deliberate steps to the back of the ambulance and felt his blood begin to chill as he slowly entered the tight space. The driver crouched to remove the sheets and Sam winced noticeably as the battered and bloody faces of Robert and Sally were revealed. Sam returned to Clay.

"That's definitely them. Robert Eckels and Sally Beeman. I know her folks live in Athens, Texas. I think his only family member is a sister, Elizabeth, in Paris."

"Texas?" Clay asked.

"No, France," Sam answered.

After returning to the café, Sam worked the rest of the day in a daze. Smidgeon gave him his space, but he spent a lot of time in the back, washing dishes.

About six that evening, Clay returned to the restaurant.

"Clay, twice in a day, I hope this isn't more bad news," Smidgeon said.

"Afraid it is, Jo. Can I see Sam?"

"Go on in the back. I think he's washing dishes."

Clay found Sam leaning over the big sink, slowly washing pots.

"Hello, Sam."

"Clay! You startled me."

"Sam, we figured out what caused the wreck. At least I think we have. Texas Rangers were already sending someone about the Smyth murder and I'm pretty sure this will be another case for them to look at while they're here."

"Huh? What do you mean?"

"The brake line was cut. Not straight through, but enough to give them a couple of stops and not realize anything was wrong, then nothing, no brakes. The driver must have panicked and lost control."

"Who wouldn't?"

"Exactly. Sam, this is three deaths in a row that all seem to have some connection to you."

"Not to mention the stuff with Smidgeon."

"What's that?"

"You need to talk to her. Somebody threatened her... twice. And slashed her tire."

"What?"

"She never told you? She said she was going to tell you."

"No, this is the first I've heard of it. Somebody threatened her?"

"Yeah. A woman warned her to stay away from me."

"What?" Clay walked over to the kitchen door and called out to Smidgeon in the dining room. "Jo, can you come on back here for a minute?"

Smidgeon hurried in, brushing a stray hair from her face. "What's the matter?"

"Jo, honey, Sam here says you've been threatened? And your tire was slashed?"

Smidgeon shot Sam a glaring look, "Yeah, meant to tell you

about it the next time you came in but, well, we were talking about the wreck so I didn't have a chance. The tire was slashed here in the parking lot in broad daylight. Billy said it looked like a knife cut right through the sidewall. I later found a note on a napkin that said, *you were warned*."

"I see. Let's go back to the first incident," Clay said. "Do you know who made the threat?"

"No, I didn't know her."

"So it was woman?"

"Yeah, didn't recognize her, and I pretty much know everybody around here."

"What did she look like?"

"Can't say much. She was dressed in black. Wore big sunglasses and a scarf. Oh, I remember red hair sticking out from under the scarf."

Clay turned to Sam, "You know anybody with red hair?"

Clay and Smidgeon both looked hopefully at him.

He shook his head, "No, don't think I know anybody with red hair." Then he looked back at Clay. "I was wondering, Clay, was an autopsy done on Loot?"

"Just a cursory report by the local examiner. We generally only request an autopsy if it seems to be needed. Why?"

"We were talking last night, you know, the four of us. Sally thought Loot's death seemed a bit coincidental. We all told her she had read too many mystery stories, but now I'm wondering..."

"Oh, you think maybe Loot was killed? Look, Sam, he was an old man."

"I guess, but he was what, in his sixties? It's not really *that* old. "

"It's an interesting thought... probably nothing, but I'll go talk to the doc. Rangers will be here tomorrow; I'll mention it to them too. You know the drill, Sam."

"I know, Clay, don't leave town."

~ * ~

"Prewash! Come here, girl!"

Lance Norton had just finished his breakfast and placed his plate on the floor. The old dog lumbered over and made short work of the few scraps he had left. The remnants of egg yolk were soon efficiently cleared from the plate.

"Good girl," he said, stroking her ears, "good girl!"

As he put the plate in the sink, there was a knock at the trailer door.

"Miss Grivois, this is a surprise."

"It shouldn't be. I thought we had a date."

"Oh, yeah, you wanted to go out riding." Lance scanned the clear blue sky. "Gonna be a scorcher today."

"The heat shouldn't bother a real cowboy and you don't have to worry about me, either. I'll be fine."

"What about Tim?"

"I told you, Tim isn't a problem. Besides, he and his mother are both a bit under the weather today. Something they ate must not have agreed with them."

"Really?"

"Oh, yes, I just came from there. They'll be fine...I think they just need to rest today. So, how about that ride?"

"Let me just call up there to be sure," he said. He'd meant to tell Tim about her request but hadn't seen him since the day he had talked to her out on the trail. He left Miss Grivois at the door while he called the main house.

"Hey, Tim."

"Lance? I thought it was your day off. Me and Ma are both feeling poorly today. Touch of stomach flu or something. What do you want? I need to get back to bed."

"That Grivois woman wants me to take her out riding. She said it's okay with you, but I thought I had better check to be sure."

"Yeah, yeah, fine...be nice to have her out of my hair for a while so I can sleep. She's been fussing around here trying to help us, almost too much. Go ahead. Just don't get too friendly with her."

Lance knew what that meant: Tim still hadn't completed his conquest.

"Okay, we'll just run out a ways, just enough to keep her happy. You rest and get to feeling better, boss."

Tim mumbled something unintelligible, and the line was dead with an abrupt click.

Miss Grivois was sitting on his couch, petting the dog.

"What's your dog's name?"

"Prewash," Lance said curtly. He was annoyed she had invited herself in.

"Rather unusual name."

"Not if you've seen her around a few dirty dishes. She lives for licking them clean."

"That's a bit gross."

"Oh, I wash them up real good. We live in close proximity all the time, so what's the difference?"

It was only then he noticed a second button on her blouse was undone, something he hadn't seen before. She was definitely showing a bit of cleavage. She was attractive enough and obviously flirting, Lance thought to himself, but there was something about her he didn't like. He was intrigued and repulsed at the same time.

"So, let's get some horses and get out before it gets too blessed hot."

"Diablo Rim," she said. "I want to ride down it."

"Probably a bit farther than I wanted to go today."

"Well, you never know how far you can get unless you just go for it, right?"

Lance chuckled, "I reckon so, ma'am."

Once he had saddled his favorite horse, Pinto, he picked one for Miss Grivois.

"I think you had Bailey the other day, but one of the hands must have him out, this one is Dobie. He has a wild streak every now and again, but he seems calm today, at least so far."

As she mounted, Lance remembered the last time he watched her ride. She obviously had some experience with horses.

They silently ambled down the rough Jeep trail toward the east, Lance leading the way. He could feel her staring intently at him as he guided the horse around the rough ruts in the crude road. A hawk soared overhead, keeping track of their progress. Eventually they approached a small trail leading off to the right of their path.

"Can we take that?" she asked. "I told you, I want to see the back country."

"Ma'am, it's pretty much *all* back country out here," Lance joked.

"Well, that's the way to Diablo Rim, isn't it?"

Lance nodded and he gently tugged at the reins, guiding Pinto down the side trail. Dobie and Monee Grivois followed suit.

They continued to ride in silence until she finally spoke up.

"You're a pretty quiet guy, aren't you, Lance?"

"Depends," Lance said. "I'm just feeling a bit awkward, I guess."

"Awkward? You're not afraid to be out here alone with me, are you?"

"No, not really. But you are, to my way of thinking, my employer's girlfriend. I mean, he said it was okay. But it still feels a bit awkward, Miss Grivois. "

"I told you, I'm not his girlfriend. I'm not sure Tim is capable of a relationship like that. I've got his number."

"Ma'am?"

"I know he wants to bed me, but I want to ride horses and see the countryside. I could spend a lot of money and go to a dude ranch I guess, but this is better, and cheaper."

Lance stopped the horse and turned in the saddle to look back at her.

"Miss Grivois, I know he ain't no prince, but I ain't never heard a woman talk that way about using a man. Not sure what you're doing is any better than what he tries to do."

She kicked her head back in a deep laugh. "You speak your mind. I like that. You know, Lance, although I've rather enjoyed hearing you stumble over 'Miss Gravois' every time you've said it, I'd prefer it if you were less formal. Please call me Monee."

"Monee... okay, sure," Lance chuckled. "You seem to know your way around a horse, Miss, uh, Monee."

She laughed at his hesitation, "Yes, I rode quite a bit as a girl. When I was young, society seemed to frown on us playing sports, so we rode horses, I guess, at least the ones who didn't dance or play piano. I'd do whatever odd jobs I could to earn money to ride on Saturdays."

"Where I grew up in Houston there was nothing like that for us. Where did you grow up?"

She laughed again. "Down southwest, around Bellaire. It was almost out of town in those days. There were a few stables not too far away."

Lance shook his head. "Different worlds I guess." He remembered he had mentioned another Houston native in the area and thought about mentioning Sam, but then, given her interest in Diablo Rim, he decided to keep it to himself.

Monee smiled and said, "Yes, different worlds. We can blame that on society too. How'd you end up out here?"

"Got me a football scholarship to a school in Abilene, and, well, I had to major in something. Animal Science kind of appealed to me. I just sort of fell into ranching once I graduated."

They approached the edge of the Rim and stopped. Monee squinted into the distance at first, then looked up and down the sloping sides of the rim.

"Seems like you're looking for something."

"Ever notice anything out here that looks flat? Like maybe a tabletop?"

Lance had played more than a few hands of cards in his life and he hoped his poker face was in good working order, because his brain was doing somersaults inside his skull.

"No, ma'am. I ain't seen nothing like that out here."

"Well, let's head on down the Rim. I want to see as much of it as I can."

"Sure thing."

Lance knew one place they wouldn't be going. He also knew one other thing he needed to do: talk to Sam.

Nineteen

One of the first things the Texas Ranger investigator did when he got to town was request another search warrant for the Tesoro Road house. By this time Sam had completed the majority of his cleanup and had moved the items he wanted to keep from the pile in the garage back into the house. The closet in the back bedroom was one of places he stored these items, although he spread some of them to other closets and other rooms. At the start of the search, Clay had introduced Sam to a tall, smartly dressed man in a cowboy hat.

"Sam, this is Tom Clausen," Clay had said. "He's the Texas Ranger working with us on the case of Miss Smythe and, of course, now, the two victims from the car."

Sam shook Clausen's hand and said, "Pleased to meet you."

He knew it was not unusual for smaller law enforcement agencies to request help from the Rangers. Clausen was polite but all business, and this time the search was more efficient.

Although it did not take as long as the first one, they did seem to spend an inordinate amount of time going through the trash bags from the truck and garage. Once again, they did not find the secret niche in the closet, but he tried not to watch them too closely when they were going through the garage. The box remained undiscovered. Sam was thankful they finally gave him permission to take the bagged trash to the dump.

The next day Clay and Clausen came into the café. Sam was busing tables and stopped what he was doing to talk to them. They sat at a table on the far edge of the dining room and the ever-vigilant Smidgeon brought them some coffee.

"Mr. Milton, for the most part I'm satisfied you are not involved directly in these deaths," Clausen said. "The latest search was primarily looking for any evidence of the chemicals used in the death of Miss Smythe, or any related medical supplies like syringes. We found nothing along those lines."

"That's a relief," Sam said.

"But," the Ranger continued, "I do think it looks like someone is targeting people you know."

"I agree, Sam," Clay said.

"We'd like to place you and Miss Toll in protective custody away from town." The Ranger's stare was cold and unmoving.

Sam looked out the window and sighed. In the distance he saw dark swirls of storm clouds moving in.

He turned back to the officers and asked, "You're arresting us?"

"No, Sam, this would be a voluntary thing, for your own good." Clay seemed genuinely concerned. "Not in jail either. You'd be put up in a motel in a secure location, with a protection detail."

"We can't afford that."

"This would all be paid for."

"I mean the restaurant. We can't close it; we'd be broke in days."

Clausen then said, "You might end up dead in a few days if you don't."

"Just can't do it." Sam's emphatic tone was unmistakable.

Smidgeon walked by with the coffee pot, "Refill?"

"Jo, sit down," Clay said and then he explained their plan.

"No way. I'm not leaving my restaurant. This is my life."

"It very well could *mean* your life," Clausen said. "I could get a court order."

"You do that. I'll fight it. Sam can do what he wants, but I'm not leaving The Mossback to rot. I can take care of myself."

"I already told them I wasn't leaving," Sam said.

Clay and Clausen exchanged glances then Clausen said, "If you stay here, we can't protect you."

Sam spoke up, "Like she said, we can take care of ourselves. So far I haven't been specifically targeted. In fact, the person who threatened Smidgeon just wanted her away from me. If somebody wanted me dead, I have a feeling I'd be dead already."

Clay responded, "We've considered that. It's Jo we want to protect more than anything."

"You gentlemen are confusing me," Clausen said, "who is Smidgeon?"

"Me. I'm both Smidgeon and Jo," Smidgeon said. "My full name is Smidgeon Josephine Toll. The old timers still call me Jo because that's what they all called me when I was helping out my dad. These days, as a businesswoman, I prefer Smidgeon, which is what Sam calls me, but the old habits, I guess they die hard."

"Oh, for a minute there I thought we had somebody else to worry about. Okay, I got it now," Clausen said.

"Maybe *she* could go. I can run this place," Sam said.

"I ain't leaving my place and I ain't leaving you to face this alone, Sam," she retorted. She grabbed his hand under the table and squeezed it.

Sam pressed her hand firmly, sighed, and looked out the window again. The approaching line of thunderheads flashed their angry intent, much closer than they had been just a few minutes earlier. Outside, swirling gusts were kicking up dust from the parking lot.

Clay asked, "Sam, you can't think of anyone else who might be a threat? We managed to talk to that woman you mentioned, Mrs. Millet."

"You found her?" Sam asked.

"We tracked down her parents in Houston. By coincidence, the next day she called them and they told her we were looking for her so she called us. She said she was traveling out west, in Oregon, on what she called a sabbatical. She said she was still recovering from her husband's death. Her parents said the same thing."

"What a relief. Glad you heard from her."

Clay stood up. "Well, I am going to have squad cars run past both the cafe and Jo's house more often. Loot's place too, I reckon. I don't agree with your decision, but I understand it. The Mossback has been here a long time, I, for one, don't want see it closed."

"You're both being stupid, but, well, I've seen it before and guess I can accept your reasons," Clausen said. "I hope you live to tell the tale."

After Clay and Clausen left, Smidgeon pulled Sam into the hallway near the restrooms and whispered, "Sam, what do you think? Are we doing the right thing? I know I always get riled whenever anybody tries to tell me what to do, but now I'm thinking maybe I went a little overboard."

"I think we have to hold our own and face this. Whoever this is has to make a mistake sometime. We do have one advantage. Unlike Loretta, Sally, and Bob, we at least know something is up."

A clap of thunder rumbled not too far away and another wind gust rattled the windows.

"Big storm coming," Sam said. "I better get the garbage out before the lunch rush starts."

"*If* it starts... bad storm might keep everybody away," Smidgeon said.

Sam gathered the trash bags from the kitchen and went out the back door. He planned to load the cans around the side of the building but once he turned the corner he was momentarily startled by an unexpected figure. A young Hispanic woman was standing there.

"*Señor*? Do you remember me?"

Sam took a longer look. "I'm not sure. You look a little familiar, but..."

"We met one time... the ice scraper... *si*?"

Memories of the event flooded Sam's mind as he remembered the girl, the old man, and the old *bruja*, who had given him the talisman.

"You're older," he said.

"*Si*. Sixteen now. I am driving," she said, pointing to a battered station wagon a few feet away. "*Mi tia*, my aunt, she insisted we travel a long way because she said she needed to find you. She's been looking. Finally she saw you and we stopped here and waited. She knew you would be right here."

Sam remembered the old woman's milky eyes. "She saw me? I thought she was blind."

"She does not have to see with her eyes, *señor*."

A car door opened and the old woman emerged from the passenger seat. The girl had said aunt but Sam thought to himself that she had to be a great-aunt. He remembered the gentle grandfather who had traveled with them before and assumed she must be his sister. The old woman at first seemed quite frail but she quickly felt her way around the sides and front end of the car and approached Sam. She looked exactly as he remembered her and her opaque eyes stared right through him as she approached. She took his wrists in her hands, just as she had done two years earlier in Fort Stockton.

He felt the natural warmth of her palms become fiery hot and a tingling sensation extended up his arms until his hair stood on end. The old woman quickly released his wrists and he could see red marks where she had grabbed him. She whispered to the girl.

"The stone she gave you. She can see that it is gone and she warns it is no longer protecting you. Although it is in the hands of another, it is bonded to you, but it is a bond you share with *mi tia*. This is what drew her back to you to warn you. She says there is a vast curse working here and, you are in great danger."

After more whispering, the girl continued, "As long as the stone remains with the other, they become more dangerous, more evil, and more powerful. There is also something about Diablo..."

The girl paused and whispered to the old woman, who whispered back. "No, I was confused by her words; it is not *the* Diablo. In truth, she says she does not understand what it means, but she is certain of her vision and says there is great danger for you in the shadows of Diablo, or so she has seen."

There was more whispering, then the girl continued. "She sees three spirits trying to protect you, but their power is weak against the great evil. You must find the stone; it can still protect you, but there is not much time."

Almost to emphasize that last statement, a bright flash of lightning and immediate crack of thunder made both Sam and the girl jump but the old woman did not budge.

"You must find the stone, *señor*."

"I don't know where it is."

"She says it will come to you, it cannot help but try to find you, but you may not see it as it will be concealed by the evil. Beware the curse, *señor*, find the stone... she says this again and again." The girl was wide-eyed. "I am frightened, *señor*. I feel this too."

The conversation was punctuated by another bright flash followed by an almost instantaneous explosion that Sam felt like a punch against his chest. The girl was obviously shaken as well but the old woman had already turned and was calmly moving around the car. As he watched her settle herself into the seat, a hard rain immediately began pelting them as they stood there. Gusts of winds with a crescendo of lightning and thunder in the background all worked to bring Sam to his senses, but the girl stood there with her mouth open, almost transfixed by the commotion. Behind her, the car horn gave a brief toot and she blinked her eyes and turned to the car then back to Sam.

She hugged him and gave him a peck on the cheek and said, "*Vaya con Dios, señor,*" before sprinting to the car in the torrential downpour. The car splashed away into the monsoon and disappeared into the haze and flash of the storm.

Sam finished depositing the trash and ran back into the café.

Chuy was standing near the back door as he ran in.

"I was just coming to get you, boss, what took you so long?"

Smidgeon came into the back just as he was saying this. "Sam, you're soaked. Don't you know enough to get in out of the rain?"

"Ran into someone outside, somebody just passing through. Was trying to finish giving them, uh, directions just as the storm kicked up."

"Lordy, Sam, honey, you're going to catch your death of cold working wet all day. You have a change of clothes here?"

He shook his head, shivering.

"Ya'll go up to the house and change, but get back here pronto." She retrieved her keys and threw them to him.

Sam dashed through the pouring rain to the car and drove to Smidgeon's house. The rain lightened up just as he pulled behind The Clunker and parked. He was thankful the deluge had abated for a moment. As he walked past the VW, he noticed what looked like the edge of a piece of paper wedged into the gap in the door. He scratched at the paper with his fingernail and worked it loose, then trotted up to the front door of the house and quickly let himself in. Outside, the rain renewed its onslaught. MamaKat curled against his legs as he shivered in the dark living room and looked at the tightly folded paper. Lightning flashed and thunder boomed as he unfolded the paper. It was surprisingly dry despite the rain.

Stark and bold uppercase block letters read:

"WE NEED TO TALK. MEET ME FRIDAY 10 PM—54 NORTH—TEN MILES. COME ALONE. TELL NO ONE."

It wasn't signed.

"More mystery," he said, tightly crumbling the note in his fist. His heart was racing. "And soon, tomorrow night. What does it mean?"

"Rowrrr?" Sam smiled at the peculiar feline interrogative inflection.

He glanced at the clock and said, "I need to change and get back." He reached down and gave the cat a few strokes and added, "Don't tell Smidgeon."

The cat purred in the affirmative and rubbed against his hand to seal the deal.

~ * ~

"I cain't get used to this fading in and out," Loot said.

Slim said, "It's part of the deal, Loot. Scamp and me got used to it and you will, too."

"It was that woman what did me in... she left the danged note, didn't she? She's trying to lure Sam out to something bad."

"Most likely," Scamp said, adding, "...best you can do is maybe nudge a thing or two but we will mostly just have to watch and wait."

"We gotta do something. Can we follow him?"

"We'll see. Sometimes you can tag along if you have a strong feeling for someone, same way Scamp did with his grandson."

"Until I found old Slim here," Scamp cackled. "All seems connected somehow though."

"Me, I've been following Sam for years. I reckon you gots the stronger bond now, so here's hoping we can grab onto your shirttails."

~ * ~

The worst of the storm had passed by the time Sam returned to the café. The lunch rush was in full swing and he tried to forget his anxiety by throwing himself into his work, busing tables and washing dishes almost non-stop. During one lull, Smidgeon came up behind him while he was bent over the sink and cuddled him. It startled him and he spun around into her embrace. He followed suit as best as he could and hugged her with his upper arms, trying his best to keep his wet forearms and hands from her body. Chuy chuckled from the cook-station.

Sam laughed. "You don't need any embarrassing wet handprints."

"Like I would care about that! I sure love you, Sam Milton."

"I love you too, Smidgeon."

He thought about the note, but said nothing. He had a bad feeling about it, but he knew following the note's instructions was likely the only way to figure out what was going on and find a way to put an end to it.

They kissed, but the kiss was interrupted by Chuy's bell.

"Order up, you love birds!"

Smidgeon tried to stifle her blush as she grabbed the plates and headed out the kitchen door. Sam followed her, but stopped and held the door open just a crack. He still liked to watch the way she moved at work, gliding around the tables in the dining room.

Chuy was smiling over the grill. "You got it bad, Mister Sam," he quipped.

Sam was a bit embarrassed by the interruption. "Don't be giving me any lip, Chuy."

"Hey, I didn't say nothing."

Sam smirked, turned away from Chuy and returned to the dirty dishes. He knew he needed to concentrate on his more immediate problem: how to go out to the rendezvous without Smidgeon getting suspicious. He had no doubt the note was from the mystery woman who had threatened Smidgeon, and deep down he knew she was the person responsible for at least three deaths.

"Maybe four," he whispered to himself under his breath.

"You say something?" Chuy asked from the grill.

"No, nothing, just mumbling to myself," he said.

"Yeah, you got it bad," Chuy chuckled.

Sam resumed washing and thinking. He thought about calling Clay and Clausen but worried for Smidgeon's safety if he called the law.

"Lance," he softly muttered under his breath. "Maybe Lance could back me up."

Twenty

"So you're saying you'll be all by yourself out on that lonely highway at ten PM?" Lance was shaking his head. "I don't like it, Sam, with so many strange things going on around here, I just don't like it."

"Yeah. But I don't know what else I can do. We gotta figure this out somehow." Sam was sitting forward in the old recliner as Lance's big dog tried to nuzzle his clasped hands.

Prewash then plopped down on the floor, as if sending a cue to change the subject.

"She seems right at home here," Sam laughed.

"Heh. She sure couldn't have done that before. I still don't know how old Loot lived here with the house in such a state."

"Yeah, it was a mess. It's been quite a job, but it's looking pretty good now."

"I almost can't believe the change, Sam. So what are you going to do, sell it?"

"Lance, I really don't know. Not right away, anyway," Sam said.

The foreman leaned forward, his elbows on his knees. "So, how you want to work this?"

"Figured you could follow me until you're almost out of sight, then swing back around and run past a few minutes later."

"That might could work. Keep circling around to keep an eye on you."

"Right."

"What will you tell Miss Smidgeon?"

"I'll tell her I need to go check the mine because of the storms."

"Seems reasonable, I guess. It sure was a gully-washer. Okay, so you want me here about nine?"

"Yeah. I'll tell Smidgeon I'm just going out there for a day."

"Sam, there's something else I need to talk to you about."

"What's that?"

"That woman Tim's been seeing; she's been hanging out at the ranch... a lot. Got me to take her out riding the other day."

"Tim doesn't mind you going out riding with his latest?"

"He's been sick. His mom too. Both been real laid up."

"With what?"

"Nausea, dizziness, short of breath."

"They been to the doctor?"

"Naw, both are as stubborn as mules. They keep thinking it will pass after a couple of days."

"How long has it been?"

"Going on a week, about as long as this woman has been hanging around."

"You know her name?"

"Monee Grivois," Lance said.

"Never heard that name before. Sounds French."

"She ain't French, but she's a pretty young thing. Trim and fit, jet black hair. A bit forward for my tastes."

Sam had been about to draw a conclusion but remembered Smidgeon had mentioned red hair.

"Black hair. I was wondering if she was the one who talked to Smidgeon but the hair color is wrong."

"Hair color ain't nothing to a woman, Sam."

"Yeah, I guess."

"Sam, she wanted to go down Diablo Rim, mentioned it by name."

"What?"

"Yeah. She seemed to know a little about the lay of the land so we went over there."

"You took her?"

"What else could I do? Anyway, out on the rim, this Monee woman said something about looking for a table."

Sam stared at Lance for almost a minute, his mouth partially open.

"Yeah, I thought you'd think that part was even more interesting," Lance said.

"How could she..."

"I don't know, but..."

"Loot's suitcase... there had to be something in there."

"So you think maybe she's the one?"

"She has to be."

"Sam, we should call in the cops, put them on this."

"Look, Lance, I'm worried more about Smidgeon if I don't go out there. She's been threatened more than once. If we call the cops now, it might push her to do something drastic. We've got a plan; let's stick to it. I know, it's probably stupid, but, well, I'm pretty sure I can take care of myself. If she wanted me dead, she could have killed me out here, or at the café, or any place in town."

"At least take a gun. I got a thirty-eight back in the trailer you can use."

"I'll have my sheath knife. I'll be okay."

"Didn't Miss Smidgeon say the woman showed her a gun? You don't want to be taking a knife to a gunfight."

"Maybe not, but remember, whoever she is, she doesn't seem to want to hurt me."

"So far, anyway. Well, if somebody grabs you out there, nobody would know for a while. I still think we should at least call that one deputy…what's his name?"

"Clay. Wouldn't work because there's a Texas Ranger snooping around too. No, Lance, there's too much at stake. I don't want to risk Smidgeon *or* the mine."

"You willing to get killed over it?"

"I don't know, but I do know this: three people have died because of me. Maybe four."

"Four?"

"Loot. I suspect he was the first."

"If she killed him, why didn't she just get the suitcase he left the girl right then and there?"

"She probably didn't know about it… yet and it may well have already been with the lawyer. Nobody else knew about it, until the will was read. Suitcase was likely already with the lawyer anyway. Word gets around in a small town."

Lance said. "Look, with Tim laid up, I need to get back to the ranch."

"What if that woman is there?"

"I'll just steer clear and keep going. So I guess I'll see you tomorrow night?"

"Yeah, about nine. I'll drive my car and you follow me in your truck just like we planned. Oh, and Lance?"

"Yeah, buddy."

"Get Tim and his mom to go to the doctor. Tell them to get themselves checked for cyanide poisoning."

"Whoa! Wouldn't cyanide just kill them?"

"I think it can be given in smaller doses, which would mimic a lot of illnesses. If this Monee Grivois *is* the killer, it would make sense because that's what killed Loretta. Anyway, this woman is obviously using Tim as an excuse to nose around the ranch and keeping him sick gives her a better opportunity. Watch your own back too, buddy."

Lance replaced his hat as he stood up. "Don't worry about *that*. I hain't trusted her from the start."

~ * ~

"Oh, *hell no!*" Smidgeon's face was red. "I don't like this one bit, Sam. I'm scared. I need you here...with me. Besides, you aren't supposed to go anywhere. No, you can't go."

"I gotta check the mine, Smidgeon. I'll just be gone one night. After all that rain, there might have been a flash flood. I need to make sure the mine is okay and still sealed. Just one night. I've already set it up with Lance...he'll drop me off and pick me up. I'll leave my car over at the Tesoro Road house so it looks like I'm just working there."

"What about *me*? The threats, the slashed tire, people dying left and right all over the place, Sam, you can't leave me like this. At least take me with you. I've always wanted to see it."

"Not this trip. I'll be faster alone. Quick in and out. I can't be long or Clay and Clausen will be wondering if they come looking for me. And anyway, what about the café?"

"I care more about you than I care about the café."

"Me too, baby, but, listen, this is the way it has to be. I think everything is going to be okay."

"It's not okay! It's not okay at all." Smidgeon stuck out her bottom lip as she clenched her mouth. But to Sam, it conveyed a begrudging acceptance.

She pulled away slightly as Sam tried to hug her, then he nuzzled her ear in a way he knew she really liked.

She squirmed and moved her head but he followed, "You're not snuggling your way out of this, mister," she said, but after just a moment's hesitation she turned and kissed him.

He ran his hands down her body in all the right ways and soon they retreated to a quieter location.

"This is not the end of this discussion," she said as she closed the bedroom door.

~ * ~

Friday afternoon, Lance had finished some repair work on one of the corral fences and drove by the big house to give a report. Monee's car was not there, but Tim was sitting in one of the big chairs on the porch. Dark rings under his eyes enhanced the sallow appearance of the rest of his face.

"Tim, you feeling any better?"

"A little. Mom too. Monee has been taking good care of us."

"That's good to hear," Lance lied. "Where is she?"

"She went to her motel in Sierra Blanca. Stayed there last night to gather a few things but she's coming back. She's going to stay here for a few nights to keep nursing us."

"I thought you two hadn't..."

"Still haven't, but since mom and me took sick she's been a big help. She's really touched me with her nursing, Lance. Mom too. She's a nice fit out here."

"Can't imagine old Tim MacGregg, getting soft on a filly," Lance chuckled. "But, seriously, you still don't know nothing about her. I wouldn't just up and move a woman into your house."

"Who's the boss here?"

Lance sighed. "At least go to a doctor, Tim."

"Don't need to. I'm pretty sure she's got some medical experience. Seems like she knows what she's doing, the way she's been taking care of us. Gives us herbal teas and stuff she fixes up every day."

"You had any of that stuff today?"

"No, not since yesterday. She'll be here later to fix us up."

"Seems like you're feeling better right now when she's not around..."

"Watch what you're saying, Lance. Remember your place."

"No problem, Tim. Your business."

"Darned right it's my business. You've done a good job with the ranch, Lance, but don't overstep your bounds, got it?"

"Got it, boss. Have at it. I gots work to go do now. Just take it easy."

Back at his trailer, Lance fixed a quick bite to eat. Before he ate, he poured some dry food into a bowl for the dog.

"Can't talk sense to some people, right, Prewash?"

As he sat down to eat, she looked down at her bowl then back up at him with hopeful eyes.

"Not yet, you can have my plate when I'm done with it, goofball dawg."

Before he left, Lance picked up his compact thirty-eight. "Sam may not want this, but I do."

He had a custom-made cradle inside his left boot where the small gun fit securely.

"Just a little insurance," he said as he smoothed his pant leg back over the boot.

Sam was standing outside the Tesoro Road house when he got there. Lance pulled up the driveway and parked behind Sam's Volkswagen.

"You look like you're raring to go," Lance said.

"Not really. I'm nervous. Don't know what to expect."

"Well, Sam, I expect she won't even show up, at least if it is that Monee woman. Tim said she's getting some stuff from her place in Sierra Blanca so she can stay a while at the house with him and his mom."

"What?"

"Yup, he's pretty much moving her into his house. He said she's been nursing them."

"Didn't you tell him?"

"Tried to, but he wouldn't hear nothing negative about her. He's got it bad, Sam. Heck, he ain't even sleeping with her, at least not yet. And get this...she's been gone all day and when I saw him a few hours ago he said he's feeling better today. Thinks it is due to some herbal crap she's been giving him."

"Everything will change after she shows up again."

"So I figure. Now, speaking of stupid people who can't see the forest for the trees, you sure you want to do this?"

"I think it's the only way to get to the bottom of things. Besides, she said she wants to talk to me. If I don't show up, well...who knows what she might do next?"

"Guess we ain't got nothing but bad choices."

"Ten miles would put us where there's a culvert. It's the landmark I use while hiking and where I head across the desert to the mine," Sam said.

"Somebody knows way too much about your business. Her interest in Diablo Rim and the table, well, you think maybe this is all just about the mine?" Lance shot Sam a questioning glance.

"I don't know. There are the threats... those have been about *me*. And Loretta and my friends Sally and Robert, even Loot, all connected to me. You spent some time with this woman, did she mention me specifically?"

"Not a word. Mostly talked about what a worthless guy Tim was."

"Means to an end. She somehow focused on the ranch. He fancies himself a lady's man so he was an easy mark. You ever get them to the doctor?"

"Nope, mentioned it but Tim wouldn't have none of it," Lance said, emphasizing the statement by shaking his head.

"Well, let's get going. We've got to get out ten miles and not too long to do it."

As Sam puttered his Volkswagen down Tesoro Road, Lance followed him into the expanding dusk.

"I still think we should have called the cops," Lance muttered to himself as he turned north on fifty-four, watching Sam's tail lights ahead of him.

The sound of sirens filtered through the road noise and he knew something was going on somewhere behind him.

"...but I think they might be busy with something else."

~ * ~

Smidgeon turned the sign in the window around to 'closed' and locked the door. It had not been a busy night.

"All cleaned up, boss," Chuy said from the kitchen door.

"You go on; I'll finish straightening up in here before I lock up."

"You sure? Don't like you alone with all this murder talk around here."

"I'm fine. You go on."

"Okay," he said as he moved to the front door. "But be careful, boss," he added as she locked the door behind him.

Smidgeon had been a part of the café her entire life but once the door was locked, she could not help but feel the same dread she always felt. In the dark, The Mossback was a spooky place. Her father Joe Toll used to joke with her about it.

"It's the same place, lights on or off, day or night, so why does it bother you?" he would ask. "What are you afraid might happen?"

She never had a good answer, so she'd learned to push past the anxiety and force herself to do whatever she needed to do.

"Still got work to do," she mumbled to herself like she always did.

She sat down to fill one of the salt shakers, knowing she was only trying to appease her nervousness because she had already filled all of them earlier in the day. While she worked, shadows danced on the walls, reflections from the headlights of cars driving down the road. These eerie movements drew her attention to the memorabilia scattered along the dining room walls, things that detailed the many scattered moments of her past.

The Mossback *was* her life. She glanced at the old calendar over by the register when one of the lights drifted past it like a spotlight. It had been there since 1971 and her dad never took it down. It was his way of reminding her. The date circled was the court date for her first divorce. Her dad had forbidden her marriage, but she had done it anyway. Less than six months later he took her back in when she couldn't take the verbal and physical abuse any more. Not a word was said about it; he just accepted her bad choice as fact and moved on.

She related her experience to her current problem and drew from the lesson she had learned. Deep inside, she knew she had to accept Sam's choice, but she didn't have to like it. She trusted Sam because she loved him, but her love didn't mean she had to stop worrying about him... or, for that matter, stop worrying about herself.

"Sam, I wish you knew how much I hate this," she said as she put her head down on her folded arms and sobbed.

Then she abruptly raised her head. She had heard a strange sound. The old building often creaked and groaned in the dark but this was different. She looked around.

"It came from the kitchen," she said and she darted to the door where she saw a glow through the diamond shaped window. The door was hot but she opened it anyway and saw flames leaping up the back wall, near the exit. She let the kitchen door swing shut and ran to the phone. It was dead. Her purse was under the counter and she grabbed it and ran to the front door where her keys still hung in the deadbolt. She unlocked it, snatched her keys and ran outside. She was out of breath by the time she got the few steps to her car. In moments she was speeding down to the nearest place she knew was open, the Dolings Motel. She threw open the door and was relieved to see Darcy was working late. Darcy, the owner, was one of her of her oldest friends.

"Darcy, The Mossback's burning! Call the fire department."

Darcy grabbed the phone and started dialing even before she managed to exclaim, "Oh, dear!"

Soon, they heard the sound of sirens and Smidgeon drove back to the restaurant. The volunteers had quickly arrived, and were hard at work. The front of the building was dark but the glow of fire in the kitchen was visible through the windows and billows of smoke rose from the rear of the building. The sound of breaking glass and a combined roar of water and steam punctuated the otherwise quiet darkness. Smidgeon was in tears as Fire Chief Lyndon McDonald, approached her.

"Jo, what the heck happened?"

"I was finishing in the dining room when I heard a noise in the kitchen and saw the flames. Phone was dead so I drove down to Marcy's."

The firemen were working quickly and she was glad for it. If Van Horn had one thing, it was a good volunteer fire department.

"I think we caught it early," the chief said, "looks like we can save most of the building but there will be a lot of damage."

In a few minutes, the fire was out, but timbers were still smoldering by the time Clay and Clausen arrived.

"Got here as quick as we could, Jo. What happened?"

She repeated her explanations and Chief McDonald walked up as she was finishing.

"I have something to show you," he said. They all walked through a sheen of mud and soot in the back parking lot. Smidgeon could still feel heat radiating from the structure but the chief pointed his light along one wall and she could see a wire dangling loose, away from the wall. Clausen gingerly held the wire so he could look at it closely.

"Cut," he said, looking back at Clay and the chief. Smidgeon shook her head.

"Yeah, I couldn't call out, she said.

"Where's Sam?" Clay asked.

"He was here earlier, but he had...well, he had an errand he had to run. I think he may be up on the ranch with his friend Lance, the MacGregg foreman."

One of the firefighters came over and whispered to the chief and he said, "We've found something else." He waved at them to follow him.

"Here, Chief," the firefighter said, pointing.

There was a scorched gas can near the back wall.

"Don't nobody touch nothing," the chief said. "Does the gas can belong to the restaurant, Jo?"

"No, what would we need gas for? I don't know why that would be there," she answered. "Never saw it before."

"Cut wire, plus a gas can, I think it's safe to say we have arson and attempted murder here," Clausen said.

~ * ~

Lance kept a close eye on the odometer as he followed the VW.

"Nine miles," he said as he drove on until he saw Sam's brake lights flash and the VW pulled over to the side of the road near a culvert.

"Ten miles... this is it," Lance whispered.

He coasted without hitting his brakes and watched Sam get out of the car. They exchanged brief nods and Lance pressed the gas pedal. As he accelerated slowly away from Sam, he kept a close eye on his rear view mirror until Sam and the VW faded into the dark.

"I still don't like this one little bit," Lance said to himself.

The plan was for him to drive several miles, then turn around and come back. He did not see any other car as he drove. He scanned his rear view mirror for any tell-tale flash of light that might indicate a car possibly coming from the other way.

He turned around and drove back, trying not to hurry. As he approached the culvert, his pulse increased as he saw the railing. He slowed to a crawl and scanned both sides of the culvert. His heart skipped a beat as a realization overtook him.

"Where's the danged car?"

Lance stopped and as he stepped out of the cab he reached into his boot and extracted the small gun. He walked around the spluttering truck and then walked over to the edge of the culvert, wishing he had thought to bring a light of some kind. The night was pitch black.

"No moon or anything tonight."

He walked across the road and repeated his search but saw nothing.

"Sam?" he said with the loudest whisper he could manage. He wanted to yell out but he figured if Sam was in trouble it wouldn't help.

He went back and took one last long look across the desert toward the Diablo Rim area. For just an instant, he thought he saw a brief flash of light but it was gone by the time he focused his eyes on the spot.

He got back in the truck and closed the door.

"I gotta figure this out. Either someone was waiting for him and whisked him away, or he's high-tailed it across the desert to the mine. I don't know what that flash could have been, but these dark nights play tricks on the eyes. Maybe he lied to me, and just hid the car and headed to the mine, but why would he head out there without a pack or a light or supplies or anything?"

Lance returned to his truck and sped south.

"I hope this old girl holds out," he said, "just want to catch up if I can, that is, if he somehow headed back south."

Highway fifty-four stretched ahead of him but he saw no tail lights.

"Think, Lance. This is not good."

"There's only one thing I can do. Gotta go to Miss Smidgeon and 'fess up. Still not ready to get the cops, but she's needs to know what's up. There's only one answer I can think of...he's gotta be headed to the mine, so I'll get back up to my place and head out the jeep trail and get as close as I can and hike down from the rim side. If I make good time I'll likely get there before him."

Van Horn flickered in the distance as the truck rattled south.

Twenty-one

Smidgeon sat in a small room at the sheriff's office and recounted her evening for Clay and Clausen. They were quite concerned about the absence of Sam. So was she, but she had no easy answers for them. At one point she seriously considered just telling them about the mine and confessing to Sam's location, but she held back. She felt they knew she was holding back too, so there was a lot of tension in the room, but she assured them Sam was in no way responsible for the fire. From the way the questions began to change, she got the impression they thought he was possibly cheating on her. She didn't entirely rule out that theory either, but deep in her heart she knew it wasn't the case.

Back at her house, MamaKat rubbed against her legs in greeting and she sat on the couch and sobbed.

"What am I going to do?" she asked the cat.

The only answer was a loud purr.

"Maybe I could call Hezekiah, get him to go out there and bring Sam back," she mused.

She heard a car door outside and her heart raced.

"Sam," she whispered to herself and she jumped to the door, but when she opened it she encountered an out of breath Lance Norton.

"Miss Smidgeon, I think Sam's in trouble," he panted.

She could see the alarm in his eyes.

"What? I mean you guys just left, didn't you? How could you know there's trouble? Sam should be out hiking to the mine, right?"

"He wasn't going to the mine. At least, that wasn't the plan. He had a note to meet someone out on the highway. We think it was the woman who threatened you. He wanted to see if he could... I don't know, get everything straight. I'm pretty sure I know who she is... she's been out to the ranch. Seeing Tim."

"Tim's mixed up in this?"

"No, I think he's just a pawn. I was a pawn too... she got me to take her out Diablo Rim. Something didn't feel right about her. Some things she said, well, I could tell she knew something about the mine. I think she was looking for it."

"Lance, The Mossback burned tonight."

"What?"

"Bad fire in the back. They're still investigating it. Found a gas can near the back wall."

"What time?"

"Started about nine-thirty."

"Plenty of time," Lance said.

"Plenty of time for what?"

"To set a fire and get out to the highway ahead of us. It was only ten miles. She could have started a fire and gotten the heck out of there. If she sped, she'd have plenty of time to stash her car. This woman is smart. She must have had this all planned out. We were so stupid. We thought she'd come down the highway one way or the other and I'd be able to come back and intercept. She must have been lying in wait."

"So you think she was waiting for Sam? To do what?'

"Miss Smidgeon, I have no idea, but I have a bad feeling. I think she figured on killing you in that fire. It must be one reason she lured Sam away."

"I do too. But now what? What about Sam? What do we do?"

"I think she must be forcing him to show her where the mine is. It's the only answer. And when she finds it, well, she's all set. Tim's got her staying up at the house."

"What? With his mom there?"

"I think she's been poisoning them, a little at a time, to make them sick so she can nurse them, ingratiate herself to them. It would give her a good cover."

"You're kidding!"

"It's Sam's theory, but I think he's right. The first woman was killed by cyanide, right?"

"That's what they said."

"Tim and his mom have both been sick for a week. Not getting better. Sam thinks she's been giving them small doses to make them sick."

"Who *is* this woman?"

"Says her name is Monee Grivois. Pretty young thing but she has a knowing air about her, like she's smarter than everybody else. She must be forcing Sam to show her where the mine is."

"Then what? Sam didn't think she wanted to hurt him."

"Miss Smidgeon, once she knows where the mine is, she don't need him no more."

"And he's all alone with her out in the middle of nowhere. We've got to help him! What do we do?"

"I'm going to go back to the ranch so I can head out to Diablo Rim from the back side. I think I can get to the mine in the dark faster than they can, so maybe I can head them off. Hopefully I can ambush her."

"Why would she be doing all of this?"

"I don't know, but I'm going to try to stop her."

"What can I do?"

"Best you can do is sit here and wait. I'm on it. I gotta go."

"Be careful, Lance."

"I will. I'll find them, Miss Smidgeon. I'll get Sam out of this. I've got to."

Lance turned and trotted back to his truck and drove off.

Smidgeon watched the tail lights fade from view and then picked up the phone.

"Hez?"

"Yes."

"I need to go to the mine. Tonight. Right now."

"I dunno...I just put ma to bed. She's doing better but is still doing poorly..."

"Hez, Sam's in trouble. We *have* to go out there. You're the only other person who knows where the mine is."

"Sam's in trouble? Whoa! Since you put it that way, I guess Ma will be okay."

"You think you can get there in the dark?"

"Sure, I've done it a dozen times. Sam always let me lead. Said I've got a sixth sense or something."

"I'll pick you up. Can you be ready to go in like five minutes?"

"I'll be waiting."

Smidgeon grabbed her daddy's forty-five and a small backpack she had seen in Sam's room. She added one of Sam's water bottles. She put on her most comfortable shoes and drove to pick up Hez.

"Thank the Lord his family lives on the way," she muttered to herself.

Hez was waiting out front when she arrived.

"What's this about?" he asked when he got in the car.

"There has been a lot of stuff going on, but the main thing is, I know Sam's in trouble. I think somebody has kidnapped him and is forcing him to show them where the mine is, then I'm sure they'll kill him. You know the MacGregg ranch foreman?"

"Yeah, black guy from back east, right?"

"Right. He's with us—he knows everything. He's heading down there from the Diablo Rim side, but I can't just sit and do nothing and I think this is more than he can handle on his own. We need to try to get there in time too. You think we can do it?"

"I can almost run the whole way. Sam was always telling me to slow down, but there ain't no moon tonight, so's it will be tricky. I'll get us there though. Fast as I can. Hey, what about the café?"

"It burned down, Hez. Just another part of all the troubles. But that means I don't have to worry about it right now." She was speeding down the highway as she continued, "I'll just park down next to the culvert where I usually dropped you two off."

"Okay." Hezekiah reached over and touched Smidgeon's shoulder. "I'm sorry about the café."

She touched the top of his hand.

"Thanks," she said, "but it don't matter now. We have to find Sam."

Hezekiah nodded.

About a half mile from the spot, Smidgeon turned off her lights and strained against the darkness to see the road.

"Don't want them seeing me quite so close."

"Yes'm, you can see the lights of the road from a goodly distance."

She pulled off the road and parked in the shallow gully that led into the culvert.

"It rains like it did the other day, my car will be ruined," she said.

Hezekiah grabbed the packs and handed the smaller one to Smidgeon.

"You packed kinda light," he said.

"A bottle of water and this," she said, extracting the forty-five. She hoped the seven rounds in the clip would be enough because she didn't bring more.

"Oh."

"I appreciate this, Hezekiah. I hate to take you away from your momma."

"Oh, she'll be sleeping until eleven. She's like clockwork. Glad I called sis, though, you know, just in case. Told her I needed to run an errand for a friend," he said as he turned and trudged off to the west.

"Yeah, just in case," Smidgeon said as she stumbled behind Hezekiah in the darkness. "Let's get this over with."

"Yes'm, just follow me and let me know if I'm going too fast for you."

"I always wanted to see this silly mine," she said, already panting. "Just not under circumstances like this."

~ * ~

Lance parked the truck and grabbed the keys to one of the ranch Jeeps.

"Hate to break an axle bouncing around out there," he said to himself. "Hope the Jeep makes it."

Tim had apparently heard him drive up and slowly staggered over to Lance.

"What's up?" he said. He coughed deeply and struggled to catch his breath.

Lance was shocked at how pallid Tim looked.

"Oh, the dog got out. I'm going to go see if she's close by. She'd likely stay to the trail or would come running if she heard an engine. Geez, Tim, you look awful."

"Getting worse again," he said. "Wish Monee would get back from town. She dropped by for a while but went off to get some medicine for us."

"So she's not here?" Lance was fishing for information.

"No, but by my reckoning she's way overdue. I hope nothing's happened to her."

Internally, Lance knew this was likely a confirmation of their theory that she was the culprit.

"Tim, go call an ambulance. Trust me. You both need to get to the hospital."

"Pshaw. Monee will take care of us."

"Listen to good advice, Tim. You both need a doctor."

Tim waved him away and returned to the house.

Lance started the Jeep and muttered to himself as the house faded from view, "Yeah, buddy, she'll take care of you, in fact, I think she already has."

There were few relatively smooth stretches on the Jeep trail that roughly paralleled Diablo Rim, but the bad parts of the road were quite jolting, especially since he was trying to go faster than he should. Lance felt as if his spine had poked a hole into his brain. The Jeep sputtered a couple of times on hard jarring impacts but it kept running and he pushed it even harder.

"It's crazy-spooky out here in this pitch dark," he said to himself.

The headlights barely creased the darkness but he managed to keep going.

"Glad it's dark," he said, "I'd never drive like this if I could see what I was doing. Just hope I don't hit a deer or something. It would be all she wrote."

~ * ~

"Ain't never seen nobody drive like your grandson, Scamp."

"Slim, he's a good boy. Just in a hurry, is all."

"How'd we end up here with him, anyway?" Loot asked.

"We never rightly know," Slim said. "Sometimes a sprit just goes where it's needed, I reckon."

"Hope this all pans out. It's Sam I'm worried about."

The crushing jolts of the rough road had no effect on them as the Jeep sped on.

~ * ~

Smidgeon was out of breath and struggling, but she continued walking behind Hezekiah, who kept up a steady pace.

"Don't fall too far back, cuz. You lose sight of me in this pitch black, you're likely to get totally lost."

"You just keep going, Hezekiah. Don't you worry about me," She panted. Deep inside, she was resolved to get to the mine and confront the woman who had taken Sam.

He stopped for a moment and let her catch up to him.

"I'll let you catch your breath," he said. "Get a drink of water."

"I'm getting there even if it kills me," she said as she retrieved the bottle from her pack. She took a drink and felt the back of her hand brush the cold steel of the gun when she put the bottle back.

"I figure we're about halfway," Hezekiah said. "Truth be told, I've never tried to hike it this fast, but then again, I'm usually carrying a heavier load."

"I don't know how you two do this."

"You get used to it," he said. "So what is this all about?"

"Well, you know Loot died, right?"

"Yes'm. Was sad to hear that. As kids we were a little afraid of him but after Sam introduced me, I kinda liked the old guy."

"I grew up hating him because there was some trouble with my dad back even before I could remember. I guess I was wrong about him. Turns out it was all a misunderstanding. Anyway, we think he was murdered."

Hezekiah had turned to put on his pack. He stopped what he was doing and spun around. "Loot was murdered?"

Smidgeon jabbed her finger up the trail, "Let's get going," she said, "we've got to get there..." but Hezekiah continued talking as he walked.

"You mean like the woman at the motel?" he asked.

"Yes, and the couple in the car wreck down the interstate."

Hezekiah whistled under his breath. "You sure one gun is going to be enough?"

"I don't rightly know, Hez, I don't rightly know." She took a deep breath and fought to keep up with her cousin, who had quickened his pace after hearing this latest news.

~ * ~

Lance slowed the Jeep, looking for the clump of mesquite he had tied Pinto to that first time he had encountered Sam. He was a little hesitant to use his lights so close to the gully, afraid Monee might see a flash and be alerted, but he felt he had no other chance to see the landmark he needed.

"Hopefully, they're still far enough away they won't notice anything, or think it is heat lightning or something," he said. "There it is," he said and the Jeep squeaked to a halt.

He checked for his thirty-eight and fingered the extra cartridges he had put in his pocket, then walked toward the rim. He was wary of flashing his flashlight too much as he tried to find the faint trail he had followed before but just tapped the button now and then to get his bearings.

"Ah," he said with a half-whisper when he spotted it, then he began his descent into the cut.

~ * ~

Smidgeon had never seen anything so black and depressing in her life. She stumbled through the brush and rocks as she struggled to keep Hezekiah's shadowy figure in sight.

"Watch out for this small dip over here," he whispered.

"How much farther do you think it is?" she responded.

"Still got close to an hour to go. Well, I think... let me check our direction again."

She caught up with him as he crouched and checked his small compass with a flashlight.

"This is tougher than usual. We always came out here when there was at least some moon," he said. "But I think we are right on track." He stood and started walking again. "Let's go."

She rubbed at her face where a mesquite branch had brushed against it. "I'm going to be a mess," she grumbled as she followed in Hezekiah's wake.

She heard him stumble a number of times and it usually gave her advance warning of some obstruction. In spite of the intense darkness, shapes loomed when obstacles were very close, allowing her to avoid things like trees and clumps of vegetation. Occasionally the sounds of something scurrying broke the silence, causing them to stop and listen. She tried not to think of coyotes or mountain lions.

"Probably nothing," Hezekiah would say and he would tromp on.

Smidgeon was tired, but she was surprised she seemed to be holding her own on the trail, but she remembered what Sam had once told her.

"You probably hike something like twenty miles every day in the café."

Thinking of that reminded her of the smoldering ruins of her family's legacy and then she thought of the danger Sam was in. Her eyes welled up with tears as she plodded behind Hezekiah,

~ * ~

"The boy knows what he's doing," Scamp said, admiring his grandson walking down the game trail to the base of Diablo Rim.

"Wish we could give him some light somehow, you know, like Kupita did back yonder."

"Slim, Kupita has a lot of experience. I've practiced and can knock a few small things over but there's no way I can make so much light. Anyway, I think he does that just to show off."

"You could be right, Loot."

"Look, Slim, he's heading up the cut," Loot said.

Slim and Scamp intoned, "Follow the devil until you see the table, turn around and you'll see the why of it."

"Will you two shut up," Loot said, "afore we lose the boy?"

Twenty-two

"Keep going."

The whisper was getting hoarse.

"This is stupid, you know that, don't you? Once I show you where it is, you can't expect to do anything with it. I've worked for years and gotten nowhere."

The inevitable, "Shut up," was again punctuated by the hard barrel of a gun being jabbed into his back.

Sam had no recourse but to continue what had become the most miserable hike of his life. He tried to keep his mind active as he walked and thought about other dismal hikes, but the tension and dread he felt eclipsed the cold rainstorms he had endured on several occasions. The thing that kept him going on those rainy hikes was the prospect of a warm shower and dry clothes at the end of it, but this time he could expect no relief. His prospects were, at best, a choice between bad and worse.

He stumbled again. It was expected on the moonless night. Somehow the woman with the gun managed to remain standing whenever he fell. Since he was in the lead, he guessed his pitfalls alerted her to any obstructions.

"Keep going." The monotonous reply was ever more guttural.

He had to give her some credit; she was good. She had been one step ahead of them, and had suddenly appeared from out of nowhere after Lance drove past. His first awareness of her was when she jabbed her gun into his back. She spoke only sporadically, always in a harsh whispered tone.

"Get back in the car, head off the road over there," she had said, pointing. "I'll tell you where to stop! Move!" she had said.

"This is nuts," he said as he tried to direct the VW through the scattered brush and cactus in the dark.

That was the first of many times she had snapped, "Shut up," at him.

She directed him to a spot where the terrain dipped. There was a Ford Bronco already there and Sam realized the ambush was well conceived. His forced march started then and continued for hours. He managed to convince her to stop a couple of times so he could check his bearings, but she allowed only a brief flash of light to see the compass and then they'd quickly move on.

Ahead, he could just make out familiar contours that told him they were approaching the ends of the cut. He began to wonder what would happen when they got to the mine. He suspected it would be the moment his usefulness would be over. She tapped him on the shoulder, a signal to stop. She removed her small pack and extracted a canteen and handed it to him.

"Just a sip," she whispered. It was almost a croak at this point. He suspected she needed it more than he did.

As he handed it back to her and she took her own sip, he considered jumping her. He was bigger, and might be take her down but the gun was a great equalizer and he silently wondered if he might be able to crawl back to the highway with a gunshot wound. He knew there was one other factor in the equation: she was a killer, he wasn't. He decided to bide his time until they got to the mine where he knew she'd likely force him down the shaft. Then they'd both be on hands and knees and she would be hard pressed to keep the gun aimed at him as she struggled with the narrow passage.

"*Then*," he thought to himself, "she'll be on *my* turf."

He kept trying to visualize the anteroom and what he might be able to use when he got there. If he could grab something quickly, he might be able to knock the gun aside and take control.

"Must be close," she whispered as they passed the spit of land Sam had glimpsed.

"Maybe a half mile," he said.

The cut was relatively flat and Sam was surprised at the seeming lack of obstruction.

"There must have been a flash flood," he mumbled. "Debris has washed away. I hope my landmarks are still there."

"The table?" she asked.

That clinched it for Sam. He knew she had to be Monee Grivois, because Lance had said the woman had referenced a table in their ride down the rim.

"What are you talking about?" he asked.

"We're close to the end now, so I guess I can explain," she said with a profound laugh.

Sam was dumbfounded when he recognized the laugh.

~ * ~

"Never ever tried to climb down a trail so steep in the dark," Lance muttered to himself as he finally reached the floor of the cut. "Go easy," he reminded himself as he moved down the open space toward the mine. "They might already be there...gotta listen."

His mind was racing. If Sam, and perhaps a captor, had indeed gone to the mine, he had no idea when they might get there, but despite the longer hike, they had enjoyed a good head start. He'd never hiked it the way Sam did, so he could only guess how long it would take them, but they had to have been hampered by the darkness the same way he had been. Although he had driven fairly close to the area, the detour to alert Smidgeon had cost him precious time.

"I'm afraid we might hit it at the same time," he whispered.

He tried to be as stealthy as he could, but in the darkness he stumbled several times. When he sensed he was getting close, he almost tiptoed forward then stopped. He heard something.

He crouched and crept ahead and the sound of voices became evident as he felt his way through the rocks.

A man's voice filtered through the night.

"I just don't understand it."

It was Sam! Lance was sure of it.

"So I was right." He silently mouthed the words to himself. "Sam *did* come to the mine." But as he squinted into the darkness he became aware of a second figure.

"There was no other way, Sam."

Lance recognized that voice as well. It was Monee Grivois! Lance skulked a little closer.

"So *this* is the table," she said and laughed. "Subtle, no wonder it took you so long."

Lance could barely make out her silhouette, her arm at an odd angle pointing toward the figure he assumed was Sam. The dim body language indicated she was holding a gun.

~ * ~

"How do you know about the table?" Sam asked.

"It was in the case Loretta got from the lawyer. Hidden in the lining. I think the case was Slim's and Loot had been hanging on to it all those years. He'd trusted Loot with it and, I guess Loot respected it as Slim's property. Just kept it and finally figured he'd find the granddaughter Slim had talked about. I mean, I'm just assuming here, but I don't think Loot ever found the note, but you want to know something, Sam?"

"What."

"I'd forgotten those cryptic details, but when I read the note, I remembered you told me, too. Years ago, in those drunken rap sessions at the bar."

"You mean at Trotsky's?"

"Right. You told us your clues way back then. If I had just thought about it, I wouldn't have needed the suitcase at all."

"But you didn't have to kill Loretta. She knew nothing of any of this."

"Of course I did. I couldn't risk her trying to come back into your life."

"What?"

"Sam, I *saw* her come to see you at Loot's old house. I was following her. I knew then she still had feelings for you. Why else would she seek you out? I couldn't have that. I had always hated her because she *hurt* you, Sam, so it was easy. But whether she came back into your life or not, I knew she had to go, just because even if you weren't in love, she *had* been close. I know you, you'd always have a soft spot. It's why anybody close to you was a target."

"What are you talking about?"

She laughed. "Listen, you've taken a lot from me, Sam. You took Godson from me because, well, you always filled his head with stories of this mine. He was on his way to see *you* when he died. Why? He wanted to see this silly mine. But it goes way beyond the mine. Remember our talk that last night in Austin after Godson's funeral? Sure, I was in shock and I was drunk but right then I realized something... I love you, Sam. I think I always loved you, right from the beginning. That's why I tried to get together with you, but you rejected me, and you basically took my self-respect too. When you left Austin all the events of our lives kept spinning through my mind."

"Moll, that's..."

"Crazy? How hurtful, Sam. Yes, Loretta had to go because she still meant something to you. Yes, the case clinched the deal. And

I figured the same with Sally and even Loot. And as for your current lover, well. I could see it was a lot more complicated. As I staked out the café and watched her, I don't know, I found I kind of liked her, which is why I tried to scare her off. Of course it didn't work because she's too strong for something like that. Which is why I brought you out here, because I sensed such a strong bond. I knew if I got close enough to kill her, you'd feel compelled to rescue her and so I knew you'd meet me when you read the note. You *had* to protect her."

"So, now you're going to kill her too?"

"Likely already done, Sam."

"What? How?"

~ * ~

As he listened, Lance shuddered with a combination of fear and rage. "She *did* set the fire," he thought to himself. And worse. She *knew* Smidgeon was in the café when she set the fire, and knew Sam wouldn't be there to help.

But he was confused too. Sam had called her "Moll" and seemed very familiar with her. Lance needed to know more so he tried to move in a little closer.

~ * ~

"I burned her in the restaurant. I knew you couldn't resist the opportunity to be the hero and confront the evil killer. It isn't hard to set a fire to smolder for a while then erupt into a wall of flame. And I knew that if you came out to confront me, she'd have to stay back and close the café."

Sam blurted out, "No!"

"Oh yes," she said, "and in killing her, I think I did her a favor because she never realized the bitter truth, Sam. For all her strength of will, for all her sweetness, for whatever she thinks she feels for you, she never realized the simple fact that no one can ever have you anyway. Nobody. Not Smidgeon, not Loretta, not Sally, and no, not even me. No one."

"What?"

"Not as long as this thing exists," she said, pointing at the rocky hillside.

"The mine?"

"I never wanted the stupid mine, Sam. I'm *going* to destroy it. You have taken everything from me and I want to take away everything from you, everything you hold dear in your life, *especially* this stupid mine!"

~ * ~

Lance saw her motion to Sam, waving the gun toward the mine.

"Open it."

He watched Sam turn toward the opposite wall and begin to struggle with what he knew was the flat rock that blocked the opening. He repositioned himself, trying to inch a little closer. The sharp "SNAP" of an unseen twig cracking probably wasn't as loud as it seemed to him at the time, but he was close enough to realize it startled the two dim figures ahead of him. Sam and Monee were suddenly illuminated by a bright flash just as everything went dark with a crash of thunder echoing in his ears.

~ * ~

Smidgeon kept pace with Hezekiah but she was exhausted. Squinting into the constant darkness was harder than she ever imagined it would be and it made her head ache. The steadfast image of Hezekiah continued to lead the way, marching a few steps ahead of her. She was thankful for his help and tried to keep him in view so she could see him when he dodged sideways to avoid obstacles she doubted she'd ever anticipate in the dark. The terrain was full of unseen obstacles and even as he would move to avoid a boulder, she would inevitably find a smaller rock to stumble over. She also worried some animal might pounce on them at any moment. The entire hike was an exercise in such pitfalls and it had left her battered and bruised. Despite her misery, she knew Sam was out there somewhere, most probably in grave danger, and she was determined to come to his aid.

They abruptly stopped when two distinctive, sharp sounds penetrated the night.

"Gunshots," Hezekiah whispered.

"Not far away, either. You think we're too late?"

"Dunno. See that chunk of land?" Hezekiah said, pointing to a dim sloping outcrop, "That's where we're headed... we've ain't got far to go. Come on." He turned and lumbered off in the direction he had pointed.

"But quietly, Hez, we need to sneak up so we can figure out what's going on."

"Okay," he whispered. "The going is pretty easy from here on in." He moved ahead swiftly, and softly called back, "Just keep moving."

The sound of the gunshots had pumped a rush of adrenaline into her body and it served to clear her head, but her anxiety increased. She was afraid of what they might find at the end of their trek.

"Gotta get to Sam as quick as I can," she whispered, panting, barely getting the words out, "...as quick as I can."

~ * ~

"Lance?" Sam said. He had unbuttoned Lance's shirt so he could dab at the warm wetness on his friend's head with his shirt-tail. He turned back to a shadowy figure holding a gun on them both. "Think maybe you just grazed him, knocked him out."

Sam felt around Lance's body, shoulders, and arms and found another warm, wet spot on his left shoulder.

"Hit him twice, once in the shoulder, too," he said.

"He startled me, sneaking up like that. How could he know we were out here?"

"I had Lance following me," Sam said.

"The truck! I should have known."

"He's a smart guy. Found me out here a while back all on his own. He knew the clues. When you mentioned the table to him, he knew. His grandpa ran with Slim and Loot in the old days. He had you pegged from the start. He just didn't know who you really were."

"I never figured he was part of your little circle, but no matter," she sighed. "You just end up losing another one of your friends. This is your fault, Sam. I told you not to tell anyone."

Sam stood. "I've got some first aid stuff in the mine," he said and he ran over and began struggling again with the rock. "He needs help. We're going to have to get him out of here."

"Forget about him. I have other plans," she said.

"He doesn't have anything to do with your plans," Sam said.

"If he is a friend of yours and you involved him, Sam, he has *everything* to do with my plans."

The rock began to tip backwards and he pivoted it down flat on the ground in front of the entrance. She played the light around the exposed cavity.

"So this is it, *the thing you love*," she said, almost spitting out the words. She pointed the gun toward the hole. "Go in. I'll follow."

Sam crouched and entered the shaft. He only had a few feet to go, then a split-second to grab something he could use once he entered the anteroom. There was not a lot of room to swing anything blunt, but he was going to have to find something. She was not expecting him to suddenly have room to maneuver and he knew he would have to use that advantage while she was still struggling in the shaft while wielding the gun.

"I need the light," he said, "I have some lanterns farther down, but I'll need the flashlight to find them. You don't need your gun either."

"Here, take the light, but I don't trust you, Sam. The gun stays."

He pointed it toward the ceiling, down past the wooden supports, so the beam would reveal only more darkness, and tried to quickly scurry down the shaft.

"Slow down," she said, trying to keep up.

Sam emerged into the anteroom and spied his small shovel along the opposite wall next to the deeper shaft. In an instant, he flicked off the flashlight and lunged for it, and spun around on his knees.

"Wait, what happened to the light? Where are you?"

"Dunno," he lied, "I'm trying to get it back on."

He knew she might sense the open space as she emerged from the tunnel, even in the dark, but she couldn't know the ceiling was low. He tried to visualize her figure and imagined her raising up while holding the gun in front of her body. When he heard her bump her head, he swung where he imagined the hand and the gun would be and there was a clang of metal on metal.

"Ow," she cried.

Sam lunged and found a body and wrestled it to the ground. She struggled against his grip but Sam outweighed her and held her down.

"Get off me, Sam, get off me. It can't go like this, it can't." She began to sob but continued to struggle.

She was smaller than he was but she was tenacious and he was surprised how strong she was. He had a hard time controlling her. He knew he would have to release his grip from one hand to reach out and try to find the gun. He shifted his weight to try to pin her against the wall so he could feel around. He thought he knew where the gun had bounced on the ground and tried to position himself to reach for it. She tried to wriggle around his grip and he knew she was trying to do the same thing.

He finally resolved to do the one thing he swore he would never do. He was going to have to hit her, try to knock her out. Hitting a woman was not in his nature, but this one time it seemed necessary.

"It is my only way out of this," he thought to himself.

He knew from his karate days that one hard punch would probably not do the trick but he hoped he could possibly at least stun her. It might give him enough time to flick on the light, spot the gun and take control of the situation.

"If you wanted to snuggle, all you had to do was ask," she said as she squirmed against his grip. "You know, all of this never would have happened if you had just—"

"It's over, all you have to do is stop now. You're not getting away with anything. Stop and let me find the first aid kit. Lance might be bleeding to death out there."

She stopped struggling against him.

"Okay," she said. "I give up. You win."

Sam knew it was a lie, but he also knew he would have to relax his grip in order to knock her senseless and find the gun. He said nothing and tried to anticipate her next move. In an instant, he let her go and sprang away from her far enough to give him enough leverage to strike out. It was the only way he was going to be able to hit her hard enough to do any damage.

When he reared back, he felt her move upright. He knew she still hadn't seen the anteroom and didn't know what was littered about. He had a general idea where she was and where the gun might be. And he knew where the exit was, and there were only so many ways she could move in the dark. He lashed out in a backhand sweep with his right fist tightly clenched. He connected with what he thought was her shoulder and heard her groan in alarm from the sudden impact. He turned to follow up with his left fist, adjusting for what he hoped was the angle of her head. He struck the hard bone of her skull and heard her head hit a wooden support beam. He followed immediately with a right fist that connected with the left side of her jaw. He heard her collapse with a moan. Both of his hands stung.

He dropped to the ground and quickly felt around unsuccessfully for the gun, but he did find one of his small electric lanterns. It needed batteries; they always did after a full weekend of use and a few weeks of sitting idle, but it did give a feeble glow of light. She was crumpled in a heap by the exit shaft. Her pack was at the end of the tunnel; she had obviously been dragging it behind her. She was slowly rocking her head and groaning. He had to move quickly. He found a candle with matches next to it and quickly lit it, providing a little more light. Ghostly shadows danced against the walls.

~ * ~

"He done good, Loot," Scamp said.

"Don't trust her, Sam," Loot said.

"He can't hear you, Loot," Slim laughed.

"Don't know that for sure. Maybe I can focus, like the Indian," Loot said. "SAM!"

"What about my grandbaby?" Scamp said.

"Oh, he'll be okay if'n they gets help soon enough, I seen lots worse," Slim said.

"SAM! SAM!"

"See? Just wasting your time."

"Time's all I got to waste."

~ * ~

Sam's hair bristled as he searched desperately and a chill ran down his spine. He was looking for three things. The gun was still his top priority but he also wanted the small first aid kit he had packed in ages ago, and he needed to find something to use to tie up Moll. The first aid kit was the easiest because he had stashed it in the corner near the deeper shaft. There wasn't much in it, but it was all he had.

He heard another moan. Moll was coming out of it. He doubted he had anything to use to bind her hands, but kept looking while he searched for the gun. Then an idea rang through his skull like something deep in his mind singing out to him.

"The straps on her pack," he thought to himself.

He lunged for the pack. She had taken his knife when she had surprised him. He reached in and found the knife and found something else, something round and hard. He pulled it out. A realization silently screamed one word through his brain: "Dynamite!"

He carefully replaced the stick and as he grabbed the knife, he felt something else in the pack, something small and oddly familiar. He pulled the two items out and after barely glancing at it, he slipped the smaller object in his pocket before using the knife to cut straps from the pack. He knew he didn't have much time. He looped an end of the longest strap around one of her wrists and cinched them together. He would have preferred to tie them behind her back but this would have to do for now. All he wanted was enough time to get out, and grab his friend and maybe get up the top of the rim where he knew Lance had to have a car or a horse waiting. It was the only way he might be able get help. He felt around for the gun, but finally decided that if he couldn't find it, she probably wouldn't find it either. He clicked the electric lantern off and crawled over the pack and out the passageway.

Lance was still unconscious and the bleeding on his wound had slowed.

"All meat, in and out," he muttered. "Lucky it didn't nick a vein or artery."

Sam fumbled with the little kit. It was mostly for the minor scrapes and cuts he expected while working, but there was a roll of gauze. He worked quickly, opening two square gauze packets and the gauze roll. He cut away Lance's shirt sleeve and haphazardly wrapped the wound. It wasn't an easy chore in the dark.

He then began to drag Lance up the cut.

"Just want to reposition you a little so if she comes looking for us, we aren't in the same spot."

Lance was not a small man and Sam was tired, but he managed about a dozen yards.

"Not much," he thought, but in the dark he knew it would have to do if Lance couldn't move on his own. He had just turned to go up the cut, intent on trying to find Lance's trail to the rim when a shrill scream rang out with one word.

"SAM!"

The voice was a terrifying mixture of frustration and rage and Sam froze. He couldn't see her, but that meant she couldn't see him either. Then he heard another sound, the faint crack of a twig snapping. He was sure it had come from the far side of the cut. He wondered if she had possibly brought somebody else, or maybe the gunshots had attracted some other unwelcome visitor like a cat or coyote. Then for a brief instant the area was illuminated by what seemed like a burst of lightning and it was followed by a boom of thunder echoing through the small chasm.

In the brief flash, Sam saw Moll silhouetted against the backdrop of the hillside wall. The remnants of his hasty binding were still-dangling from one of her wrists and her hands were outstretched, pointing up the cut away from him. The intensity of her expression etched itself into his memory.

"Not lightning and thunder," he thought to himself. She had found the gun and emerged from the mine intent on killing him. She had fired at the sound he had heard. She thought she was shooting at him.

Then a deep moan punctuated the darkness. There *was* someone else out there. Overcrowding had never been a big problem out at the mine but suddenly it seemed like Grand Central Station.

~ * ~

Hezekiah was a groaning heap on the ground. The gunshot had been so sudden and startling, Smidgeon struggled to recover from the shock. They had both heard someone scream Sam's name. They glanced at each other in surprise, then had immediately both decided to rush to his aid. Too hastily, it seemed, because Hez had stepped on the twig that gave them away. A split-second later the flash and sound of a gunshot had pierced the night. He fell hard, just out of Smidgeon's reach so she had to scamper over to his side. She put her finger to his mouth to try to stop him from making any more sound but she was relieved by one thought: if he was moaning, it meant he was still alive, at least for now.

She managed a very faint, "Shh, shh, shh," as she touched his lips. The moans stopped and she said an internal prayer, hoping his silence was in response to her urging. She managed to quietly slip her pack off and reaching inside, felt for her daddy's gun and pulled it out.

"Now, we're on more even terms," she thought to herself so intensely she almost whispered out loud. She silently thanked her father for insisting she learn how to use the weapon when she was a teenager.

"Hez, honey, I'm going after her, be quiet," she whispered in his ear.

He made no sound or movement.

Smidgeon moved to the right, toward the looming hillside of the rim. She held the weapon in front of her as she carefully stepped, feeling out with each foot. For some reason she thought of the café, and imagined herself deftly carrying hot plates between tables of screaming children, feeble older customers, and burly cowboys talking with their hands. It helped. She moved nimbly and with purpose toward the spot where she thought the scream and gunshot had originated.

The utter infuriation in the woman's voice had been telling. Sam was obviously still alive. Smidgeon was well familiar with the intense frustration Sam could instill when he focused on his own agenda. She had struggled against the same thing for two years, but for her it was a chore of love. She knew this was a matter of life and death.

She tried to slow her breathing because her heart was pounding. Not far away, Hezekiah moaned again.

"Poor Hez," she thought, knowing he was in pain and couldn't help himself.

A voice cried out again. "SAM! Might as well call me to come get you."

"She sounds really mad, frustrated, almost desperate," Smidgeon thought. "Way to go, Sam."

"SAM!" The voice was raw, losing a little of its edge.

Smidgeon continued to move toward the sound of that voice.

~ * ~

Sam tried to figure out what was going on. Moll was screaming at him, but she was screaming away from him, down the cut, in the same direction she had fired the shot. And he had heard the distinct sounds of someone in pain. He thought hard, trying to imagine who else could be out there, but he didn't like the only answer he kept coming up with. He dared not say it out loud, but one name kept popping into his head. "Smidgeon." He prayed he was wrong.

Lance's sudden appearance made sense to him. Logically, when he had disappeared with no tell-tale headlights or taillights, Lance would have realized he had headed to the mine. Lance didn't know how to find it from the highway, so circling around and approaching from the back was his only choice.

"He would have thought it was faster too," Sam thought to himself.

Sam quickly extended the thought. If Lance assumed Sam was in trouble, he would have probably gone to tell Smidgeon first. If that were the case, Smidgeon would have contacted Hezekiah because he was the only other person who knew where the mine was. It was the only answer except for one lingering side note: *who had been shot, Smidgeon or Hezekiah?*

Sam shook his head in frustration. "Maybe it's someone else," he silently whispered, not quite out loud, but he hung his head low as he listened...deep inside, he knew he was right.

Moll had screamed herself hoarse. "SAM!" The voice was raw and failing.

He squinted and tried every trick he knew about augmenting his vision in the dark, but he couldn't see her or what she was doing. He realized he should have taken the extra time to find the gun, but he had also known he had to check on his friend. He could only hope his choice had not left the love of his life dead or dying.

Then he remembered the box he had stuffed in his pocket. It had felt familiar. He pulled it out and opened it and felt inside and had one overpowering thought.

"The rock... the *talisman!*"

He picked it up and held it in his closed fist the way he had done when the old *bruja* had first given it to him and goose pimples ran up his arm. For the first time since Moll had taken him hostage, he felt empowered.

Another shot rang out, echoing down the cut, followed by another, and then a third. But the last shot had been much closer and had come from behind him.

~ * ~

After she had crept close enough to barely make out the figure standing next to the hillside, Smidgeon stood upright and fired from about ten feet away, holding the gun the way her daddy had taught her. She recovered from the recoil just enough to see the figure stagger slightly, then quickly turn and fire at her. A stinging pain in her leg shot up her spine and exploded in her brain along with the deafening sound of the actual shot. She was confused by what she thought was the sound of a third shot, but through her pain she imagined it might have been an echo. She grabbed at the pain as her leg collapsed and she fell to the ground. Almost immediately a figure was standing next to her. Even in the dark she could see a gun barrel pointed directly between her eyes.

"Well, well, well," the woman said, chuckling.

"Sam? SAM!!!!!! I've got Smidgeon. *Now* you *have* to deal with me!" The laugh this time sounded almost like the maniacal laugh one would hear in an old horror film. But as Smidgeon looked up in fear, she could see the woman was unsteady, shaking her head as she tried to maintain control.

~ * ~

Sam was flustered by a rush of adrenaline but he finally managed to whisper, "She *is* here!" Despite the fact that he had imagined it as the only possibility, it was still a hard reality for him to grasp.

"I th-think I hit her," Lance whispered in a labored breath.

In the confusion of the moment, Sam had almost forgotten the third shot. Lance was still on the ground but his hands were outstretched and trembling in front of him.

"You had a gun?"

"Keep it in in my boot," Lance gasped. "I came to when I heard you mumbling and grabbed at my gun when I saw her silhouetted in the flash of the first shot." He offered the gun to Sam.

"Take it. I'll be okay here. Did she say she had Smidgeon?"

"Yes," Sam said as he seized the pistol and stood.

Lance whispered up at him, "Be careful. Only five shots left."

Sam advanced toward the mine entrance, thinking only of Smidgeon.

Twenty-three

Smidgeon was fighting the intense pain in her leg but the woman with the gun insisted, "Get up."

"I-I... you shot me in the leg."

"Crawl, whatever... I don't care, just get moving," the woman said, and she emphasized her statement with a moderate kick.

When Smidgeon was hit, she had dropped her gun and she was fumbling around trying to find it. The woman seemed to realize what she was doing and stepped closer to stand over her.

"Where's your gun?" she asked.

"Lost it."

"Get moving, over there!" She again kicked Smidgeon, this time harder than the last.

Despite the pain, Smidgeon managed to crawl in the general direction indicated by the last kick and she became aware of an ominous gaping wound in the side of the hill.

"Sam's mine!" she thought to herself.

"Inside," the woman said and Smidgeon, following her direction, scurried inside, trying to ignore the throbbing in her leg. It was pitch black and she hesitated, but a hard cold object poked her in her rear. "Keep going," the woman urged.

She encountered an object on the floor, partially blocking the passage. It felt like a bag or a pack but responding to another painful jab from behind, she crawled over it and could immediately sense she was passing into a more open space. A light flicked on behind her as her tormentor emerged from the passage.

"Sam dropped this when he jumped me," she said, flashing the light in Smidgeon's eyes.

All Smidgeon could see for a few moments was the single point of bright light but gradually her eyes focused on the shadows and she became aware of distinct objects in the small space. She could see it had a low ceiling and items were littered about the floor. Sam had told her he had cleared out a small space inside the mine, the result of a previous cave-in. She glanced at the source of her pain. There was a red-darkened horizontal rip in her jeans and she realized she had only been deeply grazed but the knowledge didn't make it hurt any less. She tried to push the pain out of her thoughts...she had other, more pressing things to consider.

The woman was smiling as she sternly pointed the barrel of the gun at the center of Smidgeon's forehead. It was hard to be sure in the dim light, but Smidgeon was sure this was the woman who had threatened her.

"Sam will not win as long as I have you."

"Win what? I don't understand what this is supposed to be about."

The woman laughed crazily again. "I warned you to keep away from him, yet here you are. You know, I kind of liked you, Smidgeon. While I was sizing you up, watching you working. I don't know how one person could try to be everybody's everything but you manage to do it. It helped me understand what Sam found attractive. I hated you for it, but I couldn't help but like you. So I decided to be the bigger person and give you a chance. But you disregarded the favor. I guess I can't blame you, but it left me with no choice. I hoped to burn you inside that ratty greasy spoon but I underestimated you, Smidgeon." Her hand was trembling and she shook her head slightly as if fighting some inner demon, then she refocused and steadied the gun. "It was *Lance*. He told you, didn't he?"

"Yes, he warned me. You... you're that Monee Grivois woman, right?"

The woman laughed again. "Just a name I was using. You'd probably know me better as Moll."

"Moll? From Austin? Godson's wife? Sam's *friend*?"

Another laugh echoed the walls. "That's right. Sam's *friend*. I bet he didn't tell you I crawled into his bed in Austin?"

Smidgeon blinked as her face flushed in the darkness. She knew Moll was trying to confuse her, rattle her, and punish her.

"I don't know what you are talking about and you know what? I don't care. I love Sam and I trust him."

These words painted a wild look on Moll's face, and her eyes widened. Smidgeon knew she had struck a nerve. Moll reached behind her and pulled the backpack into the anteroom.

"Okay, sweetie, you can go to your death trusting him, but it's true, I did crawl into his bed. I wanted him. I had always wanted him, even after I got together with Godson, even after years of marriage. But he had something else tugging at him. He had this silly place on his mind," she said, tapping the wall with the barrel of the gun. "Oh, he was true to you, sure enough, but don't let that go to your head, sweetheart, because you will never be his first love. He'll always have another mistress, this stupid mine. Nobody will ever have his heart or his soul, not as long as this place exists."

"You're wrong. He loves me... I love him."

"Go ahead, lie to yourself, but deep down you know what I am saying is true." The gun in Moll's hand had a more pronounced quiver.

Even in the dim light, Smidgeon could see blood seeping through the left shoulder of Moll's shirt, and there was more blood on her left arm.

"Okay, here's the deal. I came out here, brought Sam out here... to... to, give him a choice. Me or the mine. It was supposed to be that simple."

"Then why all the... I mean, Loretta and Sally... why?"

"And Loot, don't forget Loot," Moll chuckled.

"You killed Loot too?"

Moll laughed again and her tone was frightening.

"Of course I did. But my goal was always... *this,*" she said, making a circular motion with the gun. "It was the only thing on my mind. I wanted to free Sam of this burden. But I had no idea where it was, so I decided to ask Loot, because he was the most logical person. Loot wouldn't give it up so he had to go...besides I was pretty sure he realized who I was. He would have warned Sam. It was expected, so I was ready. Old guy, in ill health, so I assumed nobody would suspect he hadn't just died. But when I heard about the case Loot left, I knew I had to get it. Loretta was next. Of course, she had seen me, but she was an easy one too, because, well, simply because she had hurt Sam. I was sorry for him back then, so adding a bit of vengeance made it easier for me. Now, Sally... she was one of his closest friends and I'd always been a little jealous of her. It was sad her boyfriend had to die too, but it was necessary."

"But they were never lovers, just friends."

Another wave of crazed laughter sent shivers down Smidgeon's spine.

"You obviously still don't get it. He genuinely cared for her, and that was enough for me. And now I have you. I had decided to give him an ultimatum. I was going to tell him he could leave with me, tonight, and go to Mexico, leave you and the mine and everything to come with me and we'd make a new life together. If he refused, I was going to knock him out and bury the whole place around him with dynamite. That's what is in this bag. Enough to completely destroy it. Seriously, this stupid mine was going to be blown up either way. I was going to make him destroy it if he had chosen to go with me. But now, I'll let you substitute for Sam. You say he loves you. You know what? He does, in his way. He wouldn't sleep with me. I was there naked and had invited him to, downright insisted, and he rejected me... for *you*. Now you and this stupid, cursed hole in the ground will die together. I may not have him, but neither will you and he'll live his life knowing his silly obsession caused the loss of everything in his life, especially you."

"You... you... you're crazy." Smidgeon could feel a cold sweat forming over her entire body. She was breathing fast and trying to stare Moll down. The gun barrel was still pointed right at her face. Moll trembled slightly, obviously in pain, and eerie shadows danced against the wall as the flashlight shook in her hand.

Moll put the flashlight on top of a box while she fumbled in the backpack. Smidgeon saw a chance to lunge for the passageway while Moll's attention was diverted. She assumed she'd probably be shot. But she knew she was going to die anyway if she stayed where she was.

~ * ~

"Crazy as a loon," Slim said.

"You ain't lying, Slim, uh-uh-uh. It's a shame, pretty young thing like that, too," Scamp added.

"Looks like the other one's going to make a run for it, good for her," Loot said, pointing at Smidgeon.

They were all three hovering close to the wall, somewhat between the two women. As Moll fumbled with the bag,

Smidgeon sprang for the doorway. Moll dropped the bag and began to raise the gun, but Loot moved like lightning, ghostly hands outstretched, and pushed against the air with spectral determination and Moll lurched backward, a look of shock on her face. Smidgeon reached the entrance and Moll moved again to take aim at the figure scrambling down the passage. Again Loot lashed out against the gun, moving it enough to ruin her aim. The gun flashed and the numbing echo of a shot rang down the mine walls. Moll recovered from the recoil, shook her head and took aim again.

"NO!"

The room was bathed in an eerie, bluish glow and Moll paused, confused by the sudden light and the unseen scream.

A glimmer of movement caught her eye as Loot slammed his ethereal hand down hard on the backpack.

~ * ~

Sam crept toward the last place he had heard Moll's voice, when she was urging Smidgeon to enter the mine. His imagination was running wild and he had one thought: get to Smidgeon. As he reached the entrance, he heard muffled conversation but couldn't make out the words. Suddenly there was a flash and the crack of a gunshot rang from inside the mine. A head popped into view, silhouetted by the flash. It was Smidgeon.

He grabbed her by the shoulders, pulled her out and swung her behind him in one, swift, adrenaline-spiked move. He heard her moan slightly as she landed hard and he turned to rush her away from the opening to a safer vantage point. He assumed Moll was right on her heels.

At that moment, a bright flash erupted from the mine entrance, followed by the rest of the explosion. A rush of smoke, dust, and debris poured from the opening. The force of the blast shook the ground and knocked Sam from his feet and he fell on top of Smidgeon.

~ * ~

Three vaporous figures emerged from the dust cloud, making motions as if to pat away the powdery remnants of the explosion.

"Dang, Loot, she blowed up real good," Slim said.

Scamp was laughing, "Darned if she didn't. You saved us all."

Loot seemed to be blinking and shaking his head, "I didn't think nothing was supposed to hurt."

"Me neither," Slim said. "I guess Kupita done taught you too well, danged near kilt us all...agin!"

All three cackled at the joke as they faded into the night.

~ * ~

Sam cradled Smidgeon's head in his arms. "You okay?"

"My leg hurts and I can't breathe, but, well, I guess I'll live. Did she blow herself up?"

"Looks like it. She had dynamite in there."

"Sam, she was crazy as a loon... she said she was going to blow *me* up." Smidgeon looked closely at the shadows of his face and reached up and held his head steady with her hands as she added, "She said she tried to jump into bed with you back in Austin. Did she?"

Sam looked down and nodded. "Yeah, she did. I should have told you, but that was when you were already mad at me. Look, I made her leave. All I could think of was you, told her it wasn't right. I figured she was just crazy with grief."

"Just plain crazy, I'd say," Smidgeon said.

Sam stood and helped her up. "Your leg?"

"Hurts like the dickens, but I think she just grazed me when she shot at me. I think I'm okay."

"Sam..."

The voice was coming from up the cut.

"Lance!"

"Lance is here too?" Smidgeon asked.

"Yeah, he came in from the rim side. He's shot."

"Hezekiah is shot too. I gotta go check on him."

"All the lights and lanterns blew up in the mine. Here, let's go to Lance first and you stay with him, then I'll go find Hez."

They scrambled a few yards through rocks and scrub. Lance was on his side a few dozen yards away.

"What the heck happened?"

"She had dynamite. I guess she either blew herself up or it blew up on its own," Sam said.

"Monee?"

"Actually, her real name was Moll. She was an old friend from Austin."

"Huh? I heard you say that name but I thought I just wasn't hearing right."

"I know, it's a long story. Smidgeon, you stay here with Lance. I'll go find Hezekiah."

"Somebody else is out here?"

"Yeah," Smidgeon said. "My cousin. She shot him too."

They could hear Sam calling Hezekiah's name then the night was quiet. Several minutes later he returned and immediately drew Smidgeon to him.

"I'm sorry, honey. Hezekiah... he, he... didn't make it."

Smidgeon sobbed softly into Sam's shoulder for several minutes.

Lance broke the spell. "Got a Jeep up on the rim. Maybe about a half mile. I've lost a lot of blood, but I think with your help I might just be able to make it back up there."

The three of them managed to get Lance to his feet and guided him to the bottom of the trailhead. The trail up to the rim was difficult, but they continued to make their way up to the Jeep.

"Hold on, Lance, we'll get you some help as quick as we can," Sam said as he navigated the bumps, twists, and turns of the rugged Jeep trail.

It seemed to take forever as the twin headlights fought through the black night but when they made a final turn toward the main compound and could see the lights of the ranch complex, they saw something else they were not expecting.

"Am I hallucinating?"

Lance had asked the question, but they were all thinking the same thing.

There was a circus of strobing lights in front of the main house. Sam pulled up and parked close to the flashing lights of an ambulance and patrol car.

Sam finally said, "No, you're not hallucinating at all."

Twenty-four

"I should charge you both with accessory to murder." Clausen was red-faced.

Clay was a bit more subdued. "Why didn't you call me, bring me the note when you first got it?"

The bright lights in the police station hurt Sam's eyes and he blinked in silence, trying to come up with some plausible explanation but, nothing he could think of made as much sense as the truth. Finally, he took a deep breath and spoke.

"It was the mine."

"The mine? What mine?" The ranger and deputy exchanged questioning glances.

"The Sublett mine. I found it."

Ranger Clausen looked at Clay. "What in heaven's name is he talking about?"

Clay spoke to Sam. "Sam, that old legend says it was supposed to be up in the Guadalupes. Are you saying it is on the MacGregg Ranch?"

"Yes, at least I think it is. I'd been looking for it for years and, well, I found *something*. Been working on it for a couple of years. Their foreman found me out there a while back, but so far had kept it quiet."

The two lawmen blinked at one another.

"And you say our suspect is still out there?" Clausen looked at his notepad.

"Yeah, at least what's left of her. She had dynamite."

"And this was Monee Grivois? That's the name Tim MacGregg gave us."

"She was using an assumed name. Her real name was Moll Millet, from Austin." Sam emphasized the *mill-aye* pronunciation Moll preferred.

"Her? She told us she was in Oregon!" Clay said.

"She told a lot of lies. After her husband died I think she sort of snapped. She, well, she said she wanted me to go away with her and when I refused, well, she said she wanted to take the mine away from me in revenge. Sounds nuts, I know. I've known her and her husband for years. She was my friend and I had told them about it a long time ago. I trusted them. I don't know what happened to her. We'd never been romantic but suddenly, I guess in her grief or something, she became obsessed with me. She kind of fixated on it."

"And all the other people?"

"For her, I guess you'd call it collateral damage. I think she wanted revenge. I guess anybody I knew, anybody I was close to or had been ever been close to, was a target."

Clausen and Clay again exchanged exasperated looks.

A door opened and Smidgeon came in, followed by another deputy.

"Doc treated her and sent her on," he said. "A gunshot creased her leg and she's got a few bumps and bruises, but she's okay."

She sat next to Sam.

Clay leaned forward with both arms on the table as he asked, "Sam said this was all about some fool notion of a gold mine, Jo. What do you know about it?"

"She was crazy. There *is* a mine, or, there *was*...she blew it up. I barely got out of there before the explosion. She was going to blow me up too."

Clay said to Clausen, "First deputy out to the MacGregg place after Tim called the ambulance did say he heard what he thought might be an explosion. He figured it was thunder."

"It was a clear night," Clausen said.

"Well, sound does carry awful far out there. We all figured maybe it was a thunderstorm far off."

"The mine is way down around the far end of Diablo Rim." Sam said, still struggling to see in the bright lights. "Or it was. Whatever is left of Moll is down in the remains of the mine."

Smidgeon added, "And my cousin, Hezekiah, his body is out there too."

"Wait, another one?"

Clausen interrupted Clay, "Yes, remember, they told us about that one before. We were going to get a helicopter out from El Paso and head out there to check it out at first light, remember?"

"Yes. Right." Clay rubbed at his face with both hands. "What a mess." He looked down at Sam. "You sure he was dead?"

"Stone cold," Sam said. "He was a friend too, Clay, heck, he was *family*." He glanced at Smidgeon's teary eyes and continued, "If I thought he was alive, I would have carried him out same as we did with Lance. How is he?"

"Lance Norton lost a lot of blood, but he'll probably be okay. Same with Tim, but his mother died."

"The MacGreggs were poisoned," Clausen interjected, "what do you know about that?"

"Moll said she poisoned Loot too. I figure with cyanide, just like Loretta, although I think with the MacGreggs she was using a lower dose to mimic illness. I guess she was just using the poison as a way to get in close to help her try to find the mine. With Tim laid up, she was out there a lot and even got Lance to show her around the back areas."

"And how does this all fit together?"

"She didn't know where the mine was. She tried to get it out of Loot, but he didn't know either. He and I shared a lot of confidences about it, but he didn't know the exact location. He did give me a lot of help, though. I'd hike out there on weekends and he'd drop me off and pick me up."

"You hiked?" Clausen looked as if he might be developing a headache.

"From highway fifty-four. It's a long hike but it was the only way to get in and out undetected. When she first started coming around, I guess she stalked us, saw where the drops were happening and put two and two together. That was probably when she started trying to pal around with Tim, after she figured out who owned the land."

Clay spoke up, "What about this cousin, Hezekiah? Why did he go out there with Smidgeon?"

"He had helped me in the past. He was the only other person who knew where the mine was. It was more than I could handle and we," he looked at Smidgeon, "asked him to help. I feel really bad about it. She went to him when she found out I was in trouble because she had no one else to turn to."

"Should have come to me, Jo," Clay said with a sigh.

"If I had, Sam and Lance would both be dead. Probably Tim too."

"And I don't know, but," Sam added, "probably Hezekiah would have been out there in harm's way because she would have told you he was the only person who knew where it was."

"He was leading the way and stepped on a stick or something," she said. "Sam had escaped and she was yelling his name. She shot at the sound and hit him." Smidgeon buried her head into Sam's shoulder and sobbed.

Clausen sighed deeply and turned and stared at a map of the county hanging on the wall. "Release them," he said. "We'll check the evidence and corroborate their stories with the foreman, what's his name?"

"Lance Norton."

"Right. We can charge them all later if we have to." Clausen turned around and pointed at Sam. "Do not leave town, do you hear me?"

"We won't leave," Smidgeon said.

"Sam, can you help us pinpoint the location?" Clay was looking at a standard county map.

Sam stood and pointed. "Need a better map, Clay. Do you have US Geological Survey maps?"

Clay sighed, "Is it *that* hard to find?"

"Yeah, 'fraid so. Come by the house later and I'll pinpoint it for you. I've got the maps you need."

Their interview complete, Smidgeon and Sam were allowed to leave. They had driven directly to the sheriff's office from the ranch in Lance's truck so they drove it out north to retrieve Smidgeon's car from the side of the road.

Sam pointed out beyond the culvert. "My car is out there, close to a Ford Bronco, both parked in a small depression."

"That's got to be Moll's. I guess we need to tell Clay."

"Yeah, forgot to mention it. Guess we might as well wait for them to check everything out before I try to get my car.'

"Why'd she go so crazy, Sam?" Smidgeon leaned against him then turned to face him. "You've known her for years, was she always this crazy?"

"Quite the opposite, Smidgeon, she was always the one quietly in control."

"Was it grief? Maybe she just went crazy when Godson died."

"You know, it probably didn't help, but," Sam paused for a moment as he retrieved the tattered box from his pocket, "believe it or not, it might have been this."

"Your voodoo witch charm? You found it?"

"She did. I dropped it there, back in Austin," he said, and he related the latest encounter with the old Mexican *bruja*.

"So you were standing in the pouring rain talking to the *bruja* that crazy rainy day?"

"Yeah, she sort of found me. Creepy, huh?"

"I want you to get rid of the thing, Sam, it scares me."

"I'm not sure. I think it *protects* us, Smidgeon. I don't know what to think about it but when I think about all the curse talk from Loretta's mother, I just wonder. Things started to turn around when I got it back, you know? I think I need to keep it around but just keep it hidden like I always did."

Smidgeon kissed him on the cheek, "Well, Sam Milton, if there *is* a curse, it's a curse that bites deep," she said.

It was daylight by the time they finished telling Clay about the hidden vehicles, so Sam and Smidgeon inspected The Mossback on their way to the hospital to check on Lance. They were interrupted by several regulars who dropped by to see the damage themselves.

"Sad."

"Old Joe would be crying if he saw this."

"Hope your insurance is good."

She winced when she heard the insurance comment because it had a certain amount of irony in it for Smidgeon.

"Sam, I'm not sure the insurance will be enough to cover this."

"What? Of course it will. Are you paid up?"

"Of course I am, but, well, I have just a minimal policy with a really high deductible. It's a corner I cut a long time ago when the business wasn't doing well, long before you came along. I had always been meaning to change it, but never got around to."

Sam's thoughts turned to the Tesoro Road house and the box he had hidden in the little garage.

"I might be able to help."

"What? What do you mean?"

"After we check on Lance, I need to show you something."

~ * ~

At the hospital, Lance was groggy but he smiled broadly as he greeted them. "Sam. Miss Smidgeon. Everything okay?"

"You look better than you did a little while ago."

"Lost a bit of blood, but the doc said it wasn't too bad," he said. "Flying high on these painkillers, though. They asked me about the mine, so I figured you had already spilled the beans. So, I told the cops everything I know. You think this is all over?"

"Not by a long shot. But I think they believe us. Nothing to hide anymore."

"It's too bad about the mine, Sam. I looked forward to working it with you. It was kind of a legacy to my grandpa, you know?"

"I know, buddy. The whole thing has been a part of my life for so long, I don't know what to think about it. You just heal up quick. We've got a restaurant to rebuild so we'll be around." Sam handed Lance the keys. "Your truck is in the parking lot. Hear anything about Tim?"

"Know his mom died. Cyanide, just like you said. Knowing what it was at least helped Tim, so I guess you saved him. He's been transported to El Paso in pretty bad shape, but the nurse said he'd probably make it."

"Maybe he'll let you oversee the excavation, digging out the mine."

"Maybe so, but I think I might just head back east. We'll see."

"Lance," Smidgeon said, "thank you for trying to protect me."

"To be honest, Miss Smidgeon, I didn't rightly know who I was shooting at. That woman had already shot me, so when I came to and heard shots, I just let loose. I'm hoping what hit you wasn't one of my slugs."

"No, Lance, I know it was Moll. I was already shot by the time you fired."

"Thank heavens."

They could tell Lance was getting tired so they made their exit and headed over to Tesoro Road.

"What is this about, Sam?"

"Just wait," he said as he opened the doors to the small garage. The makeshift ladder was right where he had left it. Once he set it up on the opposite wall, he climbed to the rafters and fumbled in the shadows, then climbed down with a wooden box. He fumbled in his pants pocket.

"I'm glad she didn't notice I pocketed my keys when I parked the car." He singled out the house key for her and said, "Let's go in the house."

Smidgeon unlocked the door and Sam walked past her with his load to the kitchen where he placed it on the table. He retrieved Loot's huge key ring, found the right key and opened the box. He unfolded the stiff paper covering the contents and pointed.

Smidgeon's eyes widened. "Sam? I, I, I, uh... where did it come from?"

"Found it in the house," he said. "I have no idea?"

She picked up some of the bills. "They're old."

"The box was hidden," he said. "I passed a few through the till several weeks ago just to see if they got any notice."

"What?"

"Hey, I was curious. I figured if something was wrong with them, we could claim somebody passing through used them."

"Sam Milton. Why didn't you tell me?"

"Figured it better if you didn't know."

He crinkled the paper covering as he grabbed it to pull everything out at once. "I think this must be old wallpaper or something."

Smidgeon moved box to the side as Sam let the pile of bills spread out on the table.

"It's thousands of dollars," Smidgeon said, fingering the bills.

"Surely enough for any repairs the insurance doesn't cover."

Smidgeon hugged Sam and meant to kiss him when something in the box caught her eye.

"Sam, did you see this?"

There was a note in the bottom of the box.

"No, I never saw it, but I never pulled all the money out with the wrapping."

Sam picked it up and took a long look at it. The scrawl was shaky but readable. A tear rolled down his cheek as he handed it to Smidgeon.

> *Sam,*
>
> *If you are reading this here note, I reckon I'm gone and you've found the box and I guess maybe you're probably wondering about it. Some old army buddies of mine got into a bit of trouble a couple of years after the war and came by one day and dropped this off for safe keeping. They said they snagged this cash on some kind of crazy swindle they managed to pull off in Mexico. They said they was being chased and remembered I lived hereabouts. They never came back. I heard they was killed in a car wreck or something, but I always suspected they was just murdered. I was already a pretty bad drunk by then and got scared, so I hid the money and just ignored it for years. When I started feeling poorly, I figured I'd pull a few bucks to hire a lawyer to put my affairs in order. That's when I decided to write this here note.*
>
> *Sam, you've been a good friend these last couple of years. I'd been feeling pretty lonely and useless and, well, you changed that. Do what you want with the house and with the money, but I want to leave you with one thought my*

granddaddy always told me. I've thought a lot about it as I've seen you messing with that danged mine and it seems fitting to pass it along to you as my parting advice.

If you search really hard for something, often you will find it.

But don't be surprised when the it you find is not the something you were after.

—Loot

Sam wiped away the tear and Smidgeon hugged him tight, tears streaming down her face as well. Their kiss was long, soft, and deep.

"Sam, let's go home."

He carefully placed the bills back in the box and closed the lid. "Good idea," he said.

Meet Thomas Fenske

Texas native Thomas Fenske currently lives in North Carolina where he is an IT professional managing various flavors of UNIX computer systems. He and his lovely wife share their home with a menagerie of nine cats and a ninety-something pound dog. Somehow, he manages to write despite the chaos.

Other Works From The Pen Of Thomas Fenske

The Fever

In the late 1800s, Ben Sublett was already known for his secret gold mine in the far reaches of west Texas. When Ben died in 1892, it was thought his secret died with him. Eighty years later in a central Texas jail, a dying, homeless wino named "Slim" Longo whispered a long-held family secret to twenty year old Sam Milton.

A Curse That Bites Deep

After years of frustration and sacrifice, Sam Milton's life seems to be on track. In The Fever he got the girl, he found the mine, and he hopes he'll soon have the gold, but he forgot one minor detail: the curse and its ripples are affecting almost everyone around him.

Lucky Strike

A bitter, decades-old grudge surfaces with a vengeance in a small west Texas town.

Penumbra – Reluctant treasure hunter Sam Milton and his girlfriend Smidgeon Toll find themselves immersed in the search for a missing man they have never met and end up on the trail of a cache of ancient gold in the desert southwest.

**The Hag Rider**

This Civil War memoir explores a fifteen-year-old cavalryman's transition to manhood, complicated by the spectral manipulations of a hoodoo witch sworn to protect him.

**Harmon Creek** – When political candidate Earl Swanger ended up stabbed and dead next to a bridge in rural Texas it looked like a case of homicide, right? Then why was it ruled an accident within two days? This fictional account revisits the 1930 cold case and the possible skullduggery behind the coverup.

**Harmon Creek** – When political candidate Earl Swanger ended up stabbed and dead next to a bridge in rural Texas it looked like a case of homicide, right? Then why was it ruled an accident within two days? This fictional account revisits the 1930 cold case and the possible skullduggery behind the coverup.